THE ARABIAN BIRD

THE

" 'Tis the Arabian bird alone
Lives chaste, because there is but one."

JOHN WILMOT · EARL OF ROCHESTER

NEW YORK · TORONTO

ARABIAN BIRD

By Constantine Fitz Gibbon

RINEHART AND COMPANY, INC.

*This novel is dedicated
to my friends
Fred and Margaret Wakeman*

THE ARABIAN BIRD

CHAPTER ONE

THE countryside over which they were walking so very quickly seemed to consist entirely of huge lava blocks, or perhaps of old grey coral. The uneven surface made walking difficult, particularly as the girl went so fast.

"Miss, er . . . ," he cried. But she took no notice, striding ahead, her white draperies flowing diaphanous behind her. He wondered why she dressed in the style of Isadora Duncan. Was she, perhaps, a dancer? Or was some obscure insult intended? If only he knew her name he could certainly persuade her to go more slowly.

"The noise is locus." Her voice trailed back over her shoulder. Now that she had drawn his attention to it, he saw the huge grey cloud, humming away on the horizon.

"Locusts," he corrected her. Out of breath though he was he managed to add, "locusts is the word, and the year is nineteen forty-four."

"Locust Tennant," she replied, and then of course he realised that it was his wife Louise whom he was following, struggling through the postage-stamp sweet snowstorm.

There were all sorts of stamps, all sizes, all colours, some falling through the air, others carefully arranged in albums. He wondered if the edges were perforated. He could not be quite sure, although he could see that most of them bore the head of his son Oliver, in profile, with a crown. The crown had presumably been added after they made him a major. One of the stamps had the words KEEP OUT overprinted. A real collector's item that one.

The distant wailing and buzzing was becoming more audible now that he was out of the snowstorm. But why were the quadrangles so dirty, and why had they built a tarmac road across the lawn? Presumably it was something to do with the national effort. Ah, there was Louise now, just disappearing behind the corner of the chapel.

"Lou-ee-eese, Lou-ee-eese, Lou-ee-eese." His voice grew fainter and fainter as she faded away, for she was not sitting in the chair, nor walking through the door, but perhaps in the kitchen where the electric toaster was humming. . . .

Charles awoke, fumbling upwards through the noise of the airplane. His neighbour was shaking him by the arm.

"You must adjust your safety belt. We're coming in to land."

Charles smiled at him in acknowledgement. Although this was the first time they had spoken, he had had a feeling of friendliness towards the sunburned colonel with the white moustache ever since the plane had left Casablanca. He groped for his safety belt and worked the thick clumsy buckle, still a little confused by the dream from which he had just awakened.

Charles Monroe was a man in his late forties, slightly stooped and greying, his once powerful body showing the first signs of approaching decay. His pseudo-military uniform was ill-fitting and he wore it without ease. Indeed he had never mastered all the buttons, and as he twisted his body to peer out of the tiny window a gap of white shirt appeared between the battle-dress jacket and the trousers. He was a research chemist by profession, returning now from a visit to Italy made at the request of the British Government to examine an Italian laboratory. His large grey face had that slightly puzzled look sometimes worn by a modest don. He gazed through the opaque little window at the approaching airfield.

The ground, with its improbable appendages of trees and houses, was wobbling upwards, a disconcerting sight. Charles straightened himself and waited for the bump. Despite himself he felt nervous. The whole business of airplanes, their noise and shininess and complex existence, had been hateful to him ever since that day in 1918, in France, when a plane of unknown nationality had hurtled into the ground twenty yards from the trench in which he stood. The explosion had covered him with burning gasoline. Since then he had regarded them as stupid and dangerous things and done his best to avoid them. Now he waited anxiously for this one to land, for he had read that landing was the time when they were most likely to go wrong. The plane bumped and bumped again. The colonel was loosening his belt. Humming and jolting along the asphalt runway, they finally stopped before a small low building. The silence was striking. Completely relaxed, Charles waited for someone to tell him what to do.

He had been away from England for almost two months. For the last few weeks he had been travelling, had received no letters, and consequently had no idea whether his wife was at their flat in London or at their Oxford home. When the formalities with the officials were completed, he asked if he might send a telegram. He would like Louise to be expecting him when he arrived. A small officer, accustomed no doubt to such requests, informed him that for obvious reasons of military security there were no postal or telegraphic facilities available to transient personnel at the airport. Having made this splendid statement, the small officer adjusted his hat in a highly self-satisfied manner, turned on his heel, and walked out of the room whistling a tune from *Don Giovanni*. For the thousandth time in two months Charles thanked God that he was not at the mercy of these people. He sat down patiently on his suitcase and waited for the bus that was to take them to the station.

The musty smell and dark brown upholstery of the first class carriage were as reassuring as an old nurse after the military discomforts he had just left. Charles rubbed a little of the grimy water off the window with the finger of his glove and looked out at the darkening anonymous countryside, listening to the tattoo of the wheels, thinking of Louise. The rhythm of the train seemed to repeat her name, sometimes quickly, sometimes as slowly as the length of her back.

He looked across at the bronzed colonel, wondering if perhaps he too had a young wife whom he loved; but that gentleman was busying himself with an apparently endless piece of arithmetic, a small gold pencil running up and down half a yard of figures. With a sigh Charles pulled the folded evening paper out of his pocket and held it in the path of the florin-sized ray of light.

Half-consciously he read the account of the previous night's heavy raid on an industrial town in Western Germany. His mind was elsewhere. When he got to London he would ring his little house in town to see if Louise were there. He would spend the night in London in any case, because it would be ten before he arrived.

He read his paper mechanically. A Wing Commander had observed a solid sea of fire, six miles by three, and described the raid as a capital show. He did hope she would be in London, even though he had urged her to stay in Oxford while he was away. The memory of her soft black hair, so richly curled, lay between him and the blood-thirsty Wing Commander. Charles attempted to decipher the caption beneath a joke picture which portrayed a moustachioed and gesticulating fishmonger, three housewives and a small boy, the latter caught in the very act of being bowled over by a paroxysm of mirth. He had married Louise just two years ago, and as presents he was bringing her an eighteenth century cameo from Naples and a black and gold silk square from Algiers. It was their wedding anniversary tomorrow, but he would give them to her tonight if she were in London. She was twenty-three years old. He read that the Duchess of Athlone had launched a ship built entirely with the half-pennies contributed by the inmates of French-Canadian insane asylums. When Louise opened the little box that contained the cameo, her face would have the serious expression of a Christmas morning child. Her thanks would be perfunctory, almost embarrassed, but if she liked the brooch she would wear it almost every day, for a little time each day at least. A woman in Tottenham informed the magistrate that her husband earned three pounds ten shillings a week or, according to his reckoning, nine pints a night. The skin was stretched tight over Louise's pelvis bone, his two wish-bones. A man called Stan Bussy would not be playing for the Arsenal on Saturday, and their forward line was likely to suffer in consequence. If he got a taxi from Paddington, which was unlikely, he would be home in twenty minutes. STOP PRESS was a blank. BIMBO PADS are very good for corns. They should be in Paddington in two hours. One hundred and twenty minutes plus twenty equals one hundred and forty. He glanced across to see if the colonel was still busy with his arithmetic. He was not. Charles lent him his paper.

Leaning back in his corner, Charles closed his eyes and allowed himself the luxury of thinking about Louise. She was still in many ways a stranger to him, and his vision of her had something of the quality of a deserted garden; there was in her character that which reminded him of an old marble statue, seen through wild roses, shaded with ivy. The mystery had been there before their marriage, when she was to him a pathetic, lost girl who could comfort and warm him by her presence alone. For the twenty years before he met her he had lived a life almost ferocious in its solitude. During that time, which had started when his first wife, Helen, had left him, he had at first been desperately lonely, bitterly unhappy, sick and frightened from the other war. Slowly he had become accustomed to his way of life; he had even persuaded himself that his son Oliver was in some ways a companion. Yet when the second war began and he had become reconciled to the fact that he and Oliver were strangers, his knowledge of his solitude had returned, not unbearable as in the old days, not even particularly painful, but inescapable and depressing. The war had made his work seem futile, for Charles had never regarded chemical research as being of great importance to himself or anybody else, and it had made Oxford life a more irritating microcosm of a dying world than ever. It was then, at the beginning of the war, that he had met Louise.

When he first began to realise he loved her, he was perhaps more delighted at the rebirth of his own perished emotions than anxious that Louise should return his love. And when they were married he had been, and still was, so totally intoxicated by her beauty that he could hardly see their relationship without the distorting glass of physical passion. Indeed his passion was so primary an essence in that relationship that to extract it would have led to a false picture of their emotions for each other. Once or twice, when in the great happiness of his confidence and love he had been unwrapping for her the reticence of twenty years, he had thought to see a curious, uncomprehending, almost contemptuous expression in her eyes. Yet, when he looked again, it was no longer there and Charles kissed her and forgot. He loved her. He knew she was happy with him.

Charles had first met Louise Collins at Oxford at the beginning of the war. Her father had lived there. A vague man, with slight literary and scholastic interests, he had drifted towards Oxford as a youth at the turn of the century, his simple desire being to be left in peace, his modest ambition to be mistaken for a don. A quiet and amiable crank, he had spent his interminable leisure in proving that the English were really a Jewish tribe, and in vague studies connected with lost Atlantis. Had it not been for the war of 1914, doubtless he would have continued in these useful pursuits, possibly even branching out into spiritualism, until, in advanced old age, he became one of those pleasant elders who potter about Oxford streets poking at pieces of orange peel with thin walking sticks.

The war was too much for Collins' simple mind. Suddenly, in 1914, he found that the whole nation had become as he, logic had fled and sense been banished. Far from smiling condescendingly at his opinions concerning nomadic Israelites, hard-headed newspaper proprietors were now busy proving that the Kaiser was the Anti-Christ. Eccentricity had ceased to be eccentric. The man who had stood outside the circle found to his surprise that while he stood still the circle had moved, in-

deed jumped, and like one of those rope rings in a deck game
had landed over his head to surround him. It was his hour.
Without a moment's hesitation he joined the army; and the
army, with equal alacrity, shipped him off to France. In Le
Havre he met his bride, the daughter of the proprietor of the
Café des Deux Pêcheurs. She was a formidable young woman,
and she married him quickly. In 1919 Mr. and Mrs. Collins returned to Oxford. In 1921 Louise was born. The next year
poor Collins died of an overdose of war, love, and eccentricity.
It was a minute and perhaps even an absurd speck of tragedy
in that first giant upheaval of Europe. Collins died with the
words, "My work is not completed" on his lips. He was a harmless man to be caught up in such a buffeting. He left everything
he possessed to his widow. She was delighted to receive it.

When the war of 1939 began, Louise and her mother were
still living in the musty red house in the Banbury Road. Louise
had grown into a self-contained, slightly nervous, but wilful
young woman. She had few friends. Her contemporaries in
North Oxford, the smiling daughters of dons, were, to her,
uninteresting with their pink pullovers and their mouse-like
whisperings of university gossip. Had she so wished, Louise
could have enjoyed considerable popularity with the undergraduates, for she was a very pretty girl. But her character
was such that most of the young men she met were frightened
of her. There was in her carriage a quiet purpose, a smooth
consciousness of her white body beneath her simple, elegant
dress, that made innocent familiarity impossible. A healthy
young man who had invited her to tea or taken her in a punt
on the Cherwell usually vowed that it was an experience he
would never repeat. His amiable attempts at wit were received
with the full seriousness of her dark blue eyes, and his proud

powers of conversation died away, wilting into a little trickle of "you see" and "don't you think" and "I mean," while she watched him with those great eyes, unwilling or unable to do anything to disperse his embarrassment. It was not that Louise desired in any way to spoil the young man's pleasure, and indeed, if fortified by a glass or two of light sherry, he should attempt to kiss her, she permitted it coolly, as responsive as the ivory her skin suggested. One kiss was usually sufficient. After an afternoon with Louise he returned with relief to the golden tennis-girls of Lady Margaret's Hall, the big puppy-playmates created for his slapping embraces and laughing experiments. And Louise, too, returned to the ugly red house in the Banbury Road, puzzled by the young man's embarrassment and his desire to appear so amusing.

"Tu t'es bien amusée, Louise?" her mother called from the drawing room after one such afternoon.

"Merci, Maman."

"Alors dépêche-toi. L'abbé Stephenson vient diner."

As Louise combed her hair before an open window on that hot summer evening in 1939, preparatory to a dull dinner with Father Stephenson S.J., she thought vaguely about the young man in the punt, whose face she had already almost forgotten. A weary disappointment and unconscious boredom seemed to lie on her shoulders like a heavy shawl. Yet the evening with Father Stephenson was not dull, for he had brought a friend to dinner, a young man called Roger Peacock. It was through Peacock that Charles and Louise had met, some six months later.

Peacock was a friend of Charles' son, Oliver, a friend more by accident than by design. They had been at the same college at Oxford, where they had had a number of acquaintances in common. They had both taken their finals in the summer of 1939 and in December of that year they were both at Sandhurst. When Peacock told Oliver that he intended to go to Oxford for the weekend to see Louise, Oliver, after a vain attempt to persuade him to go to London instead (Peacock owned a car), accepted his invitation to accompany him. For a number of mixed reasons—because it was almost Christmas, because he expected to go overseas soon, because he was broke—Oliver wrote a postcard to his father to say he was coming. Charles received the news without enthusiasm, divining at least that Oliver was broke. He looked out of the window into the Fellows' Garden where the sub-warden walked alone, avoiding the lines between the paving stones. It would rain soon. With a sigh he wrote down on a piece of paper, "Saturday, Oliver."

For Charles did not enjoy the company of his son. His marriage with Helen had been a time of disillusionment culminating in acute unhappiness. After she had left him he had sent Oliver to live with his cousins, while he, withdrawn from the world, tried to protect himself from his unhappiness behind a wall of reticence and hard work. For several years he had lived alone in London, deliberately discouraging intimacy in his associates, avoiding any relationships that might entangle his emotions. Yet by nature he was not a recluse, and when his son began to grow up, and Charles had moved to Oxford and a life of apparent peace, Oliver had come back to live with him. By then the gap between them was too wide. Oliver was ten, but with opinions and sensitivity developed beyond his years. Charles' fingers had grown unaccustomed to the common coin of human intercourse. His manner was inevitably stiff, and when he tried to counteract this he appeared patronizing. Had Oliver made the effort doubtless he could have bridged the gulf that lay between his father and himself. The effort seemed to him not worth the making. They drifted further apart, a vague antipathy between them, until, when Oliver was fourteen, a crisis had occurred and they had become strangers to each other.

During this visit, however, Charles was determined to be agreeable to Oliver. He did not expect to see his son very much over the weekend, and he had decided that when they did meet it would be better to do so on ground of Oliver's choosing. He knew that Oliver disliked the atmosphere of his senior common room and the company of the self-opinionated moles who inhabited it. He therefore invited him to dine at the Randolph Hotel, extending the invitation to Peacock, should the latter wish to come. Charles and Oliver had seen little of each other during the time the latter had been an undergraduate, and Charles had never met Peacock.

The Oxford streets were crowded that evening as Charles made his way to the Randolph. The vanguard of the London refugees had already arrived, and most of the university was still in residence. The Randolph, too, was crowded. There was no seat in the hall, and the lounge or drawing room was entirely occupied by the very aged, each one bolt upright and rigid in his hard chair, like the dead kings of old Peru. Still looking for his son, Charles made his way into the crowded bar. Oliver was standing alone in the corner, leaning one shoulder against the wall, his glass half tilted in his hand, staring with somewhat insolent eyes at the noisy drinkers. Charles had almost touched him before Oliver became aware of his presence.

"Oh, hello, Father. Beastly in here isn't it?"

Charles had expected Oliver to look as ragged and dirty as when last he had seen him, but apparently the O.C.T.U. had made him tidier, for his uniform was clean and pressed, and his hair was cut short.

"Peacock's coming in a minute."

Charles was slightly annoyed, although it was at his suggestion that the stranger had been invited. Oliver got him a drink, and they stood together, waiting. The acute discomfort of the place—people were continually banging into them, or waiters pushing past—combined with the imminence of Peacock's arrival, made it impossible to have any but the most disjointed of conversations. Charles suggested that they try to find somewhere to sit, but Oliver liked standing at the bar and so there they remained. The barmaids scurried backwards and forwards, slopping beer and handing out wet change. Oliver drank quickly, one pink gin after another. Men in overcoats pushed between them:

"Excuse me."

"I'm *so* sorry."

"Oops! I'm afraid I've spilled some on you."

Charles accepted all this as part of the pleasure of drinking in public. He was beginning to wish he were back in his college. But when a man knocked a little beer over his son's sleeve, Oliver did not accept his perfunctory apology so easily:

"Then why the hell don't you look where you're going, you bloody fool."

Oliver was handsome in a swarthy flamboyant way. His features resembled those of his father, save that whereas Charles' were softened by his slightly puzzled look, Oliver's were uncompromising. They were both big men with big features. Oliver's hair was jet black, while his father's was a thin mousy colour, and his head in profile was that of a self-indulgent Dante.

Charles was surprised by the appearance of Peacock,

because, foolishly enough, he had half expected him to look like Oliver. Instead, Peacock was short and blond and fat. He seemed to run into the bar.

"Hello, Oliver, you dear old drunk. Louise and I are simply panting for a drink, aren't we, *sweetie*. My dear Oliver, you'd never believe it, we've been half over England, miles and miles and miles, and just a bottle of tin-top for lunch and a little drop of whiskey in the back of the car, haven't we, *sweetie?* We went to see Lady Cranberry or whatever that cow at Henley is called, and she gave us nothing but tea, the old bitch, and the questions she asked, didn't she, *sweetie?* Nosy? Old Dr. Freud isn't in it. So Oliver, my dear, two double whiskeys quickly, right away please—or, no, listen, make it four, it's so much easier. You do want whiskey, don't you, *sweetie?* But Oliver, which of all these dons is your dear papa? Surely not the old one with the white beard whispering heaven-knows-what to the page-boy?"

Oliver looked at Peacock with amused contempt.

"Father, this is Peacock. Don't bother about what he says. He gets it all out of a book. For some reason or other he thinks it makes him sound like a gentleman."

"Really Oliver, you're as bad as Lady Blackberry." He did not stop talking as he shook hands with Charles, but addressed his remarks to him instead of to Oliver. "The questions, you've no idea. When was I getting married? Was I in the Rifle Brigade? How should I know? How was my dear sister? I was tempted to tell her, but then I remembered what they say in the army about dragging a woman's name in the mud in the mess or something. Well!"

At this point Oliver attempted to introduce Charles to Louise, but the introduction had to be postponed while a boot salesman in an ulster pushed between them and ordered eight different sorts of drinks. Peacock insisted on doing the introductions all over again after Oliver had finished.

"My *sweetie*, this is Oliver's father, Professor Monroe. Père et fils, isn't it charming? And this delightful young lady is named Miss Louise Collins, to whom I have given my heart. A common name, Professor, but an angel none the less."

She disengaged herself from the arm which Peacock had put around her waist (he was the same height as she), and shook hands carefully with Charles. Peacock drank all four of the double whiskeys, and by the time they reached the dining room was obviously drunk.

The dinner was not a great success. The dining room was cold, dank and silent, although all the tables were occupied. The surly waiter, who according to Peacock was a retired private detective who had trailed his father for years, padded about carrying tepid lumps of white fish and small pieces of hairy chicken. Peacock talked incessantly in a very loud voice, swearing frequently. Charles did not wish to restrain him, and indeed doubted if he could, but he was not unconscious that the wife of the Sub-warden of his college was making a mental record of the whole business from the next table. Louise plainly was not listening. Oliver seemed faintly amused.

When the chicken came, Peacock wanted to send it back.

"My dear, it's uneatable. It's like chewing on a very old hairbrush. No, no, Professor Monroe"—Charles was not a professor, but Peacock refused to believe this—"I won't have you dear dons martyrised by these desperadoes. Waiter!"

There was no alternative but to let the dreary exhibition run its course. The waiter came, the headwaiter. More chicken was produced and as rapidly was sent back. Peacock wanted to see the manager. The headwaiter said the manager was out.

"You stupid old man, get the manager. Christ, I know there's a war on too. Do you think I wear these dungarees for fun? Get your bloody manager."

"Roger, please be quiet." This from Louise. Charles felt intensely miserable. Oliver tipped back his chair and watched.

"I don't give a damn where he is, get him, you silly turd."

"Peacock, be quiet. Miss Collins is here." This from Charles.

"Louise doesn't mind, do you, *sweetie?* The darling little bitch is used to it."

Louise got up and walked towards the door. Peacock looked after her in surprise.

"Stupid little whore. How I hate the lower middle classes. Now you . . ." He had turned back to the waiter. Oliver tilted his chair back further still. Charles got up and ran to the door after Louise.

He caught up with her in the corridor, and apologized for his guest's behaviour. She did not seem to hear him. When he asked her if he could give her dinner at the George instead, she refused. She only wanted to go home. He walked out with her, silent in the rain to the cab-stand in the Broad. They sat side by side in the cab without speaking during the vast length of the Banbury Road. When they reached her house he apologized again.

"No, no," she said, "please don't feel that way. It wasn't your fault at all. Besides I rather enjoyed myself."

Yet, when the driver turned on the light in the taxi, he saw that she had been crying.

He drove back to the Randolph. Oliver and Peacock had gone. He apologised to the waiter, and then sat down in the

· 17 ·

hall, hoping that Oliver would return. He did not, nor did Charles see him again that weekend. Such was Charles' first meeting with Louise.

Sitting in the corner of the railway carriage, watching the flickering ribbon of occasional lights that glistened in the damp countryside, Charles remembered the empty weeks which followed his evening at the Randolph. It was then that he had first become fully aware of loneliness, of the involuntary loneliness of middle-age, so different from the deliberate painful hiding of youth. The suspicion that he was nothing to his son, save a faint pitying responsibility and a possible source of checks, then became a certainty. He had had few illusions about Oliver, yet he had always hoped that as he became older Oliver would become less savage. Charles still remembered the gentleness of his own upbringing, the kindness which was so obvious and everpresent that he had himself reacted against it and thrown it aside. He and his generation had decided that sentimentality was odious; yet now he hoped that something of that contemptible weakness might appear in Oliver. During the winter and early spring of 1940 he realised that he had been deluding himself, that Oliver's hardness was in no way a pose, as his own might have been. This discovery was painful to him, but far less so than another realisation which followed closely after the first. When, in March, Oliver's regiment went to France, Charles found that he had no reaction whatever. He had assumed that he loved his son, but when that son went away, possibly to be killed, Charles was quite unmoved. Indeed it was in some ways a relief to know that the boy was gone. As though he were standing at the rear of a ship, sailing off to sea, Oliver had been the last piece of the vanishing continent which remained above the horizon, the final lightship behind which lay the once familiar land and Helen with her new American husband and his childhood and the other war. The lightship had sunk behind the skyline. Charles was left alone, really alone now, and without choice.

To have no one to care for him, that Charles had understood, and had indeed come to expect. But to find that he loved nobody, that no one's happiness or even existence was of the slightest importance to him, this was a disconcerting discovery. It was as though he had been standing in a room full of people, at a cocktail party perhaps, laughing and talking, and unperceived by him they had all gradually slipped away, until of a sudden he was aware of his own voice re-echoing with unnatural loudness from the far end of the empty room. He had no God to believe in, nor did he attach any mystical importance to the advancement of science. His work was, at best, the harmless and interesting solving of a series of problems; from all other aspects his chemical research merely lengthened, a little, one of the paths that lead into the jungle of disconnected and explosive facts where hides contemporary knowledge. What was the purpose then of his life? He knew the obvious answer, that his work was its own reward, but he was sure that that reward was miserably insufficient. Yet, of course, he continued as before. The thought crossed his mind that he might leave Oxford. It would be a relief to be free of the burden of politeness and pretended dignity. He would like to go, but he made no effort. He had been a don so long that he had become one. He felt empty, almost unhappy.

He had seen Louise once or twice in the street, and had raised his hat to her. Shortly after Oliver's departure he was walking down the Broad one morning when he met her coming towards him. It was in front of the Sheldonian, below the

Roman Emperors, that they met. Charles intended merely to say good-morning and walk on. The memory of the evening at the Randolph annoyed him, and since he associated Louise with it, his feelings towards her were coldly embarrassed. He prepared to bow to her, when she stopped him:

"Oh, Mr. Monroe, have you heard from Oliver?"

"Oliver?"

He looked her full in the face, for the first time. He was conscious of the light beneath the white skin, the utter darkness in her blue eyes, her mouth painted like Chinese silk. Her whole face was so exactly delicate that it seemed almost unreal.

"Oliver?" he repeated.

"Yes," she said. "I heard he had gone to France. I wonder if perhaps you know where he is?"

"No, he's not allowed to say. I had a note from him about a week ago, though, and from what he writes it sounds as though he's somewhere in the north. He's not in the line anyhow."

"Oh, I'm so glad."

But she did not sound glad. Charles wondered why she should be so interested in Oliver. She seemed to divine his question.

"You see a friend of mine is in the same battalion."

Charles looked at her again. The precise tranquillity of her face, the quality which like sea-music had deafened him a moment before, was gone. She was a pretty girl asking about a soldier on a fine spring morning.

He invited her to drink a glass of sherry with him. As they walked along the Turl and across the quadrangle he began to wish he had not invited her. They walked in silence. He had nothing whatever to say to her, she apparently nothing to say

to him. In his rooms he poured out two glasses and leaned over
to poke the fire.

"Mr. Monroe?"

"Yes?" He looked up over his shoulder at her, from his
twisted position by the grate. She seemed very nervous. She
had drunk her sherry in one swallow.

"Mr. Monroe, how long do you think the war will last?"
Charles straightened himself and laughed.

"My dear Miss Collins, what a question to ask an old don
like me! I'm afraid I only know what I read in the papers. You
should ask someone who gets about in the world."

"I don't know very many people. I thought you would
know perhaps, because of Oliver. . . ."

She seemed desperately anxious, and Charles felt ashamed
of his evasive, mocking reply. Indeed he should know, and it
was perfectly reasonable of her to ask him, and smug of himself to boast a scholar's ignorance. But all he could say was:

"I'm not worried about Oliver. I'm sure it would take more
than a war to kill him off. God knows how long it will last,
though. Sir Wilfred Rumbold, the politician, lunched with me
the other day. He said that the government were not being
unduly pessimistic when they allowed for six years. But that
seems incredible."

"Six years. Thank you." Her face went blank again.

"That's only his guess you know."

"Yes, of course. I must go now, Mr. Monroe."

"But you've only just come in."

"Yes, I know, but I must go. May I call on you again?"

It was a natural enough request, yet Charles felt flattered,
for from Louise the question came oddly. Also there was an

underlying urgency in her voice. Charles' tone had been slightly flippant. He changed it and spoke seriously:

"Please do. Come anytime you wish. You'll always find me here after lunch. Please come whenever you feel like it."

He did not know what made him attach such importance to her simple, natural request, except that coming from her it sounded neither simple nor easy. And as from the window he watched her walk across the quadrangle, blown by the April gusts, he was surprised that he had so unquestionably fallen in with her mood of subdued hysteria. He shrugged his shoulders slightly as she disappeared through the big grey gates. Two weeks later the German armies attacked in the West.

As soon as he heard from Oliver he wrote to her:

> Gloucester College,
> 13 June 1940.

Dear Miss Collins:

I received a letter from Oliver this morning. He arrived back from Belgium two days ago, and I am glad to say that he is all right. But I am sorry to have to tell you that Roger Peacock and Harry Tennant, whom perhaps you also knew, were both killed. Oliver wrote only a postcard, and if I hear more about these tragic things I shall write to you again, should you so wish.

> Very sincerely yours,
> Charles Monroe.

She came to see him again that afternoon. He was about to go for a walk, when he heard her foot on the stairs. He opened the door before she reached it.

"I was just going for a walk, Miss Collins. Would you care to come with me?"

They were out of the college and a few yards along the Broad before she spoke.

"That's all you know about it, I suppose—what you wrote me in your letter?"

"Yes, that's all Oliver said, just that they'd been killed."

He knew that this pluralization of Peacock was absurd, but he would not intrude.

"It was kind of you to write and tell me."

After a pause she asked:

"Where is he now—Oliver, I mean?"

She walked with her head lowered, not looking at him. He had to slow down in order not to hurry her.

"At Tidworth. At least that's where the postcard came from."

They turned into the front quadrangle of St. John's. The golden baroque stone was marvellous in the sunlight, four-square and solid in its certainty of moral values.

"Do you think I can go and see him?"

Charles looked towards her, but she kept her eyes on the ground.

"I don't see why they should stop you."

"I must know, you see."

They were in the garden now, and he turned to the left toward the rockery. She looked up at him.

"I think I loved Roger Peacock and he was going to marry me after the war."

Charles mumbled something and led her to a bench half shaded from the brilliant sun by a sweeping elm. The situation had become unreal to him, a half tragedy in this baking afternoon. She thought she had loved him—surely a strange way to speak of a lover just dead. The silly face of Peacock, too, kept interfering in his mind. How could he be connected with death and the tragedy of Andromache or Cressid? Yet Charles knew his prejudice to be false. Hamlet can be fat, and Romeo has worn a beaver hat.

"Louise, I hope it hasn't hurt you too much." A stupid thing to say, but she did not seem to think so. She looked at Charles puzzled.

"That's what I can't understand. It doesn't seem to have hurt me at all. If I were unhappy, I'd know, wouldn't I? I mean, I might be numb and not realise for a little while, but I would know if something awful had happened, wouldn't I?"

Charles said nothing. Would she? How could he tell? He would. He had known at once when he received that note from Helen, before he had even opened it he had known the awfulness. Would she? He supposed so.

"And yet," she went on, "I was half expecting it, this or something else. Perhaps this is best for me, but they shouldn't have killed him."

Charles bent down and picked up a twig.

"They should have just taken him away, not killed him," she went on. Her voice sounded quite flat and rather loud.

"Did you want to marry him?"

"Yes."

She paused.

"But if he were alive after all, if Oliver had made a mistake, and he were still alive, I don't think I'd marry him now."

Charles understood then about women who are booty in war, about Trojan women happy with Greek husbands, Sabines with Romans. Louise was looking straight ahead at two butterflies playing above a flower. He wondered if she understood too.

"Does your mother . . ." he began.

"I never told my mother about Roger. I shall leave Oxford now and go to London for a while, but first I must see Oliver at Tidworth. Mr. Monroe, is it unnatural for me to feel so heartless about poor Roger?"

"Yes I think it is," he said, "but I do not think that you are to blame or can in any way change that."

"I suppose I always expected it," she said, "I suppose it's going to happen to all the women in the world now; their lovers will either be killed or else they will almost despise them."

She looked at Charles and half smiled.

"I don't think it will be as bad as that," he said.

She stopped smiling.

"It is bad, isn't it?"

"Yes, very." They sat in silence for a few minutes. Then he said:

"Louise, will you write to me from London?"

"Yes, I will. Thank you, Mr. Monroe, for listening to me. I'll write to you, or come and see you."

They walked out of the garden, back through the unchanged yellow quadrangle. Louise left him at the gate. Charles walked slowly back to his college. He felt unsatisfied, as though he had failed Louise. He wanted to go back and find her again and tell her all the little he knew of the brutality of emotion. But he did not. He waited, through the summer, the hope that he would hear from her fading, while his memory of her became closer and more intimate. In the winter she wrote to him. A little over a year later they were married.

Seated now in the corner of his railway carriage, Charles stirred with unease at the memory of that remote garden conversation, the conversation which had formed the first basis, the substratum, of their understanding and love for each other. The emotions of that summer of 1940 had not become false, but they were perhaps unique, unrelated. And yet in some ways Louise's generation had been born for nothing else.

The colonel across the compartment handed back the newspaper. It was folded so that a single word of exaggerated destruction blared at him from the headline.

"Thank you very much," said the colonel.

"Not at all," said Charles, with a polite smile.

The train gave a loud hoot, and shot under a bridge. They were entering the outskirts of London.

CHAPTER TWO

THE engine slowed down outside the station, gradually coming to a grinding stop. The train rattled for a moment as it came to rest. Up in the front, by the engine, the driver knocked the dust off the palms of his hands and began to pick his teeth in a nonchalant manner. Blankly the passengers looked at each other and out of the windows onto the darkened tracks. It was very quiet until, forty yards away, a tube train skittered past showing little streaks of light through its imperfect blackout. Charles tried to see his unilluminated watch, annoyed, resentful. Sometimes, he had heard, they stopped like this for an hour or even longer, just outside the station, a few yards from Paddington, a long second in his life away from the waiting taxi and the warmth of home. Another tube train went by and another, and between them rose the hum of blackened, dirty London, washing like the waves of a stone sea, waves reaching out from the bright glass in the standardised pubs, from the night factories, from the big buses crawling between the changing traffic lights: and between the waves came the little inaudible ripples of sound, from the small box-like rooms where millions go on living despite war, from the men standing smoking at street corners, from lovers kissing damply at the edge of the park, from the newspapers blowing down the streets, and the rotten fruit lying in the gutter. Then the tube rushed by again and London was blotted out. Slowly the train started, crawled into Paddington Station and came leadenly to a stop under the hysterical blue lights.

As Charles walked down the platform, pulled over a little by the weight of his suitcase, he could feel the grime under his fingernails, the thin layer of dirt squashed between his gloves and the skin of his hands. This dirt had been with him for hours, but it was Paddington that made him conscious of it, for in Paddington, like a corpse under a glass sheet, lay the memory of the lonely years after Helen had gone.

Sick, poor and unhappy, he had started to study chemistry at London University, living alone in an ugly room in Bayswater near Paddington. That was the station where, in the old days, he had caught the train to Gloucestershire and to Helen, and it was to that station that Helen had gone when she left him. It was cramped with memories. Charles, when he had lived nearby, had worked with frenzy, forcing his mind to master the strange subject which he had chosen because of its strangeness, because there was nothing in chemistry which would make the ghosts walk. Seven hours, eight hours, twelve hours a day he had spent at the University or reading in his room, until the stiff sentences became meaningless, until the equations, the formulae, the laborious explanations of quaint phenomena had made his mind limp as a storm-racked ship coming to anchor. Then, with a certain pride in his day's work, he would go out, to a pub perhaps, for he avoided his club, or for a walk, or occasionally to a music hall. He would be tired and contented until, as he sat alone or listened to the polite and boring in-discretions of a stranger, the achievement of the day would dis-appear, and the old nightmare would come crawling back.

Always during those first three years after Helen had left him, his way had led back through Paddington Station. And always in Paddington came the recurring question: where was Helen? It was eight o'clock. She was perhaps sitting down to dinner, smiling at some stranger, a blank egg-face across the table from hers; and as she smiled in Charles' mind, her face, too, faded away and only the consciousness that she was no longer for him had remained. It was half past ten as he walked back through Paddington from a theatre, and where was Helen? In somebody's flat, where the egg-faced man was un-buttoning her dress and she was saying, "Darling. . . ." Then Charles had to force himself to look at the people hurrying down side streets. He would try to remember anything, any-thing he could, the paradigm of a Greek irregular verb, the date of the battle of Lepanto, the names of all his platoon sergeants in France, but there at the back of his mind was "Darling . . . ," and he knew that he would have to think about it all, all of it, every horror, every corrupt debauch of his imagination, every past humiliation, until that "Darling . . ." had become unreal, until that gramophone record had been worn smooth. And the next day, when he had worked until he could work no longer, then it would be a new jealous record of misery to be played over and over. That had happened twenty years before, in and about Paddington. That was why he felt the dirt under his gloves as he walked towards the telephones.

In the dark corner, only faintly lit by the distant blue lights, the half dozen phonebooths were full, while outside two soldiers waited, shapeless in their greatcoats and equipment, leaning on their enormous dufflebags. The faces of those within the booths were just visible, a faint smudge of white, moving, talking, listening. An old woman came out of one box, a string bag in her hand, muttering to herself in some foreign tongue. The tense feeling went out of Charles, the mysterious figures telephoning became merely the usual handful of shoddy individuals clogging his way in wartime London, queuing for a bus, blocking up the exits, shouting for taxis. A minute or two more and he was in a booth, but when he dialed his number it gave the busy signal.

He had made no allowance for a busy signal. He had been prepared for almost anything else, for Louise to be at home alone, to be in Oxford, to be away. He was even prepared in theory for some absurd sort of Maupassant situation. Now he was confronted with an unexpected vision of Louise sitting in the yellow armchair, telephoning, probably with a cigarette in her hand. Telephoning and smoking. The two dull actions, superimposed over his desire to be with her, calmed him, brought back that banal element in their relationship which he had forgotten during the weeks in Italy and the journey home. He pressed button B; the pennies dropped noisily; he waited for the ticking in the earpiece to stop and dialed his number again. It was still busy. He walked out of the phonebooth and checked his suitcase at the luggage room. With his little canvas bag containing his night things in his hand, he went back to the phones. After waiting a few moments he dialed the number again. It was still busy. This was becoming absurd. Either Louise was having a very long conversation or else she must be telephoning everybody she knew. He shrugged his shoulders slightly, faintly contemptuous of Louise and her telephone.

With an unwitting feeling of superiority he went to the buffet.

The bar was crowded and there were no spirits. Charles bought himself a light ale and leaned resignedly against an imitation marble pillar. To whom could Louise be telephoning? Her mother perhaps? The thought of her mother exhausted him, that caricature of Louise. Madame Collins' empty chatter, her eternal preoccupation with the comme-il-faut, table napkins, calling cards, gloves to match shoes, her vacuous mind. Sometimes in moments of unkindness, he wondered whether Louise's reticence, her apparent tranquillity, masked any more profound feeling than was revealed by the superficiality of her mother's frankness. The black and ivory image of Louise, which had been like a charm in the foreground of his mind when he stepped off the train, had vanished; so much had his mood changed. Charles gazed about him in an absent manner, observing the A.T.S. girls in their square mud-coloured uniforms, the pimpled soldier with the enormous yellow teeth drinking a furtive ginger ale, the crowds pushing through the swing doors, men wiping their hands across their mouths, a poor squashed clerk reading the evening paper. Charles looked at them and suddenly felt old, too old to struggle through the crowd back to the telephone, too tired to face a homecoming to Louise and the inevitable small difficulties and emotions of their readjustment, too tired even to love Louise. He knew that this feeling would pass, for he had had it before. The knowledge did not make his discouragement any less real.

It had been a long journey, and his head was beginning to ache. He moved his shoulders heavily, leaning back against the pillar. His momentary, tiny loss of faith in Louise exacerbated him. He felt irritated with his own weakness. Why should he suddenly have a *volte-face* of that sort beyond his control? It was something in his mind that happened like a little land-slide; a mental boulder became loosened and went careening down into some distant valley in that deserted part of his brain where the pine-trees and the prickly pear grow. But this was nothing, this momentary annoyance with Louise and her mother. It was almost gone already. Still, he would stay in the bar for a minute or two. He glanced round again.

The soldier in the corner reminded him of Oliver. Oliver had presumably gone to India by now. Charles was relieved to think that he had gone, even though he had seen very little of him since he had married Louise. She did not care much for Oliver. He seemed to embarrass her a little, for he apparently regarded their marriage as something of a farce. The first time they had seen him after their marriage, Oliver had got drunk and made a number of pointless, sneering remarks about his pretty step-mother and evergreen hearts. Charles was glad now to see Oliver so seldom. It had become difficult for him to see any connection between the leathery, sardonic army officer and the little boy he had tried to love ten years before. That little boy had perhaps existed, but Charles had never really known him. For the first three years after Oliver came back to live with him at Oxford—until the school speechday—they had played, rather half heartedly, at being father and son. After that speechday they had both silently given up, first Oliver then Charles. From that time on Oliver had ignored his father, and had finally stopped even being polite. Charles' mind went back to the day at the school. That had indeed been a mental land-slide; this little pique of annoyance with Louise and exhaustion with himself was nothing by comparison, nothing at all.

It had been a hot June day in 1931. Oliver had won a

prize, and his father had come to the school to see him receive it. Oliver was then fourteen years old.

The prizes had been handed out by a boozy, bucolic-looking peer. A number of inaudible speeches had been made. The O.T.C. had paraded, the parade being slightly marred by a false word of command which sent one platoon wheeling into the spectators. Lunch was a cramped, unsuccessful affair with much jelly and whipped cream. After the meal the gathering had drifted out to watch the cricket match. During lunch Oliver had suddenly seemed very grown up, almost the same age as Charles. His face already had a hard, lined look. His eyes, too, had become very bright, glittering light blue against his browned skin. Charles felt shy of his son.

They had sat in the shadow of the oak, on Charles' grey waterproof carefully spread against the latent moisture of the ground.

"Did you have a good trip, Father?"

"Not very, Oliver. America is a pretty difficult sort of place. I always feel a bit of a fish out of water there."

Oliver may have thought that his father was a fish out of water here too, watching a match as though he were looking at a water-colour. He said nothing. The afternoon was very hot. An occasional gust of wind could be heard, coming from afar, rustling from one scattered, full-branched tree to the next.

"Do you like this school, Oliver?"

Impossible question. He might as well have asked his son if he liked weather. The boy thought for a moment, almost decided to say what he felt about the school. But it was too hot.

"Yes."

They sat in silence. The click of the strokes seemed very distant to Charles, the white figures, running prettily between the wickets, very unreal. The murmurs of the spectators were polite and infrequent.

"Sanderson, he's in my house you know, hit a six right into the top of that tree yesterday."

Into the top of that tree. The words struck an echo in Charles' mind, a distant flash of light on the waters of memory. Painfully he searched for the elusive vision, and suddenly, painfully it was there.

The summer of 1918, when he had been on leave, was the last time that he and Helen had been happy together. Oliver was less than one year old. A hot day, like this, in the garden of the Gloucestershire house, and Helen had said:

"Sometimes I think that if you wanted to, you could jump right into the top of that tree."

She had turned and kissed him, and he knew for that moment that she loved him. He knew too that in a few days he would be going back to that frightful place in France where he was almost sure to die. Well, he had not died, nor had he ever jumped into the top of any tree. Helen had left him after the war. The marriage had been nothing but a sort of wartime loan from Helen to him. Before the war she had been a child, and almost as soon as the war was over she had gone. Perhaps women have a prescience as to mortality. Anyhow, Helen had picked a living one for the duration. A live one, but no high-jumper.

He looked at his son, half him, half Helen. Where was Helen's half, he wondered. But can one tell with children? He tried to remember what he himself was like at fourteen. It should be possible, yet only a random collection of incidents, meaningless, almost idiotic, remained. Half him, half Helen. Pavlov says environment counts most. In that case Oliver should be part him, part his cousins, no part Helen, but he's not. Perhaps Pavlov and those others are right for beetles and bugs and guinea pigs, but how can they know about human beings, how can they know as much as, say, Balzac? Yet that morning in Gloucestershire had existed. Charles moved uneasily.

Oliver knew that his father was looking at him. He wished speechday was over. It seemed so pointless to be sitting here with a bound copy of *Lorna Doone* under his arm, beside this intruder. His father in the holidays was a distant man, spending all the day away or in his study, and in the evenings listening patiently and politely to Oliver's little chronicles of birds nesting and rabbit shooting. But at school he became the symbol of freedom, of clothes other than this dingy blue suit, of swimming way out to sea, and of reading in bed as late as he liked. He became magnified into a way of life. By appearing at the school he brought the symbol somehow into disrepute. Not that Oliver was in any way ashamed of him. It was a purely personal, introspective, and indeed unconscious reaction.

Yet he had a certain measure of affection and a certain amount of respect for this cool and detached man. He was grateful to his father for not interfering. Although fortunate in that he lacked most of the ghastly shyness of early adolescence, he had enough of the pains of growth to realise that any probing into his being would be painful. And this his father spared him, largely out of a respectable indifference, partly for fear of what he might find there and the memory of Helen.

Oliver knew that he was deficient in that feeling of awed wonder which so many of his schoolfellows felt for their fathers. Richardson, for instance, whose father was a soldier, was forever inventing improbable anecdotes to illustrate Colonel Richardson's legendary courage and ability. Urquhart would talk for hours about how rich his father was, although if the truth be told, he was only a moderately successful stockbroker. Oliver never felt tempted to glorify himself by means of his father. In any case, his father's talents as a research chemist were not of the type that impress little boys. Furthermore Oliver felt sufficiently self-confident to stand up without any props. So he kept his father as a private symbol for himself. In the holidays he regarded him, with complete equanimity, as the man in the study, the source of good things, and occasionally as a friend. But here he did not know what exactly the relationship was. His father became a stranger, and therefore he wished the day were over before any incident should occur.

A burst of clapping cheered someone's century. The field returned to its bee-like humming.

"Would you like some ice-cream, Oliver?"

They got up, Charles leaning down again clumsily for his coat. Oliver was standing a little apart. The noise began at that moment and in a second the airplanes were overhead. There were nine of them, three groups of three each in a V formation, flying very low. They were jet-black without any markings whatever. Suddenly they appeared over the trees, their evil blackness filling the sky, their thundering roar killing all the living world. The helmeted inhuman heads of the pilots were visible, each staring straight in front during the few seconds that this alien black mass of noise tore through the silken air of summer.

Oliver saw them at the same moment as his father, and he felt the same cold touch of nervous agony. He was still enough of a child to look to Charles for reassurance in the face of this frightening explosion. His father, half stooped for his coat, had turned his face up towards the sky. Graceless in this twisted posture, his mouth open, his face bore an expression of complete and irresistible terror. Oliver had looked for support. He had looked to his father as the essence of his own stability. Instead of a man he knew or even a stranger, he saw this inchoate mask of emotion, of an emotion which he had been taught all his life to regard with contempt. With a rumble the planes were gone.

The cricket field reappeared, but shrunken to the size of a pocket handkerchief. The heat of the sun had become dull, almost unfriendly, the song of a distant blackbird loudly noticeable. Charles picked up his coat. His face was still very white.

"Well, Oliver, how about that ice-cream?"

Oliver said nothing as they set off toward the road. His father had more or less regained his composure, the habitual gentle distance which he put between himself and the world.

"Do you know what they were?"

"Yes," said Oliver, "bombers. Night bombers. That's why they paint them black."

The bar closed in upon Charles, but the cold terror and shame of that afternoon remained. He finished his beer and walked out again into the station, where a metallic voice announced the incomprehensible names of towns for which a steaming train was about to leave. Here in the station he was anonymous, anonymity the next best thing to death; out there, outside the great dark enclosure, he was expected to do something, to act, to comprehend the position of a middle-aged man with a young wife, of a father with a contemptuous, arrogant son, of a don whose words were anxiously listened to and often believed. Yet, who would believe him about the black airplanes? Now, perhaps, they would, now that the pretty toys were coming home, some would think they understood the superficial imagery, but all they would really understand would be their own fear of bombs. Even Louise would not understand, not now, and Oliver probably never would.

The phonebooths were full again. Charles watched them for a little while. Then he gave up. He walked out onto the arrival platform and immediately secured a taxi.

The mouldy old car turned round in its length and rumbled off. Going home. *Die Heimat.* He remembered the long column of German prisoners he had seen marching to work in the hot African sun, tow-headed and bronzed, singing of their homes, those wonderful soldiers' homes, unchanged since Caesar's legions tramped across Europe. Home, where the birds sing sweeter and the girls are prettier; home, where the wine is cool and the butter yellow, and the forests stretch away forever under the azure sky. Charles realised in the taxi how lucky he was. He was ten minutes from home, while the men with whom he had eaten yesterday had months or even years to wait, while those big Germans would perhaps never again hear *die Voeglein im Walde* of which they had sung. The consciousness of his luck and happiness was huge within him. And yet, he thought, he was complaining and grumbling and frightening himself with memories of ten or twenty years ago. The taxi honked

and turned down a side street. Charles held on to his little
canvas bag as though it were the symbol of his happiness.
In der Heimat, in der Heimat. He felt very excited as the
car entered the park.

Charles' mind habitually avoided the centre of his
thought. He stayed near the edges, much in the manner of a
timid man walking through a field full of cows or horses. Such
a man may know that he is not frightened of cows, that they
will not under any circumstances hurt him, yet he prefers to
remain near the hedge. Thus it was with Charles, who would
probably have acknowledged it. The biggest external phenom-
enon of his life—the series of wars—was a subject on which
he now had literally no opinion, except that he disliked it. He
could not bring himself to see the war as a clearcut issue, and
indeed the more he listened to other men's views the nearer he
stuck to his hedge. The desire for simplification which was
manifest in so much he heard, the war described as one set of
concepts versus another, seemed to him interesting but hardly
convincing. Nor could he explain it away satisfactorily as a
plot to cheat some group of society, nor as a crusade to destroy some concrete manifestation of evil, nor even as a huge
and pointless bonfire lighted by lunatic incendiaries. It was
just there, the war, smashing about in the middle of the field,
ferocious maddened herds stampeding up and down, bellowing
slogans, kicking up such a cloud of dust as to be almost in-
visible.

On occasions he had met men who were regarded, and who
considered themselves, as responsible figures in the activities
of mankind, men who talked of the affairs of humanity with
the prescience and certainty of a wholesale grocer discussing
figs. Facts they marshalled together, arranged, sorted out by

size and types; incidents, the characters of prime ministers
and presidents, accidental dislikes and unfortunate misunderstandings, all were accounted for and fitted into a pattern from
which came a program, a shifting and weighing on which was
based a continual course of action. Orders were given, heels
clicked, salutes exchanged, and dutifully masses of men walked
up gangplanks or queued for bread tickets. Charles, on the
rare occasions when he was privileged to listen to such men,
preserved a discreet and somewhat incredulous silence. He did
not actively dislike them, the iron-jawed air marshal with his
master bombing plan, the sharp-eyed economist who spoke so
glibly of starvation, but he found it difficult to believe in them.
Their interlocking minds, which by a careful pruning and
selection had become fitted together like shields, had no connection with his. Mass human activity seemed to be, in spite of
the master minds, fortuitous, and perhaps because of the
master minds, usually odious. He stayed near the hedge, near
the gate, and hoped that the cattle would not stampede in his
direction. He was a man without ambition or conceit.

His years of solitude in the twenties had accomplished
that which he had intended. He had become a successful
chemist, but this was merely secondary. More important, the
smashing chaos of his war years and the destruction of his
own life, when Helen had left him, had been hidden, a rubbish
heap behind the high wall of those lonely years, the plain even
ugly wall which he had built stone by stone, smooth and blank
as the side of a prison. When at last it was completed and he
felt the courage and ability to look over the top, he found
that the twisted metal and mountainous refuse had rusted,
subsided. The jagged edges had disappeared and only the odd
shapes and occasional protuberances of those green mounds re-

mained as an indication of what lay beneath. Yet when he built
that defence against the evil memories, he shut out the countryside as well. Beyond lay the golden fields, the fabulous brooks
of his childhood, the foxglove hollows of his early youth. Had
his been an introspective nature, had he not avoided the centre
of his thoughts, he might have been enabled to cover the painful memories as an oyster covers a pearl, but he could not.
He could only attempt to blot out, to shut away.

When he began to emerge from this prison of his own construction he was nervous, careful. He was still anxious to avoid
emotion, for he felt insufficient strength and, furthermore, he
was conscious that he had been a failure. Other men had seen
worse war than he, had been more thoroughly deceived and yet
had not collapsed, had at least not run away from human
intercourse as he had. Even a drunkard maintains his life as a
social man of sorts. Gradually, inevitably Charles had built
up a new background for himself to replace what lay behind
the prison wall. The old agony sank farther and farther out
of sight. Sometimes he did not think of Helen for a week. The
new war had not revived the old to any appreciable extent.
His second marriage had been so entirely different from his
first that so far as he was aware there were no hidden connections, no subterranean rivers.

The action of birth is presumably as difficult and painful
for a child as for its mother. Charles had attempted a second
birth and had largely succeeded, at the cost of considerable
suffering. The break in his life was not of course in any way
complete. Oliver remained, and much else besides. Yet in essen-
tials Charles had managed to withdraw himself, heal himself
without anaesthetics, and emerge again, a somewhat shaky
creature, a middle-aged newly-born. Once born again, as it

were, once married to Louise and engaged in the normal commerce of daily life, he still remembered those lurking monsters of long ago and he avoided them as best he could. Hence his refusal of ambition and his reluctance to identify himself with the emotions and beliefs of strangers, hence his determination to stay near the hedge.

In his relationship with Louise he had preserved a similar reticence. Although he had been as open with her as he could, although he loved her deeply and fondly and kept no part of himself deliberately aloof, yet somehow he had preserved the last drawbridge, had forbidden the final intimacy. Forbidden is too strong a word, for had he been capable of giving it to her he would certainly have done so, but he could not. He was compelled to keep some corners for himself. As a result he had towards Louise an attitude which was fundamentally a little detached, and this detachment, which was purely subjective, he used to prevent himself from seeing Louise too clearly. The edges around his vision of his second wife were faintly blurred and his doubts, which were slight, had no hard shadows. If he were almost an old man, almost a husk, if he were too old and tired for Louise—and she had never given him the slightest reason to suppose such to be the case—then he preferred not to think about it. And he did not. He preserved a considerable discretion towards her. For example he never asked her about her relations with Peacock or any other man. He had no wish to learn of her old emotions, although at times he was curious. He was still basically frightened, and, like some animals, when he felt fear approaching he remained motionless. With Louise he was happy, happy for the first time in many years, and he was determined to do nothing which could spoil that happiness.

As the taxi turned into the square, his happiness seemed almost tangible on the old leather seat beside him.

Charles and Louise had rented a small house at the end of a mews. Though called a house, it consisted in practice only of one long low room, for the ground floor was a garage which at present stood empty. Their part of the house contained a small hall downstairs and the big room upstairs which was divided in two by double doors, one part being used as the bedroom. Off the bedroom was the bath, off the drawing room the kitchen. The entrance to the mews was hard to find, for it lay behind an arch. The driver had difficulty and Charles had to shout directions through the glass panel.

As they drove up the short, cobbled street Charles looked up at the windows, but could see no light. This meant nothing in view of the blackout. He paid the taxi which turned and drove away. For half a minute, perhaps, Charles looked at his house before putting the key in the lock.

"Louise!"

The hollow cry fell through the empty house.

He turned on the light in the hall and hung his bag on the hook behind the door.

"Louise!"

He expected no reply, yet one was forthcoming. Far away on the other side of London, the sirens began to blow, faint and almost gentle at first, advancing with giant strides towards the yellow-lit hall where Charles listened.

He ran up the stairs and opened the door to the drawing room. The electric fire glowed a malignant red. He turned on the light and saw that the telephone lay on its side, off the hook, ticking. He replaced it. On the green mantelpiece the little china clock pointed at five to ten. The room was still impregnated with Louise's light perfume. On the low table by the sofa were two empty glasses, a bottle of gin, a bottle of Angostura bitters. The sirens were now blowing at full force, rocking the city with their hideous wailings.

Charles opened the door into the bedroom. It was not necessary to turn on the light. Across the bed lay a uniform, crumpled as it had been thrown, a battle-dress jacket and trousers with blue braces. Boots were at the foot of the bed. On the floor was an opened suitcase with a shirt trailing over the side, men's hairbrushes and a razor in the lid, a pair of khaki socks beside it on the floor.

The nearest siren had stopped. The noise was less deafening. Quietly, as though leaving a room where a corpse was laid out, Charles closed the door and went back into the drawing room. He stood still for a moment and then sat on the sofa. The sirens were fading away now, quietly dying in North London, sinking almost gracefully into silence. The last one or two could just be heard above the distant traffic. Charles buried his face in his hands.

CHAPTER THREE

WHILE Charles was telephoning at Paddington Station, Oliver and Louise were finishing their dinner at the Café Royal. Oliver leaned across the coffee cups and lighted her cigarette. She looked up at him over the flame of the match.

"I'm still surprised that you should have come to see me, Oliver."

"Are you? As a matter of fact I'm rather surprised myself. Shall we call it sentiment?"

"I don't see why we should."

He laughed.

"No, I don't either. Still, it was sentiment of a sort. Besides, I wanted to sleep on your sofa."

She settled back in her chair while the brandy was poured out.

"Charles will be sorry to have missed you."

Oliver tasted his brandy.

"Good brandy." And after a pause: "You don't really think that, do you, about my father?"

"In a way I do. Even if he doesn't seem to enjoy it when

he does see you. I think he'll be sorry if you should leave for India while he's away."

"Well, there's nothing I can do about it."

"No, of course not."

There was silence between them for a moment. The Café Royal was beginning to empty. Oliver and Louise were dining on the balcony and he looked over the edge.

"Do you remember Rivière?" he asked her. "I think he was a friend of Peacock's. He's down there."

She looked over the edge. The Frenchman looked up at the same moment, and, seeing them, waved. Louise remembered him faintly, something to do with an enormous luncheon party in Christ Church. Oliver was watching her as she stubbed out her cigarette.

"Louise, may I ask you an impertinent question?"

"I'd rather you didn't, if it's very impertinent, though I don't suppose I could stop you. What is it?"

"It's not very impertinent. I want to know if you like being married to my father.'"

She laughed at him, straight into his eyes.

"Really, Oliver, it's not a bit impertinent, but what a funny question. Of course I do. It's obvious. There's nothing *wrong* with our marriage, if that's what you mean."

"No, that's not what I meant, but let it pass. Cigarette?"

Louise saw that Oliver was annoyed with her, and felt that it was foolish of him. Did he expect her to discuss her intimate emotions as she had done once, that summer's day when she came to see him after Peacock's death?

"You know, Oliver, I've grown a lot older since that evening we spent together at Tidworth."

Oliver smiled.

"Three years and a bit. That's not a lot."

"You've grown older too."

"You're very perspicacious."

"You seem less . . . less harsh than you used to be. I think you have become kinder, perhaps."

"Louise, you mustn't become pompous with me. I asked you if you were happy with my father, because you've always interested me and because when you married him I thought you were both crazy. Now I want to know if I was wrong. I hope I was. But for God's sake don't give me a lot of nonsense about kindness and the Christian virtues."

"But, Oliver, those virtues mean a lot to me."

"They didn't use to."

It was Louise's turn now to get annoyed.

"You talk as though you'd known me intimately for years."

"So I have."

"You have not. Except for that afternoon at Tidworth we've hardly ever talked to each other."

"Perhaps not. But I was with Peacock a lot, you know, and he wasn't exactly reticent."

"Oh."

Louise looked wooden, which amused Oliver, so that his good humour returned. He thought of that afternoon, sitting in the corner of the dirty pub near the barracks, while she asked him about Peacock's death and they talked about the dead man. Oliver had never understood why he had portrayed Peacock to Louise as a better man than he believed him to have been, as a better man indeed than she had thought him to be. Louise, too, was remembering the dingy bar and her own voice going on and on about Peacock and love and death. Oliver had said little, and that little had usually been mere agreement with what she said, yet he had let her talk herself out of her first confusion. Remembering that afternoon she smiled at Oliver:

"Your father . . ." she began.

Oliver watched her, his hard face impassive. She tried again.

"After all, Oliver, you hardly know your father."

This was not what she meant to say at all. She had no intention of justifying Charles to his son. Indeed, what was there to justify?

"Why do you keep telling me I don't know people? I know my father well enough to feel there's not much more about him for me to find out. But it's not that I dislike him—as a matter of fact I rather like him—it's just that I don't understand why you married him."

"I married him because I was in love with him, and I still am."

"Louise, please. Let's leave the housemaid words out of it. I assumed you married him because you were lonely and tired of trying to be yourself in a world where everybody wanted you to be somebody else. Deep calling to deep . . . or not so deep."

"Did you?"

She had frozen again. Housemaid, indeed. Oliver took no notice.

"But what I can't understand is why, when a weak sensualist like Peacock was not strong enough for you, an equally weak recluse, ascetic, whatever you call him, like my father should . . ."

He was interrupted by a hand on his shoulder. It was Rivière.

"Mademoiselle Collins and Oliver, what a delightful surprise. I had no idea . . ."

Rivière was a sallow man of medium height, dressed in the uniform of the French airforce, much bedizened with Lorraine crosses. His voice was smooth, expressionless, his English as perfect as that of a B.B.C. announcer, an accent of such clarity and refinement as to be almost inhuman.

Oliver rose to his feet. Louise greeted the Frenchman affably. Oliver's voice assumed a malicious edge as he corrected Rivière.

"You are wrong, Rivière. I have the honour these days of addressing Miss Collins as Mama."

"I beg your pardon?"

"I lost a friend and gained a mother."

Rivière looked blank.

"I married Oliver's father," Louise said flatly.

"But how delightful!"

The three of them were caught in a strained silence, impaled on Oliver's disagreeable fantasy. Rivière would have asked about Peacock, had he not felt the question to be indelicate. Perhaps for this reason Oliver hastened to bring the subject up.

"Peacock was killed, you know."

Rivière's face assumed a mask of false tragedy. He had known Peacock slightly and had always somewhat disliked him.

"Oh, how very, very sad. I had heard nothing . . ."

Oliver watched him sardonically. Poor Rivière was embarrassed. He could hear his own voice pronouncing the platitudes apposite to death and bereavement, and he didn't know how to stop. Nor did he know where to look. Oliver was almost grin-

ning, and to address his condolences to Louise would be in
the worst possible taste. So he muttered on about "dear,
dear . . ." and how he had hoped to see Peacock, and . . . and . . .
Oliver cut him short.

"I don't see why you should be so upset about it. After
all he was no particular friend of yours." And then, as an
afterthought, "He was rather a beastly little chap, really."

This was altogether too much for Rivière. Changing the
subject hastily he talked for a moment about the war, invited
Louise and Oliver to join him downstairs, and went back to his
own table. From the balcony they could see him shaking his
head as he explained to his blonde companion the awkwardness
of his recent conversation. Louise and Oliver looked at each
other and burst out laughing simultaneously.

"Oliver, you shouldn't," she said, still laughing, "really
you shouldn't."

"Louise, my darling," he replied, "you shouldn't encour-
age me. You're a thoroughly bad influence on me and always
have been. Among other things you drive me to the bottle.
Waiter, two brandies!"

Before the drinks came, and before Oliver had a chance
to revert to the subject of Louise's emotions, she determined to
steer the conversation into new channels.

"You know, you have changed, Oliver. Perhaps it's the
fighting you've been in."

"You keep saying I've changed. You must be the sort
of person who tells children they've grown, even if they've
shrunk."

She laughed and felt relieved that Oliver had apparently
retreated.

"And anyhow I haven't been through a lot of fighting, as

you call it. I've either been in England or in Cairo and my
engagements have been remarkably unmilitary. Even if I had
been fighting I don't see that that could have changed me,
other than by blowing bits of me up."

She lit a cigarette and said:

"Like a duck to water?"

"No, not really, at least that's not the point. Of course I
dislike being shot at or being uncomfortable, although not
unduly. But that's nothing to do with it. It's that a battle is
incredible, and afterwards I don't believe it ever happened."

"How funny you should say that. Charles doesn't believe
in it either, even when it's going on, the raids I mean. A bomb
for him is like a noisy dog."

"He must be getting dotty then. I know what it's about
enough when it's happening. It's afterwards that I can't remember. Like making love. You know what it was like, but
you can't remember. At least I can't. A girl once told me
women do, but I don't believe they can either."

The waiter bringing the brandies and emptying the ashtray had overheard the last part of Oliver's remarks with
obvious interest. Oliver turned to him:

"Do you believe women can remember?"

"I don't know, Sir," said the waiter: "I'm Swiss." And
he walked away.

"We should have gone to the Grill Room," Oliver said.
"The waiters down there are more experienced."

He twisted his glass between his fingers and smiled at
Louise.

"Are you glad I came to see you?"

She looked at him quite seriously, almost sadly.

"Yes, Oliver, I am glad."

Oliver's face, too, had become serious, and she saw behind it that other face of his, one afternoon in the high summer of 1939.

They had gone out to lunch at an inn in the country, near Oxford, she, Oliver, Peacock and a girl called Annie. It was a few weeks after she had become Peacock's mistress. He was still living in rooms in the High Street, although term was over, and she had gone to see him one morning after breakfast. Peacock had already begun to assume a faintly contemptuous attitude towards her, which she realised later was a form of self defense. When she entered his room he was wearing a purple silk dressing gown, eating raspberries for breakfast.

He had not stood up when she came in. The sunlight poured through the window, almost tangible bars of light falling to form a square on the Persian carpet.

"Hello, Puss," he said. "Have some raspberries."

She sat down. Peacock was thinking of becoming a Catholic. He described a dinner party he had attended the evening before at which a monsignor had been present. Louise listened carefully. She was reluctant to speak for she could not understand Peacock's apparent enthusiasm for the church. To her the religion in which she had been brought up meant little; l'abbé Stephenson was not for her a solid rock on which to rely, nor had the Catholic chapels of Oxford ever seemed places of transcendent beauty. She had, under Peacock's auspices, read a book by Maritain. It had interested her, but was not relevant to Peacock or herself. While he talked on, becoming visibly irritated by her failure to show much interest in what he was saying, she thought to herself suddenly, He wants to become a Catholic because he is so ugly.

She laughed. Peacock stopped talking and frowned at her.

"I don't see anything funny in what I've been saying."

Her face became still again. She wished she had not laughed.

"No, no. It's just something that crossed my mind."

Peacock looked at her with distrust.

"In that case I shall leave you to your reveries. I'm going to shave."

He went into the bedroom. Louise walked over to the mantelpiece and looked at the Cocteau drawing which hung there, a Greek profile with a large eye and curly hair. Peacock had once told her that the line of the neck held all the tragedy of the romantic. She wondered what he had meant, if anything. A little Wedgwood bowl was filled with cigarettes. She was lighting one when the door opened and Oliver came in.

"Hello, Louise."

"Oh, hello, Oliver.'"

She still felt a slight embarrassment at being found alone in Roger's drawing room, even though Oliver usually ignored her. He appeared surprised to see her.

She said, "I didn't know you were still in Oxford."

"I'm not. I came up from London last night. Where's Peacock?"

"Shaving."

Oliver walked through to the bedroom. He left the door open.

"Hello, Peacock."

She heard Roger mumble through the soap.

"Have you got anything to drink? I've got a girl downstairs. She seems to have a hangover. I told her you'd have some champagne we could give her."

Peacock mumbled again and Oliver walked back through the drawing room and downstairs. Louise thought that perhaps she would go, but before she could make up her mind Oliver and Annie were back.

Oliver's introduction was odd.

"Miss Collins. Annie." Then he went over to the corner and began rattling bottles.

Annie was a yellow-haired girl with a big mouth and large breasts that bulged ominously through a black suit. She wore a lot of jewellery of which she seemed conscious, for she was forever twisting her rings or fiddling with her necklace. Her flesh looked slightly green through her dark brown make-up.

Oliver rang down for ice, but Annie insisted on drinking the champagne before it was cold. They put another bottle in the icebucket. After a few drinks Annie felt well enough to talk. She was on the stage. She knew a great many titled people to whom she referred first by their nicknames and later by their titles, sometimes even adding their claim to fame. Thus she described a visit to the "Nest" with Woozy who turned out to be the Marquess of Oakhampton, the famous foot-fetichist with a collection of over a thousand pairs of boots. Louise decided she liked Annie, for she was so clearly enjoying herself. She was the sort of girl who is always happy when drinking champagne.

They drank three or four bottles and all felt very cheerful and young. Peacock suggested they drive out to a little pub by the river for lunch. With much squealing from Annie, they got into the car and drove off. Annie liked being in a big car, but at the same time she wished it were small enough for her to sit on Oliver's knee. Peacock drove very fast and well. He acquired a kind of dignity from his car, and when he took his hand off the wheel to touch Louise's knee, she forgot his irritating affectations and warmed towards him. When they arrived at Minster Lovell, Louise smiled at Peacock before getting out of the car. She heard Annie chattering in the back, yet she knew that Oliver was looking at her.

The sun was hot now, blazing down on the little pub which crouched between the smooth green hills and the river. They had soon finished lunch and sat by the river drinking their coffee. Annie had become somewhat flushed. Louise closed her eyes and leaned back, listening vaguely to Peacock's voice. The heat lay like a blanket over the valley. The conversation became spasmodic. There were long gaps of silence, filled only by the murmuring of bees and the occasional splashing of water. In the distance a cow lowed. A door slammed inside the pub. When Louise opened her eyes she was alone.

She got up and walked to the wide balustrade at the water's edge. It was surmounted with stone gargoyles, crudely carved and worn away by many winters until they had become hardly recognizable. Lichen had taken root in every crack. She leaned back on the balustrade and looked towards the pub. Oliver came out and walked over to where she stood.

"Where are the others?" she asked.

"Gone for a walk."

"Shall we go and find them?"

"If you like."

They walked along the river bank, through the lush grass yellow with buttercups. Even the birds seemed oppressed by the heat. The path led through a little copse and then turned where the river turned, back into the meadows. Far away a hare scampered to safety. An old rowboat was tied to a tree, rotting in the river, three quarters filled with water. Peacock and Annie were sitting beside it on the bank. Annie waved to them as they approached.

"I want to go for a swim," Annie announced almost defiantly.

"Why not?" Oliver looked indifferent.

"Will you swim, Louise?" Annie seemed to be avoiding Peacock.

"I'll swim with you," said Roger and got to his feet.

"How about you, Louise?" Oliver asked.

"No. I don't like swimming in rivers."

"Neither do I," said Oliver.

Peacock had already begun undressing. He was soon down to a pair of yellow silk pants which made the rolls of flesh upon his belly look pinker and whiter than ever. His face, by con- trast, was a blotchy red. He stepped awkwardly down to the muddy river edge and waited for Annie. She took all her clothes off, hanging them carefully on the branch of a tree as though in a wardrobe. Her elastic belt had left a red ring around her hips. She stroked her flanks and stretched out her arms with satisfaction, delighted with herself, hoping no doubt for compliments from Roger or Oliver. The latter was light- ing a cigarette. Roger was feeling the temperature of the river with his toe. Annie walked down to the sunken boat, her body, unaccustomed to the lack of restriction, swaying heavily. Louise thought that the two by the water looked curiously self-conscious and unidyllic. Oliver echoed her thoughts:

"This sort of thing makes one understand what the missionaries meant about Mother Hubbards."

A scream from Annie broke the splash as Roger dived in. The boat lurched and they were both in the river.

"Shall we continue our walk?" Oliver asked.

Louise got up and they went on along the path. The splashings and Annie's shouts became fainter. They did not walk far, but the landscape changed with that suddenness which is one of the charms of England. From lush meadow it became moor, almost swamp, the home of plover and snipe. The hills closed in nearer the river, hills wooded with oak and snarled with bramble. Within a few hundred yards of leaving Roger and Annie they had traversed as many thousand years of history. This was the England which had existed before the Romans came.

Their path led towards the hills.

"Shall we take it?" said Oliver.

Louise looked back as they left the marsh. She could see a white shape on the river bank which must be Annie. Peacock was standing over her. She turned and they entered the wood. Her mind washed clean by the heat, conscious only of the slight sadness of the trees, she walked ahead of Oliver.

The undergrowth was less thick than it had appeared, with here and there a large boulder, moss-covered, lying among ferns. Ahead of Louise a wood pigeon rose from a high branch and disappeared, whirring. Louise stopped. Oliver was immediately behind her. She turned towards him to say something about the pigeon. He did not listen to what she said, but took her arm and pulled her towards him. She saw the hard blueness of his eyes.

"No!" she said, and twisted away from him. He frightened her, but she thought she was offended at being used in this casual manner, and she remembered the red line around Annie's big hips. She walked on deeper into the woods, Oliver's footsteps near and loud behind, the trees closing in like an enemy.

"Louise."

She stopped and turned.

"Come over here and sit down."

She followed him to a flat grey stone. There was a little open space before, covered with brown leaves, dappled with sunshine. Oliver looked at her intently and her feeling of fear was gone. She thought nothing. He would kiss her now. But he did not. He said:

"Not just a boozy afternoon, Louise. It's not . . ."

"I know, Oliver, but we mustn't. I mean, I mustn't. Besides . . ."

Surely now he would kiss her. He was staring at the ground between his feet. She leaned over and touched his sleeve.

"I'm sorry, Oliver."

Though for what she was sorry she would have been hardput to say. Oliver took her hand and kissed it. He got up from the stone and pulled her to her feet and into his arms. A loud crackling in the undergrowth made him let her go. A man with a gun under his arm was standing beside them.

They were trespassing. Feeling heavy and depressed, they retraced their path back to the dry marsh.

"We must go back to the others," Louise said.

Oliver took her hand again. She squeezed his before disengaging her own.

"Come on, Oliver." She looked up at him and tried to smile.

"Louise . . ." he said.

"No, Oliver, you see it can't be."

He said nothing and followed her back. Roger was peevish and cold. Annie's legs were covered with river slime. They all felt rather ill as they drove back to Oxford. Oliver and Annie returned to London that evening.

As she looked across the table in the Café Royal, it was his face as he pulled her towards him on the path that she remembered. The hardness of his eyes was the same, although they seemed less blue. The certainty in his face had faded a little, chipped a little perhaps. She had thought often enough of what might have happened had that gamekeeper not come. She was not going to think of it again now.

"Whatever became of Annie?"

Oliver must have been thinking of that same afternoon, for he answered immediately.

"She married a man called Williams in 1941 and was killed by a bomb three weeks later. So you see we're the only ones left."

She could not be sure if he meant what she thought he meant by that last remark. Also it was not true, since there were now others. Charles for instance, apart from whatever Oliver might have created. In any case she had no wish to follow Oliver's train of thought to its dangerous conclusion.

"Let's go and talk to Rivière before this place closes, shall we?"

Oliver had no desire whatever to talk to Rivière, but he knew that Louise had made up her mind. His annoyance returned, exacerbated by the brandy he had drunk. Why was she so stubborn? The problem which had periodically puzzled him during the past four years was as insoluble as ever. Why Peacock? Why Charles? She was as slippery as an eel about it. Still, there was nothing more he could say, up here on the balcony under the eye of the lurking waiter. He paid the bill and they walked downstairs together.

Rivière was pleased to have them join his table. He seemed to be having a heavy time with his companion, a blonde lady of

indeterminable age with a fixedly bright expression. He jumped
to his feet, made the introductions, sat down again, jumped up,
signalled to the waiter, and finally relapsed with a little sigh
against the red plush bench.

Oliver felt that the move downstairs had made a subtle
difference in the relationship between Louise and himself. On
the balcony they had been two people come together, facing
each other across a table. The strings of their past lives
stretched out behind them, directly away from each other. If
those strings had at one time been entangled, that entanglement
was distant and might have been forgotten. Here, downstairs,
they had come in together, a pair, a young couple. They were
on one side of the table, Rivière and his friend on the other.
Oliver glanced at Louise to see if perhaps any consciousness
of the change were visible on her face. There was none. She
had rested her chin in the palm of her hand, nodding her head
slightly while Rivière talked. The feeling of irritation which
had come over him upstairs remained with Oliver. Louise was
ignoring him, evading him.

Rivière was talking of the old days, parties and what not.
Oliver listened to the end of one sentence.

". . . and from those gay and carefree days came all the
heroism of Dunkirk and the Battle of Britain. The German
officers drilled and drilled, while the men who were destined to
beat them were drinking champagne and reading James Joyce
and voting for pacifism. Remarkably satisfying."

Rivière looked remarkably satisfied as he leaned back.

"James Joyce?" said Oliver incredulously.

"You know what I mean," said Rivière.

"I'm afraid I don't. And as for heroism, I don't remember
much heroism in 1940. A lot of confusion and exhaustion and

ignorance and fear. I don't know anything about the airforce, but the bit of the army I saw wasn't particularly heroic."

"But you were against such terrific odds, and you did make it," Rivière said.

"We were going home. We knew that and that's what kept us fighting. It was the only thing we had to hang onto in all the confusion."

Louise looked at Oliver coolly.

"I think you would refuse to recognize courage. It would be against your beliefs."

Oliver lit a cigarette. He saw an implied insult, for if he did not see visible virtue he was presumably duller than, say, Peacock or Charles, who doubtless reverenced the abstractions in their different ways. He remembered the dust and heat, the noise and the continual hot tiredness behind his eyes, the stench of the dead men and the dead cattle, the eternal marching in the noise and fly-blown heat. He had seen some men show remarkable powers of endurance. Louise had been cherishing the legend of courage, the myth of the lion. Now she was almost insulting him, insinuating that he was either blind or dishonest. All right. He flicked out the match and put it in the ashtray.

"I saw a lot of very strong emotions," he said; "and I saw some men who either through insensitivity or self-control seemed to have very few. I also saw one or two men perform crazy acts, while temporarily out of their minds. I never saw anything that fitted the newspaper idea of heroism."

He spoke deliberately, towards Rivière, "Did you?"

The question was rhetorical. He did not give Rivière time to answer.

"You may or may not know, but Peacock was made out to be a hero, to have died like Horatius on the bridge. I heard that they wanted to get him a Victoria Cross. With about forty men he held a key position against two German battalions for over twenty-four hours. They were bombed intensively and they went on fighting until they are believed to have had no ammunition left. Then he was killed. It's a fine story and, as I say, I don't see why they didn't give him a V.C."

Louise was looking at Oliver steadily. This was what he had told her at Tidworth. And of how the last time he had seen Peacock, when Roger was cut off and probably going to die, he had spoken to Oliver of her. She had imagined Roger transformed, with the expression which she had sometimes seen when he drove his big car very fast, the superficiality and self-ishness gone, as it had apparently gone from so many of that generation during their finest hour.

Oliver was talking carefully, making a pattern of wet rings with the bottom of his glass on the marble-topped table as he spoke.

"I saw him during the period of his heroic action. It didn't seem particularly remarkable to me."

"Why not?" asked Rivière's companion.

"I'll tell you what happened, if it won't bore you. You might like to know this, Louise." He looked up at her quickly, and then down to his glass again. Her eyes were fixed on his face.

"I was in charge of the carrier platoon at the time. There weren't any carriers left, so I didn't have much to do and the colonel was using me as a messenger. We were covering the brigade withdrawal and it was all very confused. One company had got lost, and the colonel was not sure where another of his companies had got to or if they knew their orders. That was A Company, the one Roger was in. The colonel sent me out to find them, and make sure they were in the right place and knew what they were supposed to do. I went a mile or so along the road towards where they should have been. There was a ruined farmhouse off to the right with a certain amount of shooting going on, so I went over to see who was there. I walked in through a hole in the wall and found Roger.

"He was sitting on a sofa, drinking out of a bottle. All the other officers in A Company had been killed or disappeared and most of the men too. He was sitting there with a platoon sergeant-major and another sergeant. I remember the sergeant-major was cleaning his brasses. It seemed rather an odd thing to be doing. Roger was fairly bleary and looked surprised to see me. He thought I was a ghost at first.

"We drank some brandy and I tried to tell him what was going on, but he couldn't really follow what I was saying and kept getting his map upside down. He was pretty drunk. So I got the P.S.M. to stop his fool polishing and come and listen. He kept saying, 'Yes, Sir!' and pretending he understood but I don't think he did. Roger sat on that busted horse-hair sofa singing a song about a woodpecker. When I'd finished, the sergeant who was there asked me if the Germans recognized a white flag as a signal of surrender. Roger woke up a bit at this.

" 'All these buggers want to do is surrender. I won't surrender. I won't.' He almost shouted it at me. I was afraid he was going to cry. The sergeant-major had gone back to his polishing and was starting on his boots. The other sergeant suggested I might like to go round the position. It all seemed strange and unreal. I was dead tired myself and everything looked flat. It felt like being on the screen of a movie instead of watching it. Besides there was an awful lot of noise. I followed the sergeant, I think he was called Manning, out into the little courtyard. He didn't want to go any further.

" 'It's the men, Sir,' he kept saying. 'They want to surrender. They don't think it's right, sitting here and being shot for no purpose. They say Mr. Peacock's a Jew and that's why he won't surrender, Sir.' I told him that to my certain knowledge Roger wasn't a Jew, and shut him up before he said any more.

"The soldiers looked sullen and frightened, but they cheered up a bit when they saw me. They had thought they were surrounded before I arrived. I told them a lot of lies about how the battalion was to attack in the morning and relieve them. I don't know whether they believed me or not. I'm sure Manning didn't.

"When I got back to the farmhouse, Roger was washing his face. He had pulled himself together a bit and wanted to know when he could withdraw. I had already told him it was the next night. Then he wanted to know if he could come back to battalion headquarters with me to get orders and leave the P.S.M. in charge. I told him that I had been sent up to give him his orders and that if he came back to battalion headquarters before his company withdrew I was pretty sure the colonel would have him shot. Our colonel was a rough fellow. This depressed him and he went back to his sofa and had another drink. Then he had an idea:

" 'Sergeant-Major!'

" 'Yes, Sir.'

" 'I want you to shoot the first man who tries to leave this position or surrender.'

" 'Yes, Sir.'

"I don't know what good Roger thought that would do, but it was no concern of mine. Sergeant Manning started to go out then. I called him back. I wanted to get out of this crazy place, but there was too much shooting going on.

"I sat down beside Roger and had a drink myself. He began talking, mostly about women, about how he loathed them for sitting on their big behinds in England and sending him out to France in an ugly uniform to get killed. It was all pretty incoherent and I didn't make much attempt to follow it. Then he began rambling on about the Catholic church and how he wanted to find a priest so that he could go to heaven when he was killed. But after a while he got confused about this too and said that the priests were as bad as the women, which was why they wore skirts, and that they were all in England sleeping with his girls and that they were killing him. Depressing stuff, and I wondered how long he had been talking like this. Quite a time, I imagine, because neither the P.S.M. nor Sergeant Manning bothered to listen. In fact the P.S.M. had gone to sleep, and I had to wake him up when I left. I took Manning with me, as I was sure he'd surrender right away if he stayed there, and I wanted Roger's company to go on fighting so we could get away.

"I don't know what happened after that. They held out for another twenty-four hours. Whether the Germans killed Roger or whether one of his own men shot him, I don't know. Anyhow I think he should have got the Victoria Cross."

He looked up from his glass. Louise had not taken her eyes off him while he had been talking.

"That's not what you told me at Tidworth," she said.

Oliver looked at her steadily.

"At that time I didn't think it was any concern of yours."

"Then why do you tell me now?"

"I've changed my mind."

Faintly they could hear the siren beginning to blow outside. The waiter came with the bill, and Rivière paid. Louise and Oliver were still looking at each other.

"You should have told me right away."

"Yes. I should have."

They got up and slowly made their way out into the foyer. After a certain amount of talk, Louise and Oliver decided to go to a small club in Chelsea, which was underground and which stayed open until twelve. The raids in the spring of 1944 seldom lasted more than an hour or two. Rivière said he would join them after he had escorted his lady to her door, provided the raid were not too severe.

They all walked along Regent Street together. The searchlights were crossing and recrossing in the sky. Rivière's friend found them very beautiful. Far to the south the banging of the anti-aircraft could be heard. The people in the streets were hurrying for home.

Oliver and Louise left the other two and walked down a sidestreet towards Piccadilly. Oliver felt all the annoyance and irritation gone out of him. In the Green Park a huge searchlight arched quickly in a giant curve across the whole sky, lighting up the dark buildings. The drone of aircraft was faintly audible as they hailed a taxi. They drove off.

CHAPTER FOUR

CHARLES sat on the sofa, smoking cigarettes. He would smoke one half through, stub it out, light another. The sirens had stopped, and London lay quiet, awaiting the bombers.

Jealousy grows like a tropic flower, a lush and highly coloured growth, stretching out strange tentacles from a pale centre. Roots feel down, grasping and curving at the deep stones, forcing a path through old rock-fissures, drawing new strength from long covered cesspools where old guilt and dead immodesties were once indecently interred. The roots inch out, sucking the long festered juices, the crapulous shames of childhood, the secretive haste of adolescence, the mean action in the corner of a foreign city. The fruit and flower is fed by the piecing together of the torn-up letter which lies among the apple cores and cigarette ash in the garbage can; sheets are examined for tell-tale marks; the furtive hand reaches behind the books, behind the crockery, behind the once friendly furniture; the nimble brain spins a web of crazy innuendo. There are strange cracking noises in the woodwork, and the patch of damp on the plaster ceiling mocks the poor madman.

Sitting there alone in the empty flat, Charles watched the hideous flower blossom in his mind. It grew, a crime against reason and dignity. He sneered at himself for his past folly in trusting Louise, he pitied himself for the dishonour in which he now felt himself to be, he hated himself for the faith which had so recently been his. Immediately and without thought he began making absurd and childlike plans. He would shoot them, killing them both with one bullet, as in some old romance. He would leave at once, taking all his money, which he would squander in curious debaucheries. He would write an incriminating note and blow his brains out. Carefully, as though avoiding the eye of an enemy, he examined the drawing room, holding up the two glasses, measuring the amount of gin left in the bottle, feeling down the sides of the sofa. In an armchair he found an old handkerchief, one of his own. Inconsequentially, he poured a gin into one of the dirty glasses and drank it down in one. It burned his throat and misted his eyes. The slight shock partially cleared his brain, and he entered the bedroom.

He knew at last, by examination of the label, that the suitcase belonged to Oliver. Therefore he had been a fool. Therefore he must conceal the traces of his recent insane spasm. Accidentally the jealousy of twenty years ago had been revived. The plateau on which he had been living, the floating island of his second marriage, had narrowed to a peak during those minutes when he sat on the sofa. The peak had become a promontory, a knife edge above the seething waters. On the left Helen, to the right Louise. As a tightrope walker, a second Blondin, he must make his way to some cautious piece of ground. It had been a near thing. He would have something to eat.

He walked into the sitting room and through into the kitchen. As he moved he heard the noise of his own clothes rustling; when he stopped, the silence, like squares of felt, lay against his ears. The tins of food in the kitchen were shiny, forbidding. A loaf of bread lay on its large side in its proper box. He turned out the light in the kitchen and walked back through the sitting room, avoiding with his eyes the battle dress on the bed. He closed the bedroom door, and in the sitting room the silence again lay along the side of his head, only accentuated by the faint throb of an airplane. He stood then, with his back to the door, and looked at the white room. When the raucous telephone began to ring he jumped as if he had been touched. He watched it ring, three, four times and then he picked it up. His heart was beating painfully.

"Taxi-rank?"

"No, *no*, NO!" Charles almost shouted the last words. He put the receiver down hurriedly, as though a small cheat had been done, and straightening himself, walked over to the far corner of the room, where a magazine lay on a table. He went to pick it up. Beside it stood a half empty jar of peppermint humbugs. They were slightly soggy from age, and a little stickiness remained on his fingers, but the taste was unmistakable. He was back in his childhood, eating death. This was the sensation he wanted, the persistent memory that would help cover the recent fissure of the earth's hard skin. It was peppermint.

In 1904 Charles was just nine years old. It was his second term at school, an expensive red-brick private school. On the afternoon of January 31st he and twenty-nine other little boys were playing football in the rain. The cold Januaries of early childhood! The wet wind screeched horizontally through his red and black striped jersey and against his blue knees. A ferocious, giant master urged the boys on, with much blow-

ing of whistles and slangy shouting into the teeth of the wind.
The crowd of boys ran up the field, slipping in the mud, falling
against each other. Scarcely half a dozen understood the purpose of the game. But here was that monstrous man again,
with his hairy arms, gesturing violently, shouting unintelligible
instructions. The pink lights of home lay only four days
behind, four days from that late afternoon when the yellow
fire became weird with the distant adventures of Henty's
wonder boys. Charles looked across, through the dripping
cheerless pines, to the little house outside the school grounds.
Perhaps behind the pines, even in this cruel end-of-the-world,
perhaps there was a fire lit and crumpets soft with butter. He
put his icy fingers inside his trousers for warmth.

"Hi, there, you Monroe, you're slacking! Get in the
scrum there!"

Obediently he tried to forget about the warmth and the
lights. The great slimy leather ball suddenly shot out of the
heap of kicking boys, shot out skidding straight towards him.
For half a second, perhaps, he was panic-struck. But he picked
it up, heavy as a cannon-ball with its thick layer of mud. Now
he knew that he must run with it. He ran straight towards the
goal posts, as fast as he could, carrying the hideous thing
held out in front, with both hands, like a tea tray. Behind
him he could hear the panting of the other boys, but he ran,
faster and faster, the cold wet air rasping his throat, his heart
beating, running for ever until suddenly he was there.

He had run the wrong way. He had placed the ball between
his own side's goal posts. The master was furious. The other
little boys stood in groups, blowing on their fingernails, not
caring in the cold and wet, nor wishing for anything save the
end of torment. And then back again and again and again to

the middle of the field, until all life had become this hideous, senseless cold, this exhausting running between whistles and shouts and kicks. Sometimes the ball would come near Charles, but he had learned now and he never picked it up. Suddenly there was a miraculous relief.

Another master had appeared on the sidelines and was beckoning to the tormentor. The master ran off the field, and immediately the game came to a halt, the boys standing stock-still staring at the two big men, or kicking at the ground with their blunted boots.

"Monroe!"

He looked around quickly. This other master had doubt-less come to punish him for running the wrong way. It was Mr. Stephens, the maths master. He ran over to where they stood.

"Monroe, you're to go to the head-master's study right away."

Mr. Stephens patted him on the shoulder. He stood quite still looking up at the two men, indistinguishable to him, giant representatives of the enclosing, bitter world into which he had been so cruelly pitch-forked.

"Run along, laddie," said Mr. Stephens.

"Yes, Sir."

Then he was running again, across the field and up the lawn, onto the gravelled drive through the winter-dead black-ish laurels, into the front of the school. He knocked at the study door.

The light and warmth were very sudden, but to children actions last so much longer than they do to older people that by the time he had reached the fire he had almost forgotten the football game.

"Sit down and warm yourself, Charles."

It was natural that he should be called by his real name, now that he was sitting in a proper chair in a real room. Monroe was the name for inky class-room forms and blackboard-screeching chalk, playboxes and iron-shoed stampedes down half-lit corridors. It was right that the old man should call him Charles here. The use of the name made him see the head-master as a human being, a white-haired frail old gentleman, trying to be kind in a clumsy way.

"Would you like a sweet, Charles?"

"Yes, please."

Mr. Blakeney got up and walked over to the heavy mahogany desk. Charles examined with pleasure the huge deer's heads, with vast marble eyes, which flanked the fire. He wanted to climb up and stroke their noses, but he was afraid this would be wrong. Mr. Blakeney was still fumbling in a drawer. Charles noticed the loud ticking of the clock in the corner. He felt sleepy, and his hands were tingling with the change from cold to warmth. He pushed his feet nearer to the fire, and his boots began to steam. The clock ticked.

"Here you are."

Mr. Blakeney handed him a round box full of peppermint bull's-eyes. Without any waste of time Charles put one in his mouth.

"Charles, I'm afraid I've got some bad news for you."

Tic-toc, tic-toc. The bull's-eye was delicious. Charles did not understand what bad news meant.

"You must be a brave boy, and take it like a man."

"Yes, Sir," said Charles dutifully. But now what was the old man talking about? How could it be bad when it was so obviously good to be warm and comfortable with a bull's-eye? He looked up vaguely toward the impassive deer.

"Charles, you'll never see your father again. Have another bull's-eye."

"Thank you, Sir."

He took a sweet. Of course he'd never see his father again. He was to be here thirteen weeks. Isn't that for ever? And he never saw his father here, or his mother either for that matter. What then was Mr. Blakeney talking about? Tic-toc, tic-toc.

The old man looked at the happy little boy. He hated this sort of business, and Charles seemed to be particularly unimaginative. Well, he'd have to say it, he'd have to use the word.

"Charles, your father's dead."

"Oh no, Sir, he's not. He's sick."

He remembered his father as he had last seen him, in bed with all the funny little bottles full of different coloured liquids on the bedside table. He had arranged them by size, like the elephants on the piano. But for some reason he was supposed to make less noise, and the strange white starched woman, whom he *hated*, had taken him out of the room. That was how he had last seen his father, sick. And before that, back into the dim mists of four or even three years old, there had been his father, a huge dark-grey man, his waistcoat covered in gold chains, his black moustache tickling Charles' cheek at bedtime. His father who had carved a thousand roasts, his father with a curious unique smell, sitting under the lamp in the evening reading magazines, setting off to work in the morning, once inexplicably slapping him. That was only once, last year, and his mother had become suddenly hard and stiff and had said:

"Harry, just because you've been foolish, I see no reason for you to work it off on little Charles."

He had pulled out his watch and left the room.

Once his father had made him a swing in the garden, but since he had made it Charles was almost afraid to use it. He knew his father best from Sunday evenings and the incomprehensible chapters of the Bible. Still, fifteen minutes Bible was well worth the following quarter of an hour when Charles could choose the book.

Mr. Blakeney was beginning to get troubled.

"Charles, he *was* sick. I received a letter this afternoon from your mother. He passed over on Tuesday evening. Your mother will come down next week and take you away for a few days. Do you understand me?"

"Oh yes, Sir!" Charles' joy was perfectly obvious, since he made no attempt to conceal it. Mr. Blakeney looked into the fire and sighed deeply. It was no good. Furthermore it distressed him to be reminded once again how much the boys hated his school. The food, he knew, was good and sufficient. Mr. Macleod was very good at organizing the games. Ah, if they'd only been to the monstrous schools of the 1850's they'd realise how lucky they were. Surreptitiously Charles popped another bull's-eye into his mouth. How far away was next week? Where would they go? Father, presumably, would not be there, for Father was dead. It almost began to mean something, but not quite. Not until he saw his mother's grief would he realise what death was, and that it could cause heartbreak.

"Now then," Mr. Blakeney was saying, speaking pointlessly with the dull conviction that he must say something: "You had better go and change or you'll be late for tea. You're a brave little man, and I'm sure you'll look after your mother now that she's all alone. You haven't got any brothers or sisters, have you?"

"No, Sir."

"You run along then—and here, have another sweet to take with you."

"Thank you, Sir." For many years, in fact until the war, the word death always brought to Charles a vague recollection of peppermint.

He gave a last longing look at the deer's heads and went out. First came the head-master's hall, softly carpeted, then the long winter corridor and the steaming changing room. The football game was just over. The room was full of naked boys, smelling like mice, pushing each other under the showers. They crowded around him as he came in.

"What happened, Monroe? Did you get a whacking? What did old Blakie say? What happened, Monroe? What happened?"

"He gave me some bull's-eyes and told me my mother's going to come and take me away and my father's dead."

A partial silence fell on the boys, and the older ones who had heard of death moved away. Then they all began shouting again, and Mr. Macleod came in and told them to shut up. Monroe's friend shyly said he was awfully sorry. Charles had a shower, but when he came to get dressed he found that both his shoes were quite full of water. What could he do except put them on, wet as they were? They squelched on his feet as he ran down the corridor with the other boys to tea. Sausages for tea.

He swallowed the remainder of the sweet and looked around the room. How had that little boy become this nervous, middle-aged man? What connection was there between the little boy with the bull's-eye and the frightened man with the peppermint humbug? He lit a cigarette. The little boy was more sensible, he thought, for he did not know the expected reactions and did not feel them. In fact, why should he really care if Louise had been unfaithful to him? Louise and Oliver, suppose they had been lovers, it would be they who should suffer for their foolish coupling, not he. It all seemed minute, seen through a reversed telescope. His childhood memory of forty years ago was more real than the memory of his horror twenty minutes before.

He would like to visit the school. It was presumably still there. He and Louise could lunch at the . . . No, not Louise, for Louise might no longer be with him. Yet that was wrong too, for the suitcase in the other room belonged to his son Oliver. Oliver, then, had not left for India, but had come to London, had presumably changed his clothes in his father's flat, which was perfectly understandable, and after drinking some pink gin with his step-mother had taken her out to dinner. It was all as simple and straightforward as that. After all, it is only to be expected that one's son might wish to stay with one in one's London flat. He could sleep on the sofa. That he had never done so before, that was no reason why he should not sleep there now, no reason at all. Perhaps they could all three go down to the school tomorrow, Sunday. It was only an hour from London by train. It would be a pleasant outing, that's what they call it, a family outing. He could tell them about the peppermints, and they would all laugh. It would make a good story if he could tell it as clearly as he had just remembered it. But he knew he was fooling himself. Oliver's face rose up before his mind, and he heard in his ears his son's deliberate voice. There would be no family outing, and Louise would not laugh at the story of the peppermint bull's-eyes.

No, there would be no family outing. That schoolhouse could only exist in his unique memory, an incident beyond the

good or evil of cruel decision. This left him again opposite his
own reflection, shut up in the mirror-flat, hearing the distant
guns as he looked at his watch, and seeing that it was only half-
past ten. A bomb, falling three quarters of a mile away,
crunched out three houses, an irrelevant comment, the idiot
external noise which for thirty years had provided the cacoph-
onous accompaniment to his own crossed life. Charles lit another cigarette and waited, listening.

There would be no family outing, no picnic, no jolly party
with red nosed comedian and fat elderly lady shrieking at mice.
For Charles there had hardly ever been such innocent gaiety,
since they had all set out for the grand international sporting
holiday, bands playing and colours flying, in August 1914.
That had been the great jamboree, the climax of jubilees and
cockney jokes. All organized festivity had paled in the recollection of those hot kisses and farewell champagne suppers.
How fine, if it had all been over by Christmas. The tin-pot
heroes would have returned: for the older, a slight wound, perhaps a becoming limp, and a knowledgeable twisting of a grey
moustache: a more dashing game of polo, a mountain of winkles
for the younger. How fine that might have been. Yet it had all
gone wrong from the start. The stage had been well lit, the
actors handsome and young, the audience appreciative, and the
curtain had gone up to a great burst of music revealing a mass
of colour and high emotion. Then, almost immediately, the play
had faltered, the fine actors dropping in the first few minutes
to be replaced by squalid rat-figures and creeping sightless
agonies sprung from some crazy pantomime. The claps of the
audience had become howls of derision or wailings for torture,
indecent shouts scarcely audible through the crashing of the
tuneless accompaniment. And on and on and on it had gone,

the play without a plot, meandering from act to dirty act, boring and hideous, disseminating only a feeling of conceit for the stupid, of guilt and fear for the sensitive.

It had cast a flickering, lurid light over all their lives; deafened as they were by the noise, an occasional word pronounced during accidental silence had had the clarity of a trumpet call, the weight of all literature. And this for thirty years. Guilt had become a Siamese twin to joy for most of mankind. A few lucky ones could avoid the unconscious responsibility, but Charles was not of these. The simple-minded spoke of escapists and passed on with a sneer to their games of fancy halma. The profound embraced absurd religions in the far corners of the earth. The artists perfected their technique and went blind with too much punctuation. The station platform became the trysting place of lovers, for the trees in the parks were all cut down.

For Charles, the guilt of his generation had come quickly. He had seen it first in that twisted echo of a happy courtship which had led to his marriage with Helen. That was the last jollity, the silhouette against the flaming background. It was a dance in 1916.

There had been some doubt as to whether it were right for the dance to take place. It was Helen's eighteenth birthday, and her parents had invited all their friends who lived nearby. Charles was on leave from France and was staying with them. Many neighbours had raised their eyebrows at receiving the invitation. Was it right to dance, while men were dying? Were there, indeed, enough men left to dance with? And then, the morning of the party, the telegram had come to say that Bill was dead. Bill and Helen were not, in fact, engaged, for Helen had refused him a definite answer. Yet was it right that they should dance that night?

"Do you think it right, Charles?" Helen's mother had asked him after breakfast, among the roses.

He had not noticed what his answer had been, vague words drifting down the autumn wind. They had walked among the flowers, and Helen's mother had said:

"We have no gardener any more. The house, too, needs attention, particularly the roof. Helen wants to be a nurse, but surely she's too young?"

Charles thought of the Belgian girl on the sofa in the upstairs room of the cabaret, her white breasts still those of a child, her eyes greedy to give her body to another soldier. Charles said something to Helen's mother, and again his words were lost with the feathers of smoke from the grey chimneys.

And then Helen herself had come out, walking bravely across the terrace and down the curved steps, holding herself as carefully as a water-diviner might carry a rod. She had not waited for her mother's anxious questions, but unasked had insisted that the dance be held. Then she had gone back towards the house, and as Charles watched her firm hand push open the French window, he knew such a sweet longing for her strength and beauty that he could scarcely reply to her mother's soft questions.

At the other end of England, when the wind blew from the east, men could hear an echo from the guns in Flanders. Here in Gloucestershire there was no such echo, save the avoidance of a dead man's name, and the certainty for Charles that in three days he must return. And so, after watching Helen disappear through the bright window, he walked down the garden, past the stone bird bath and the fake Greek statue, and out into the fields. Taking the lane for the village, he went a mile or two until, breasting a small hill, he saw in the valley beneath him a body of marching men, clerks in khaki, and instinctively

turned off into the fields, as a schoolboy who, when holidays
are nearly over, quickly shuts an accidentally opened cupboard
where hangs his school uniform, so Charles turned into the
field that he might not be forced to think of the future.

For it was of Helen that he wished to think, Helen the
châtelaine, the breath of life amid the chintzes and chrysanthe-
mums and cut glass of this golden afternoon house in the
Western countryside. When Helen picked up an ivory paper-
knife, Charles understood why elephants are killed; when she
stooped to rearrange the roses in the silver bowl, he knew the
feeling in the fingers of the Italian who had made that bowl.
She moved through the old house, an explanation that also
justified. She wore the outside world as a renaissance lady
might wear velvets. Once, a year before, when she had closed
a book and looking at Charles, had asked some question in
which lay the suicidal, uncomprehending anxiety of baffled
youth, Charles had been so surprised that he had almost
laughed at her. Doubt had no business with Helen. Yet, since
she was alive and young, there must be some connection between the firm picture of her blonde head and the shadowy
killing that echoed across the North Sea. For she was not a
girl to love only at certain hours of the day or night. But, try
as he might, when Charles re-entered the garden he had not
discovered where the connection lay. And as he watched Helen
over the luncheon table, he knew only what he had known for
weeks and months—that he thirsted for her and that in his
desert world, now, she was the only vision that was not a
mirage.

Charles did not usually enjoy balls, and this one was no
exception. Since it was Helen's birthday, she danced with all
the men in turn, the pimply subalterns from a nearby regiment,

rubicund old gentlemen who trod on her feet, an occasional contemporary of Charles'. She danced one waltz with Charles,
during which they scarcely spoke. Then he was thrown back
on the company of Lady de Romble, a hawk-eyed dowager with
pendulous cheeks and strong views about "conchies," "the
boche," and so on. Charles listened to her politely, but he
could not help it if his eyes followed Helen. Dressed as she
was in scarlet silk, all the other figures in the room seemed pale
and shadowy by comparison. At last he escaped from Lady de
Romble, only to be entrapped by a Mrs. Effingham-Courtney
who wanted him to present a medal to a girl-guide. Charles
made an excuse and walked into the garden with a glass of
champagne in his hand. It was getting late. The clusters of
candles in the glass chandeliers had made the ballroom too hot.
The party would be breaking up soon. Sitting on the stone
balustrade at the edge of the terrace, he watched the silhouettes
of the dancers thrown against the French windows.

There was no moon. Charles rested his untouched glass
on the balustrade beside him, and traced the black outline of
the house, blacker even than the clouded sky. Pencils of light
poured from the windows, but none came near him. He had sat
there for perhaps twenty minutes when he heard a rustle on
the steps that led down into the garden. Even in the darkness
he could see the faint glow of Helen's dress.

"Helen!"

She stopped on the top step, and said, very quietly:

"Charles, where are you?"

"Here."

She walked over to where he stood.

"Where have you come from?" he asked.

"I came out through the library."

She put her hand on the balustrade.

"Look out where you sit," he said. "There's a glass here."

He found the champagne glass. She reached out for it.

"Oh, give it to me. I'm so thirsty."

She drank it down in one swallow, and sat down beside him, putting the glass back on the balustrade on her other side.

"Helen!"

"Yes, darling, I know."

He kissed her for a long time, a long kiss, a great draught for his parched lips. She was, indeed, no mirage. They sat in silence, their fingers interlaced.

"Helen . . ." he began.

"Don't say anything. Later, darling."

They were silent, her perfume almost tangible to his senses.

"I must go in now. Kiss me, Charles."

He kissed her again and he saw that at first her eyes were open, but when she closed them, he too closed his, and behind her the glass toppled over the edge of the balustrade and fell tinkling onto a rock below. He let her go. She gripped his hand very tightly for a moment.

"Helen . . ." he began again.

But she had stood up and was going towards the house. He thought he saw her wave to him before she entered the beam of light that came from the French window, the same French window through which she had passed that morning, twelve hours ago, another lifetime.

Charles smoked a cigarette before following Helen indoors. The dance was breaking up, departing guests loud in their expressions of gratitude to their hosts. Charles walked through to the dining room to get himself another glass of champagne. He was afraid that his hand must tremble, and, as he passed a mirror, he glanced in to see whether his face showed any reflection of what had happened. In the dining room a man whom he had known slightly for several years, a man named Crichton, was standing alone.

"Hello, Monroe. Looking for a drink?"

Crichton was slightly flushed.

"Hot in there, isn't it?" said Charles.

"I don't know. I've been out here most of the time."

"Don't you dance then?"

"No. Can't."

Charles glanced down and saw the stick with which Crichton supported himself.

"Stupid of me. I'd quite forgotten."

"Nothing much to remember, is it?"

Crichton looked at him savagely for a moment. Then his face relaxed, bored, slightly petulant. Charles took the glass which the servant handed him.

In the garden, he thought. In the garden it had happened. I must not think of that now.

Crichton was speaking again.

"Who's that noisy old woman who looks like a bloodhound?"

"Old Lady de Romble? Did you get her too?"

"For about half an hour. Told me the Germans have a factory for getting oil out of corpses. Damned ingenious, I think."

"What's ingenious, Bobby?"

Helen was standing in the doorway, excitement flickering in her eyes, her breast rising and falling.

"By God, you look stunning, Helen," said Bobby Crichton.

"Thank you. But what's ingenious?"

"Corpse factories," said Charles.

"Oh, *that*." She walked over towards where they were standing, not looking at Charles.

This is just a play, he thought. Make-believe. Sur le pont d'Avignon.

A perceptible shade of sarcasm had come into Bobby's voice when he said:

"Damn nice dress, Helen. Almost does you credit."

She ran her hands over her hips, as if pretending to be a model.

"Do you think so?" She turned to Charles, "Do you think it does me credit, Charles?"

He caught the full look of her, the strength of the desire behind her eyes. It was not a play, not at all a play. A thunderbolt crosed from Helen to him and back again in the half second before he replied, lamely:

"You look lovely."

"Scarlet woman," said Bobby, coldly.

His voice had broken the tension. The noises from the rest of the house became audible again.

"You *are* rude, Bobby. Rude and tiresome, both of you. Go back to your corpse factories."

She began to turn, to leave the room.

"I don't have to go anymore," said Bobby. "Charles goes back on Tuesday."

She half stopped for a moment, but did not turn back. She had left the room.

"Did you know Bill?" Bobby asked.

"Yes, quite well." Charles was finishing his drink.

"He was my closest friend, you know."

"Was he?" Charles put his glass down on the sideboard. "Goodnight, Bobby."

"Goodnight, Charles. Sleep tight."

"Not as tight as you will."

"Bloody prig," said Bobby to himself. Charles just heard the words.

The last guests were now leaving. Charles said goodnight to Helen's father and mother. Helen herself was standing a little to one side, joking with an old gentleman. Charles waited until she was alone.

"Goodnight, Helen."

Her face was impassive.

"Goodnight, Charles."

He waited for a second, but she did not look at him. He walked out of the room and slowly began to mount the stairs.

"Charles!"

Her whisper was loud. He came down three steps and leaning over the bannister, was bending down to touch her cheek, when he heard the tap of Crichton's stick.

"Goodnight, Helen," said Charles.

She turned toward Crichton, and Charles went on up to bed.

Later, much later, when the dawn was beginning to outline the bedroom windows, Helen said to Charles:

"You must promise me not to get killed."

He ran his hand along her back.

"When shall we get married, Helen?"

"Darling, whenever you like. But you must promise me not to get killed."

"I promise, Helen. You're quite something to live for, you know."

"Bill didn't think so."

She turned onto her side, away from him. There was a long pause, and Charles was beginning to think she must be asleep, when she said:

"Are you glad Bill was killed?"

"No."

"You should be. This wouldn't have happened if he'd been alive."

He remembered Crichton's face then, not Bill's.

"I don't think it would have made much difference."

"Don't you?" She turned back and put her arm around him:

"I'm sorry, darling."

He kissed her, and she said, her voice muffled by his lips:

"I talk too much."

He watched the dawn brightening and heard the first half-attempted song of a blackbird.

Bill is dead, therefore. . . . That is what she had said. Bill's body was even now decomposing in a French cemetery. Charles lay beside Helen in fine linen sheets and stroked her firm breasts. The one fact caused the other. Yet he, Charles, was merely incidental, the man who was there. The war had given him Helen as it had given an occasional fortunate businessman a million pounds. He was a robber of the dead, a profiteer from another man's death, and his profit, the loot of his robbery, was in addition an insult to the dead man, an insult almost to himself. Immediately he realized the absurdity of what he was thinking. He had in no way encompassed Bill's death. He loved Helen and would have loved her equally had

Bill been alive; in fact he had loved her equally while Bill lived. Therefore there was no connection. Or was there? Was he being honest when he said he had loved her equally? It was only tonight, after Bill's death, that they had lain together. And was his love for Helen relevant, if he were only the lucky businessman who had bought a bleach factory? Was he, in fact, being honest when he said he was sorry Bill had died? Was he a prig?

Helen was sleeping. Quietly, careful so as not to awaken her, Charles got out of bed and put on a dressing gown. He walked over to the window. The garden was in full daylight and down below the terrace he saw glitter the champagne glass where it had fallen the night before.

If he had been killed and Bill had lived. If, if . . . He shook his head, irritated by his inability to disentangle the confusion in his mind. If one man lives and another dies, what does the living owe the dead? Only death equals death. The only way he could repay his debt to Bill would be by getting killed himself. Perhaps Helen had had some intuition of this. Yet Charles knew that he felt no such compulsion. He knew, apart from anything else, that death was absurd, grotesque, and that to attempt to see it in any proportion, to fit it into any scheme of thought was for him impossible. Therefore he could only ignore Bill's death. Yet that he obviously could not do. He could therefore pretend to ignore it and gradually forget about it. He could leave it in the back of his mind, the unpaid debt, better forgotten. He might be killed himself, very soon. Dead men's checks are valueless. But he might live on, and if he lived he would have forever the guilt, conscious or unconscious, of that unpaid debt.

Even though he had not asked that anyone should die,

even though he knew death in war to be as pointless and futile as war itself, yet some died and some lived. And if the whole generation must bear the guilt, as with a few exceptions it must, then those who live have their own guilt and that of the dead too. Even though a man may profit nothing from the misery and suffering of others, yet for that misery and suffering he is individually as responsible as is the blown-up newspaper shouter, or the whining, hypocritical hero-politician.

Charles looked out over the garden, and then at the sleeping girl on the bed. He had made no evil, he had merely inherited it. For him, death no longer tasted of peppermints, but love was still a secret between two people.

Such then were two incidents in the life of Charles Monroe. Sitting in his flat in London, that spring night in 1944, while the bombs were falling outside, he remembered the schoolboy, but forgot the young soldier. The layers of the years are curious in their refractions. The child was distinct after forty years, but the photograph of the man of 1916 showed to Charles a stiff, improbable stranger, and Helen in her scarlet dress was no longer a figure of flesh and blood. The years with their train of subsequent events had distorted his memory of her, and had made of her a symbol of the jealous frustration which he was experiencing again that evening with Louise. A symbol, but more than a symbol, for her memory opened wide the gates of misery, even as doubt itself picked the rusty lock of memory. Therefore Charles, on his knife-edge above the boiling waters, avoided Helen and looked back to his childhood. Yet somewhere, at the back of his mind, that old guilt which had followed so swiftly on his first passionate embrace of Helen still irritated and embittered. Crichton might perhaps have laughed to see him now; he would certainly no longer call him prig.

CHAPTER FIVE

THE taxi in which they were riding towards Chelsea seemed to Louise a curiously self-contained place, almost a home. They drove faster than is customary in a London taxi, for the driver doubtless felt that in speed there was some obscure protection from the threatening airplanes. Outside, the streets were still wet from the rain which had fallen earlier in the evening, and the damp asphalt reflected the few occasional lights as thin streaks or milky patches. Louise had lost the feeling of nervous tension which had been with her all evening.

When she had opened the door of her flat and had seen Oliver, defiant on the step, a feeling almost of panic had passed quickly through her. Then, as they sat drinking pink gins, she had experienced a premonition of tragedy, a clumsy and awkward dread of she knew not what. During dinner at the Café Royal this had disappeared. Louise had, superficially at least, regained her composure; she had been able to talk to Oliver, safe in the assurance that she was Charles' wife, a virtuous, married woman of simple tastes and limited understanding. She had refused to identify herself with Oliver and had certainly failed to grant him that spiritual *droit de seigneur* which he seemed to claim.

The story of Peacock's death had changed all that. It had suddenly made her life with Charles seem unreal, a ghostly spinet played in a deserted house. And because what she might have called her other life, her life with Charles, had become unreal, her present moment had become entirely clear and simple. Now, in the taxi, she felt completely at peace. Now there was no reason for doubt or dismay, nor need she continue to play a part for Oliver other than that which he expected. Therefore the taxi became for the time being a natural home, the driver and the London streets her household gods. Perversely, perhaps because it was the opposite of what she felt, or perhaps merely because she enjoyed stating the obvious, she said:

"It seems strange to be in a taxi with you again, Oliver."

If Oliver had intended any reply, his words would have been lost in the loud and sudden anti-aircraft fire that crashed around them. Away in Hyde Park all the rockets went off and, even through that noise, the sound of an aircraft engine could be clearly heard. It was flying low. The driver accelerated, and as the taxi turned into Cale Street, Oliver was half thrown from his corner against Louise.

At that moment the German pilot overhead was told by his bombardier that the bombs were away, and headed for home. He never reached the coast. His charred body lies buried in Essex.

The driver of the taxi turned out of Cale Street just as the bomb hit, a hundred and fifty yards away. For an intolerable time he had heard its screeching fall. He was a resourceful man who in 1916 had once picked up a fizzing German grenade and thrown it to safety, and now while the whistling became louder, closer, he calculated where the bomb would fall, examined the houses along Cale Street, noticed two strong buildings with a narrow lane between, and, accelerating, turned into it. All this took about three seconds.

Louise and Oliver, being inside the taxi, did not hear the bomb until almost a second after the driver had begun to evade it. Then Oliver's reaction was as deliberate as was the driver's. First he acted for himself, an inconsequential gesture: he turned up his coat collar. Then he reached over to Louise, silently, where she was beginning to crouch in her corner. All this time, of course, the bomb-whistle was getting louder. He took her by both shoulders, noticing the crispness of her silk dress over her skin, feeling even the shoulder straps of her brassière. Half rising from his seat he pushed her down onto the floor. She initiated no movement of her own, but obeyed his slightest pressure. The shriek of the bomb was now very loud as Oliver allowed himself to fall across Louise, covering as much of her body as he could with his own. The taxi, wheeling into the alley, forced them against the front of the seat. They heard the bomb smash into the building. It exploded.

First of all came the flash, then the taxi was slowly lifted up and dropped onto its side, to a tinkling accompaniment of falling glass. A short gasp came from the taxi driver and a distant scream was audible from among the crashing masonry. For what seemed again to be a long time they lay still, Louise and Oliver almost standing on their heads, such was the angle they had been thrown. Finally Oliver opened what was now the top door and pulled Louise free.

"Are you all right?"

"Yes. Yes, I think so. My neck hurts. Oliver!" She held onto his shoulder.

The driver had been partially thrown from the taxi, but one leg was caught under the front mudguard. Oliver pushed up the taxi. The driver began to swear, but curiously using no swear words.

"The brutes, they smash my fine new taxi, they half kill me, they break my leg. They and their fine airplanes. I seen them. The swine. I know who they are. I'll get them, the brutes."

It was meaningless, just as though he had been using the customary invocations of excrement, the divinity and unnatural vice. Oliver thought at the time how odd it was that the man should have such restraint. He wanted to ask him if he were religiously inclined, but there was too much to do. He pulled him well away from the taxi, onto the wet pavement, and almost immediately two men came with a stretcher and carried him away. From down the street they could still hear his voice going on, swearing at the top of his lungs but never using a word which might shock an old lady.

Oliver led Louise to the steps of a house. They sat down and he put his arm around her:

"Not frightened now, darling, are you?"

His voice was very tender. Louise leaned up against him. She was confused and for a moment thought that it was his father speaking.

"No darling, I'm all right. Oliver, I mean. I'm all right. Are you?"

"Never better, thank you. Makes you beastly sober though, doesn't it? And so quickly."

She looked up into his face, and bending down he brushed

her lips with his. She turned her head half away from him, and placed her hand flat against the stone step. It was damp and cool against her palm.

"Come on, Louise. Let's go and get a drink. That club's just around the corner. Here, take my arm."

The bombed building had begun to burn, little red lizards of fire darting from the black hulk. There were a lot of people in the street now in addition to those of the A.R.P.

"Please get out of here. You're in the way." It was a warden of some sort, in a steel helmet covered with white lettering. Oliver said nothing and he and Louise walked off, down into another street where the glow from the gathering fire was no longer visible. Louise was quite heavy on his arm during the two minutes' walk which took them to the club.

She walked down the stairs, still on his arm, looking, in the electric light, shaken and somewhat tousled. She left him immediately to go and powder her face. Oliver went to the bar and ordered some brandy. The bar was fairly crowded. He waved to two people he knew. They gestured to him to come and join them, but he shook his head.

"Good evening, Mr. Monroe, good evening."

The sour-faced proprietor gave what was intended to be a welcoming smile. "Noisy outside?"

"Not half as noisy as it is in here."

The gramophone was at full strength, Tino Rossi against the Luftwaffe. Rossi was winning.

"I've just been blown over by a bomb, Henri. So give me two brandies, real ones from the bottle you don't water."

The walls of the bar were decorated with faint sub-sexual jokes, the fumbling laugh of the female officer and the football blue. Oliver had looked at them all a dozen times before, but none the less he put his hands in his trouser pockets and examined them again. His jacket felt slightly uncomfortable, and he realised that he had forgotten to turn down the collar. Then he noticed a dusty streak along his cuff, and was brushing it off when Louise came in. All this had enabled him to avoid the eye of a blonde young woman whom he knew only too well and who was now dining with a naval officer in a far corner of the room.

"Here you are, Louise. You need this. Drink it quickly, and we'll have another one with soda in it."

"Thank you, Oliver." She smiled up at him, a strangely coy smile such as he had never thought to see on her face.

"I think, I should drink to you, Oliver, since you practically saved my life."

"Good God! Here give me your glass. I'll get you another one and then you can drink to me all over again."

Louise watched his back as he leaned over the bar, pushing through the people. From the numbness which had descended on her after the bomb, she was beginning to emerge more excited than she ever remembered having been. She felt completely happy, gay as the people in gay advertisements. She wished she were a character in a witty comedy, and she was conscious that she was beautiful, a fact which seldom crossed her mind.

"Here's to you, Oliver."

"Shall we sit down?"

There was a table free and they took it, Oliver sitting with his back to the blonde in the far corner.

"Well, Oliver?"

"Bombs seem to agree with you."

"I feel wonderful now. It was really very exciting."

"You can do something for me, then."

"Anything you say."

Oliver glanced at her and smiled:

"Oh, nothing as serious as that. Just solve for me the mystery of what happened to you between Peacock's death and your marriage."

She laughed. "There's no mystery. I'll tell you all about it if you like."

She could say that now because it had ceased to be real. This evening several years of her life had dropped away and become irrelevant, like the white squares on a draughts board. She could look back, in detached understanding, at the shadow game that someone with her name had been playing. The music in the bar continued to be much louder than the air raid outside. People were crossing and recrossing in front of their table.

"Tell me, then."

She told him as much as she could remember that seemed true. She was interrupted once or twice while he went to get drinks, or while they got up to dance. She told him about the summer of 1940 and the winter that followed.

That hot summer of 1940 had been, in Europe, a time for love. There were then few quarrels, but many farewells. Lovers remained together until wrenched away. The brassy sky lowered over the rumbling continent. Men and women turned to each other, the only sure footholds on a cracking cliff face.

Louise had come to London and had got a job in the French section of the B.B.C. She lived alone in a furnished room, and every morning and evening she rode on the bus for twenty minutes. Almost immediately she had stopped thinking about Roger Peacock. Indeed it was then, when she first came to

London, that she stepped sideways out of the real context of her life, the context which seemed real as she sat beside Oliver in the underground drinking club.

During that summer of love and fear, when she had had no love and when she sometimes believed that she was scarcely alive, she had learned to watch and to make patterns of what she saw. In the streets, when the paving stones were cooling after the hot day, she had studied with a growing fascination the complexities of the great city, the dissimilarity of gestures, the careful cornice stone that finished the grey building, the quarter world of names and edges which she had always previously ignored. And in the park on a Sunday she watched the pigeons and the few remaining children, the faithful lovers and the old men with sailboats. The world she saw came more and more to resemble a fantastic toy-shop in which she was responsible for the display. When her day's work was finishing, she would wait with an anticipation that was almost its own reward for the solitude that enabled her to pursue her explorations and arrangements in her newly found world. For a month or six weeks after her arrival in London she had hardly spoken to anyone apart from the people in her office building.

"One of the people who worked with me was Johnny Pym. He worked for the translators and was, I suppose, about eighteen and very polite. He was full of little pieces of knowledge, the sort of thing you get from the back of cigarette cards. He was studying history and English literature by post. I liked him, and we often had lunch together. His home was at High Wycombe, where his father worked in a bank. Have you ever noticed how intelligent and kind the people are who live in small country towns like High Wycombe?"

Oliver nodded.

"One day in late July or early August Johnny came into the office, where we worked, in a high state of excitement. He had won the prize in a magazine competition. One of those semi-facetious things at the end of the weeklies. The prize was two seats for a theatre, any theatre, and he wanted me to go with him. My immediate reaction was to say I couldn't go. I liked him well enough, but I was enjoying my evenings alone so much that I hated to waste one. Also I imagined Johnny must have a lot of friends. He was such a gay boy that I assumed he spent his evenings with a heap of funny Dickens characters. But I was wrong. And he looked so sad when I said I couldn't go that I had to change my mind.

"We went to a revue. You know, Oliver, you and Roger always assumed that I was almost as knowledgeable as you two. As a matter of fact I had hardly ever been to the theatre in London. Once or twice with my mother to see Ivor Novello, once with Roger to the Mercury, and that was about all. Johnny knew even less about London-by-night than I did. It was great fun, that evening. We had very good seats in the stalls and drank gin and lime in the intervals. Johnny found all the jokes very funny, and so did I. He pointed out a man he said was a film star. We had a lovely time.

"Afterwards we went and had supper in Soho, at a little Italian restaurant that was pretending in a half-hearted way to be French. I'd told Johnny once that I liked good spaghetti and he'd taken the trouble to find the place. It was almost empty. A big, motherly woman brought us our food and insisted that Johnny have a second helping. He told me all about his family, about his sister in the A.T.S. and his father's stomach ulcers. I asked him when he was going to be called up. He looked quite blank and said he thought in about a month or two. It seemed to me somehow pathetic to think of him working away in London when he knew he was going to be called up in a couple of months' time. I think if I'd been a man I'd have done like you and Roger and joined the army right away when the war began, without waiting for them to conscript me, but it seemed to me that evening to be a fine thing the way Johnny just ignored it all. Do you see what I mean? It seems to me that in many ways Johnny was right, that it's better to regard the war as a sort of fate, like death. I admire people who can go on with their daily life when they know they have a fatal illness that will kill them in six months. You and Roger used the war as an excuse to get drunk. Johnny didn't know about society. He was like the pigeons and the corners of the buildings that I told you about."

Johnny had received his call-up papers earlier than he had expected. During his last few weeks in London he and Louise had been together a great deal. When the bombing started in earnest, his mother had wanted him to return to High Wycombe, and had it not been for Louise he would probably have gone, for he hated the raids.

"I showed him what I thought I had discovered about the city. We walked about a lot together, and he took me to the sort of places I wouldn't have gone to alone, Wapping and Limehouse and Stepney. We used to have a sandwich when we left the office and he'd tell me everything about himself and about the places we went to. He was going to write a novel. Before he met me the heroine had been tall and blonde. Now she was to be small and dark. I don't know when he could have been writing it, because he spent all his evenings with me and had even got behind with his correspondence courses. I'd never really had a friend before. I enjoyed those evenings so much.

"Then he had to go to the army. He must have known for several days before he told me, but he said nothing about it until our last evening together. We were sitting outside the 'Doves' at Hammersmith when Johnny told me. I had known, of course, that he would be going soon, but it was a shock all the same, and I think I cried a little. He had always been so gentle and so gay. That last evening he told me that he loved me and wanted to marry me. I couldn't tell him that he was just a little boy. We sat side by side until it got dark and then we walked back to where I 'lived and he kissed me goodnight. It was the first time we had ever kissed each other, I promise you."

Oliver lit a cigarette to cover Louise's awkward pause. Then she went on:

"I missed him very much. The night bombing became heavy as soon as he had gone, and when I watched the places burn down that he and I had walked through together, I felt as though it were Johnny that was being hurt. He wrote to me two or three times a week, long letters all about his sergeant and how much more pleasant it all was than he had expected. He never said anything in his letters about love or marriage, so I began to believe that he realised there was nothing in it.

"After a couple of months he came up to London. I hardly recognized him in his uniform with his hair all cut off and his face quite brown. It was late autumn then. The office in which I worked was about to be evacuated to the West Country and the day he came in everything was upside down. All the girls were flattering to Johnny and clapped their hands and said how wonderful he looked. He was pleased with this, of course, and I too had to say how handsome he looked, though I didn't think so. I had liked the way he looked before he went into the army, pasty and yet healthy; now I thought he looked brown and rather unhealthy. His eyes seemed to have got closer together.

"That evening we went out together, but it was too cold for walking about now, and anyway I don't think Johnny would have wanted to do that. We went to the Brasserie Universelle in Piccadilly Circus. It's a noisy place, and Johnny kept looking around at all the people and sort of shouting. He seemed an entirely different person from the boy I'd known. But later on we went back to the Italian restaurant in Soho, and there he became more like his old self. All the same, the evening was not like the other ones had been, and I was glad when I could say that it was time for me to go home. I thought we'd go by bus, but Johnny insisted on taking a taxi. Then he began talking again about getting married. I told him I thought it was a mistake. He was holding my hand and he dropped it, but he didn't take any notice of what I said and went right on talking about how he'd written to his parents about me, that he'd had an awful time persuading them he was old enough and that they had agreed to ask me to come and stay with them at High Wycombe. Johnny wanted me to go there with him the next day.

"I should have had the courage either to go with him or else to tell him definitely that it was no good. But somehow I couldn't bring myself to hurt his feelings, and as a matter of fact it was impossible for me to go to High Wycombe in any case, on account of the office move. So it was postponed until his next leave. His letters became fewer and fewer, and less and less personal, and again I thought that he would let the whole matter drop. It was becoming a sort of crazy nightmare to me. I couldn't understand why he kept on writing to me at all. I got so I dreaded his letters and those awful false replies I used to send him. Yet I couldn't break it off by letter. And it was nothing, really, nothing. I don't understand why Johnny wanted to hang onto me so. I wrote to Charles then, just after I had left London."

"I remember his writing to me that he had seen you. It was the first letter I got after I reached Egypt. I read it sitting on a packing case in the sun."

Charles had come to see Louise in the little West Country town where her office was situated. He had stayed for the weekend at the comfortable, old fashioned hotel. His tolerance and unselfish interest had enabled Louise to see the apparent impasse with Johnny in its true proportions, a simple misunderstanding. The cold tail end of winter blew down the steep mediaeval streets and past the flash-fronted Woolworth's in the square. Louise and Charles sat in leather armchairs by the fire after Sunday lunch and talked intermittently over their coffee. He came again three weeks later, and it was as though he had only been out of the room for five minutes. It was then the beginning of springtime. He and Louise walked out of the town, across the still wet fields under the scudding white clouds. Gradually she regained her peace of mind, not as a spectator in the toy-shop of the previous summer, but as a passive actor in the countryside.

She had not heard from Johnny for two or three weeks, when she received a letter saying that he would arrive on Friday for four days, and that his mother and father were coming to meet her on Saturday. She engaged a room for him at the same hotel in which Charles had stayed and went to meet him at the station, her actions seeming to her as improbable as an afternoon dream.

"Can I have a light, please, Oliver? Johnny had just got a commission. His uniform was very new, and he kept tugging at the leather belt. He was growing a small moustache. We dined at his hotel. I found it impossible to connect him with myself in any way. I was sure I had never seen him before, and for a moment I had a feeling of panic that someone was impersonating my Johnny and doing it very badly. For one thing he didn't seem to be able to understand what I was saying. I'd speak, and then he'd reply more or less on the same subject but really about something quite different, and then I'd try to talk again, and again he'd go off. It was like a shaky boat tacking in a high wind.

"After dinner we went to the bar and he was rather rude to the bartender. I don't think he meant to be rude, the way Roger Peacock used to, but he was rude all the same. Then I told him that I couldn't possibly marry him, that I was sorry but it was absolutely no good. He didn't seem to care at all, except that he'd look such a fool before his mother and father. Apparently it was too late to tell them not to come, and if they had lunch without meeting me they'd feel they had wasted their railway tickets. I felt the least I could do would be to help him out with his lunch, so I went.

"His mother had, I imagine, formed a sort of Delilah picture of me and I think she came all prepared to dislike me. Anyway she was obviously relieved that Johnny was not going to marry me. In fact everyone was relieved. We had a pleasant lunch, although I couldn't really enter into the conversation since it was entirely about people in High Wycombe. Mrs. Pym wore a very large hat, I remember, and her husband tried his best to be gallant towards me. Johnny boasted a bit about girls and how well he'd done in the army. His parents were very proud of him and they were right to be. There was only one thing that made me regret having given him up. If only I could have told him to cut off that moustache, his parents could have been even more proud of him."

Louise leaned back in her chair and took a long swallow. She smiled at Oliver, who asked:

"So that's why you married Charles?"

"Yes, it is really. After that lunch I felt so light hearted and relieved, that I had to talk to somebody. I went to Oxford the next weekend. I was so happy and gay I wanted to sing all the time I was in the train. I told Charles about the luncheon party. I think perhaps it was the first time we had ever laughed together."

"He doesn't laugh much, does he?"

Louise frowned for a moment.

"No. That's one of the things I like about him. After all, there's not such a lot worth laughing at, is there?"

"Doesn't he laugh at you then?"

Louise looked up and smiled at Oliver.

"Do you?"

"Yes, of course I do. But what happened to Johnny?"

"He wrote me a stiff little note asking that I return him a book he had once given me. I did so and never heard from him again."

Oliver lifted his glass to her, and said again:

"And so you married my father."

"And so I married Charles. Is the mystery solved?"

The words sounded peculiar to her. She had had quite a lot to drink and that, combined with the taxi smash, had excited her nerves until every sound seemed new and strange, every object foreign, everything with the exception of Oliver's face, the eyes of the face on the woodpath, the link back across the untrue years.

"And so I married Charles."

But who had married Charles? Not the Louise in Peacock's drawing room, perhaps the girl who sat on the No. 39 bus with Johnny, certainly not the woman who was now talking to Oliver, who had nearly been killed forty minutes before.

"I've changed," she said. "Didn't you say in the Café Royal that children sometimes shrink? I've shrunk."

"Come on, Louise, we'll dance."

She got up and they began to dance, but she could not follow the music. Her legs seemed to become entangled with Oliver's. After a few moments they sat down again.

"I think I must be a little tight, Oliver."

"Bless you, my love. We'll have another."

Oliver got up from the table and walked over to the bar to order some drinks. Absent-minded, waiting for his turn at the bar, he gazed around the crowded room.

In the far corner the blonde girl waved to Oliver. The naval officer who was with her looked round.

"Who's that, Katie?"

Oliver waved back. Katie finished her whiskey.

"For God's sake get me a drink."

Her companion looked at her doubtfully.

"Don't you think you've almost had enough?"

"Oh, God. All right I'll get it myself."

The naval officer got up. "No, no. I'll get it."

"And make it a double."

The naval officer, on his way to the bar, passed Oliver who

was returning to Louise with the drinks. They nodded with the constraint of Englishmen who have not been introduced. Oliver sat down again, opposite Louise.

"I don't think it's becoming for you to see your mother-in-law under the influence of alcohol. Can I have a cigarette? I'm talking too much."

"You're not my mother-in-law or step-mother or whatever it is. And as a matter of fact you're not talking nearly enough. And here's a cigarette."

She lit her cigarette and looked at Oliver somewhat craftily.

"Oliver, have you ever been in love?"

Oliver blew out a cloud of smoke before he answered.

"I have never been able to understand what that expression means—so I suppose I haven't."

"But if you were you'd know, wouldn't you? I mean, you might not realise it right away, but you'd know something had happened, wouldn't you?"

The words reverberated like an echo in her head as she said them, a distant echo, something different, somebody else in another place. She half shook her head. Oliver was talking:

"Why ask me? You should be an authority on matters of the heart by this time."

Louise was feeling more and more excited. She talked very quickly.

"But that's just it. I'm not. I don't understand at all why I love people, or even if I really do. Perhaps I don't really, perhaps I haven't really."

That was what she had wanted to say. Somewhere, far off in her mind, a heavily rusted door was opening slowly. In a little while light would come in. Oliver was smiling at her. She smiled back.

"Ne t'en fais pas, ne t'en fais pas," he said.

"Ah, on parle Français." Rivière stood at the table.

Oliver and Louise looked up startled, almost as though they had been caught in a robbery. Oliver was the first to recover. While he was fetching Rivière a drink, Louise looked at the Frenchman with care, while they talked politely of the air raid and the taxi smash. The near revelation which she had experienced just before his arrival was fading now, and the question which she asked herself was not really pertinent: why Charles, Roger, Johnny Pym, rather than Rivière or. . . .

"Well, Rivière," said Oliver: "You look more like a breath of old Paris than ever."

"What, the Pont Neuf?"

"No. Saint Philippe du Roule, more."

"I thought Paris for Englishmen was the Pont Neuf or the Boulevard Raspail."

"You forget Henry James and Henry Miller."

"Americans, my dear Oliver, both of them." Rivière gave a toothy smile.

"Right. You win."

Now what are they talking about, thought Louise. A slight alcoholic cloud interfered with her view, like those tattered pieces of fog that sometimes come round London corners in the autumn. Louise wanted very much to talk about herself, love and desire. This stupid conversation about Paris was still going on. Rivière was saying:

". . . because if you try to find the centre of Paris, its Piccadilly or Unter den Linden, you are inevitably caught up in the super-imposed systems of Napoleon or Haussmann, basically foreign. The old circular cities were built around their city Gods, in this case the high altar of Notre Dame.

Paris, instead of expanding in even ripples, became multiform. Napoleon set up a rival Godhead at the Etoile, Louis Philippe at the Bourse . . . we've had as many Parises as we've had beliefs. You English, who have never believed in anything except the danger of belief, once your city broke out of its ring, it could just sprawl over half your country for all you ever cared."

Louise could stand no more of this. The elation of earlier in the evening was still with her. She was regretting her silences of the past six years.

"Monsieur Rivière, just before you arrived Oliver and I were talking about love."

"Forgive me for having interrupted the most fascinating of all conversations."

"No, no. That's not what I mean. I just wanted to ask you: you have been in love, haven't you?"

"Almost continuously, ever since I was twelve. Except once, for a week in nineteen hundred and thirty-eight, I have always been in love."

He bowed towards her. Damn him, thought Louise. This was not what she wanted at all. Yet she was not going to back out now.

"Oliver says he never has."

Rivière looked towards Oliver and smiled slightly.

"My dear Miss Collins—I beg your pardon, Mrs. Monroe . . ."

"Louise," she interrupted.

"Thank you. My dear Louise, men sometimes boast that they have never been in love. Sometimes they allege the opposite. They usually mean the same thing."

Oliver was examining his finger nails.

"Well, Oliver?" said Rivière. He too had a small revenge to extract, a residue of the conversation at the Café Royal.

Slowly Oliver put his hands on the table and looked up at Louise.

"Would you care to meet a friend of mine?"

Louise now felt a little frightened. She had not said much, since Rivière's arrival, yet she realised at this moment that in her relationship with Oliver her position was so weak that it was folly to offer him battle. Besides, she had no desire to fight him. All the same, she could see no retreat.

"You haven't answered Rivière's question."

"Rivière hasn't asked me a question. I shall answer yours, though."

He rose and walked to the far corner of the room where he spoke to the blonde girl who was dining with the naval officer. Louise felt an almost tangible constriction of her throat when she saw that they were coming back with Oliver. He introduced them, Miss Katherine Farr and a Mr. Tremont. Louise smiled at Miss Farr while being introduced, and received in return a look of such undisguised dislike as to freeze the polite words of greeting on her lips.

CHAPTER SIX

OLIVER'S reasons for bringing his ex-mistress, Katherine Farr, over to their table were not entirely disingenuous. She did not know that she was no longer his mistress, nor indeed was he quite certain of that fact. Yet during this visit to London he had decided to avoid her, and when he had seen her across the club, he had made up his mind not to speak to her unless she first spoke to him. Since she was dining with a man whom he did not know, this was easier than it would have been had she been alone.

On his last trip to the bar, to fetch Rivière's drink, when she had waved to him and he had waved back, he knew that it was only a matter of minutes before she came over to their table. Therefore he determined to make the best use of her presence, to conjure her up, a shapely djinn, when it suited his purposes. He had no wish that Louise should be indiscreet before Rivière, lest in retrospect she blame her own indiscretion on him. Thus a diversion of some sort seemed desirable to Oliver. Furthermore, he feared the evening might become an impasse since Rivière had joined them. He had no more desire to listen to Rivière's theories about city-organism than had Louise. He was sure that the injection of Katherine into the party would, for better or for worse, dissolve the polite core. In this assumption he was correct. Also he wanted to impress Louise.

Katherine sat down opposite Louise. Tremont was between her and Oliver.

"I thought you didn't like this place, Oliver," she began.

"I don't much, but one does meet old friends."

"Jolly nice, I say," said Tremont. "Cracking music."

"Then I was wrong to think that you are avoiding old friends?" asked Katherine.

Louise watched her carefully, not as she had watched Rivière. She decided Katherine's mouth was too big, her hair certainly bleached, too much lipstick. Also her voice was too husky. In fact, affected and probably a slut.

"Only some," said Oliver, and then, turning slightly towards Tremont, "Stationed in London?"

"Good Lord, no. I'm just up on a spot of leave. Damn lucky to get it too. I was telling Katie here how we were just off East when we went and dented a propeller. Damn good show, if you ask me."

"Wasn't that true, then, Oliver, what you told me about going to India?"

Katherine was lighting a cigarette as she spoke. Louise felt a sensation of resentment at Katherine's assumption of authority.

"Yes, as a matter of fact it was," replied Oliver. "It's been postponed again, that's all."

"It's so difficult to know when you're telling the truth."

"I say," said Tremont, "how about a drink apiece? Same all round? Three brandies, two whiskeys?"

With the excuse that he was going to help carry the glasses, Rivière accompanied Tremont to the bar. Louise remained silent. It was precipitating faster than Oliver could wish. In an attempt to delay what he now realised to be an inevitable explosion, he said to Katherine:

"Who's the sailor, then?"

"He's called Tremont."

"I gathered that."

"He's not my new lover, if that's what you mean."

"That's interesting, but it isn't what I meant. Tell us about him, his hopes, his dreams. Did you meet him on top of a bus?"

Katherine was momentarily mollified.

"I've known him since we were children. About once a year I go out to dinner with him and he tells me how he has his bottom scraped. It's something that just happens to sailors."

Katherine turned to Louise.

"I've heard such a lot about you. Do you mind if I call you Louise?"

"Please do."

"I thought you were married to a don."

"Yes, I am."

"Then why aren't you in Oxford? All dons' wives should be in Oxford."

"How about Cambridge dons?" asked Oliver. "Rather hard on them."

"It's all the same," said Katherine.

"Katherine, for God's sake," said Oliver.

"Oh, all right. Why don't those stupid men bring the drinks?"

"You mustn't call Rivière stupid. He's not, and even if he were, he's French, so you couldn't say so in London."

Katherine was still looking at Louise.

"You're half French, aren't you?"

"What a lot Oliver must have talked about me."

"He has."

Katherine's voice had grown even huskier. Louise was beginning to feel cornered, for she had not the wit to see that Oliver was on her side. Katherine went on:

"Yes, he's talked a lot about you to me, although I don't suppose you've ever heard my name before."

"No, as a matter of fact I haven't."

For a half second Oliver thought that Katherine was going to throw something at Louise.

"Why not wait for the drinks, Katherine? A full glass goes through the air better, as you may remember."

She looked away from Louise to Oliver:

"Thank you, my dear. We mustn't forget our dignity, must we? Ah, here they come. Is that the right drawing room comedy note for you?"

Tremont, smiling foolishly, and Rivière with his nose in the air, were coming back carrying glasses.

"Cheery-by!" said Tremont, as he took a swallow.

The drinkers in the club had now all reached that state of near panic which afflicts the far-sighted English at thirty minutes before closing time. The problem is how to procure at least three more drinks before the bar shuts for the night. Desperately the barmaids pour watered gin over imitation bitters; frantically the pot-boy hands out three quarter full glasses for pints of beer. With the knowledgeable certainty that this has happened every night for the past ten years, the proprietor gives change sixpence short, while in the back of his mind the hotel which he will build at Bandol receives a new wing, the curves of the ladies who will console his old age become plumper and more expensive. Occupied though he be with primitive thoughts of greed and lust, Henri can by long habit yet encompass all that is passing in his bar. The couple over in the corner have been kissing for three minutes. Since the man is in the American airforce, and will pay the highest price for the worst whiskey, Henri will allow them another two minutes' embrace before interrupting. The two painters under the clock have drunk only one pint of beer apiece since nine-thirty. Next time they come he will make it so difficult for them to order anything that they will go elsewhere, *canaille*! The table of Mr. Monroe looks quite quiet. A few minutes ago he had feared a possible fight there. The blonde is drunk, but what a girl! As for Henri, he likes English girls drunk, not too drunk of course, but these English, they need a little something before they are any good. His mind oozes on in its familiar channels as he gives eight shillings change on a ten and nine-penny bill.

He was right. At Mr. Monroe's table the tension had somewhat relaxed. Rivière was paying Gallic compliments to Katherine while wondering when he could press her knee. He moved his chair a little closer, and to his surprise it was she who put her hand on his thigh. Tremont, Oliver and Louise were talking in a desultory fashion: Tremont about the Navy, Oliver about nothing, Louise in monosyllables while she wondered if perhaps she had imagined the virulence implied in Katherine's rudeness. She half decided that she had, for it seemed to her so utterly gratuitous.

Katherine was drinking quickly. She turned to Tremont and said:

"How about getting some drinks?"

"But you haven't finished the one you've got."

She picked it up and swallowed it in one draught. The whiskey caught in her throat and she began to cough. They all stopped talking, and watched her while she shook her head, trying to regain control of her throat. When she finished coughing they relaxed.

"All right, Katie?"

"Yes, thanks. I must just go and spend a penny."

Her face was still red from her spasm, and she rose somewhat unsteadily to her feet. When she was out of earshot, Tremont said, fatuously:

"I'm afraid Katie's had a drop too much." And then, with anxiety, "I hope she's not feeling queer or anything."

"Nonsense," said Oliver. "She's perfectly all right."

Tremont looked appealingly at Louise. She said:

"Should I go with her?"

Oliver drummed a little tattoo on the table. Tremont said:

"That would be jolly decent of you. I feel sort of responsible, you know."

Louise looked at Oliver, but he kept his eyes fixed to the glass which he was turning between his fingers. She looked back at Tremont and then, rising, went towards the door marked LADIES.

She had to push through the people at the bar, for the lavatory was near the entrance to the club. She did not know quite what she was supposed to say, as she opened the door and entered the tiny, rather dirty vestibule off which were the two water closets.

Katherine was standing with her hands against the walls of a corner, the attitude of a little girl being punished. Beside her was a rickety table, covered with a soiled cloth, on which lay a dirty hairbrush, the property of the club. Katherine's head was bent forward, her shoulders shaking. She made no move to turn when Louise came in. The music from the gramophone was very loud in here, with the circular persistence of a French fair.

Louise stood for a moment before making a shuffling noise with her shoe on the floor. Katherine made no move; her sobs were regular, like the echo of an axe a mile away on a cold winter's evening.

"Katherine!"

She turned slowly. She did not attempt to cover her face, nor to hide the ravages of tears. She looked at Louise, her face leaden:

"What do you want?"

"I don't know. I thought I might be of some help. I didn't know it was . . ."

"Help? Oh God! That awful freemasonry of women."

Her voice had been small when first she turned towards Louise. It was now huskier and to Louise sounded more normal. Katherine took out a handkerchief and began to dab at her eyes.

"Well, you've seen me crying. Are you satisfied now?"

"Why do you talk to me like that? I don't want to do you any harm."

"She doesn't want . . ."

Katherine dropped her hand from her face and stared at Louise.

"By God, it's probably true. You poor little creature, you probably don't want to do me any harm. That almost makes it worse. Why in Christ's name couldn't you stay in Oxford with your don?"

Katherine sat down quite suddenly on a small kitchen chair. Louise said:

"Do you want me to leave you in here?"

Katherine said, "It doesn't matter any more. But it hurts you know." She looked up at Louise. "I knew he didn't love me, but I did try to make him go on wanting me. And now, when I thought he'd gone away, to find that he's come to London without even letting me know, that he cared so little that he'd even come here with you, here where he's almost sure to see me. . . ."

Katherine took out her powder puff and began dabbing at her face. Louise felt a small, unrecognised flicker of pride. Women of Katherine's type had always somewhat frightened her. She relapsed into the obvious.

"Perhaps he was going to phone you tomorrow?"

Katherine ignored this. She was talking more to herself than to Louise.

"I had made such silly promises to myself. I thought that perhaps if I never went to bed with anyone else while he was away . . . Oh, I don't know either. I'm probably well out of it." She put her powder puff away and looked at Louise.

"Maybe I should thank you for making it all so clear."

"But it's nothing to do with me."

"Nothing to do with you? Listen to me, you innocent blue-eyed baby, I've had to hear about you from him for over two years. Oh, not often directly, but I loved him a lot you see, and I learned to know how his mind worked. He admired this woman's hair, he thought so and so had such lovely manners or something. It all fitted in—it made up a fine picture of his blue-eyed step-mother, of you. Once, when he was drunk, I asked him about you and he told me the whole story. We were staying at a pub in the country and after he'd fallen asleep I sat up for most of the night thinking up ways to kill you. I'd like to make you a present of that night. It'd interest you."

"Why do you tell me this?"

"Because I think it's about time you woke up from that schoolgirl dream of yours. I wish to God he *had* gone to bed with you when you were having an affair with that other man— maybe he wouldn't still be mooning about you. Maybe he'd realise I'm a real woman too."

"But I've never had anything to do with Oliver."

Louise knew she was lying. Yet that afternoon in the wood by the river was so slight. It was really nothing. Still she knew she was lying. Katherine got up from the wooden chair.

"Oh, no? You just couldn't let him alone. You even had to go and marry his father."

"This is absurd."

Katherine straightened herself. She was trying, not very hard, to regain her lost self-control. The look she gave Louise was almost pitying.

"Look, I don't know how women usually behave in these circumstances and I don't care. Let me just tell you this. I love Oliver and I think that I always shall. Maybe I'm fooling myself, but that's what I think. He wants you and he has for years, and if you don't know that you must be even stupider than you look, which I can hardly believe. Therefore if you're going to be honest, either go to bed with him or leave him alone. Do you understand me? God knows, I don't care what happens to you. If I read tomorrow that you'd had your throat slit, I'd probably laugh. Furthermore, I don't believe that Oliver will ever want me any more, and so that's all over. But . . . this long range flirtation that you do is no good for Oliver, it's about bitched up my life, and I don't suppose even you get much pleasure out of it. For everybody's sake, including your own and that of Oliver's future women, try and see what's going on."

The two women looked at each other for a few seconds. Louise could see Katherine's hands, clenching her handkerchief. The music from the gramophone was very loud. Louise said:

"I'm sorry. . . ."

"Oh, for God's sake!"

Katherine pushed past Louise and walked out through the door, back into the bar.

Louise stood for a moment. Then, with a look of total absorption, she began hunting in her handbag for her compact. Carefully she began to powder her nose.

Back at the table, Katherine wasted no time at all.

"Looks like you should make her tonight, Oliver. Anyhow I told her so, and I expect she does what she's told."

Tremont's lower jaw dropped slightly. He said:

"I say, Katie. . . ."

Oliver said, "Most thoughtful of you, my sweet." Katherine in a rage really did look magnificent. His memory flitted over that afternoon on the Welsh beach. How she had scratched! "Most thoughtful, but I think I can manage my own affairs best, all the same."

Tremont said, "I say, Katie, don't you think we ought to be toddling along?"

She turned to him quickly. "Shut up!" And then to Oliver: "But when you've had enough of her to sicken you of invalid food for the rest of your life, don't come back looking for me because I won't be there."

"Don't fool yourself," said Oliver: "Of course you will."

"Look here," said Tremont: "Really, you know, you can't . . ."

Katherine twisted in her chair again.

"Shut up!"

She almost screamed it. One or two people at nearby tables turned to look. Oliver and Katherine stared at each other steadily. Rivière tapped Tremont on the shoulder.

"You'd better do like the lady says, and shut up."

Tremont said, "I can't understand it. I thought we were all having such a good time."

Oliver said, carefully, "When you realise, Katherine, that being a loud-mouthed bitch is not always acceptable as honest comment, you'll be better company."

"Look here," said Tremont: "You can't just sit there and call Katie a bitch."

"Go home," said Katherine in a tired voice, without even looking at Tremont.

"You're wrong," said Oliver. "I can. In fact I just have."

"Why don't you do what she says?" said Rivière. "Go along home."

Tremont stood up, uncertain, his eyes beginning to pop a little. He said, to no one in particular:

"By God, if you were outside I'd knock your head off."

Nobody accepted the offer. Nobody even said anything.

"Are you coming, Katie?"

"No."

"Bounders," muttered Tremont. He looked around the table and caught Rivière's eye. Rivière winked. Making a noise that was almost a snort, Tremont turned on his heel and headed for the door.

"Oh, Oliver," said Katherine.

"Bad luck, Katherine," said Oliver.

Louise, emerging from the ladies' room, saw Tremont stride past her, out of the room. Her few moments of solitude might have enabled her to adjust herself to the situation, had she been either quite sober or of an introspective nature. But since she was neither, she could hardly evaluate Katherine's loud statements, let alone prepare herself for the situation which, after all, was not really so new to her. She could only continue on her course, buffeted by characters more powerful than her own.

Her feelings, when Katherine had left her, had been neither those of anger nor of surprise. She had not even asked herself whether Katherine had spoken the truth. Her first reaction had been one of weariness, an exhausted unhappiness such as Alice must have felt in Wonderland, when the beasts did tease so. Louise was lonely and unarmed among liberated emotions whose violence, since she had never experienced similar anguish herself, she could scarcely comprehend. It seemed an unfair cruelty to her. It was a feeling not dissimilar in quality to that of a shy, nervous girl when first she finds herself at a rowdy, pinching school. For a moment the girl is desperately alone—there can be no surcease, since there is no one in the world who does not hate her. Then she remembers her mother and father. So Louise remembered Charles.

She did not precisely remember him. Rather did she visualise an interior, with herself and Charles as the figures. The sunlight pouring into the room and lighting the corner of a pile of books. The books stood on the large desk between the window and the fireplace. Charles was writing, every now and then consulting the big volume which lay open on his knees. Louise herself was sitting on the much upholstered sofa, with some sewing half on the seat beside her. It was all as neat, light and dull as the standardized Dutch interiors which line the museums of Europe.

She longed for such dullness, such domesticity where even politeness is unnecessary, where long silences, expressive of nothing, form the flat backing for the slight and easy tapestry of contentment. She longed even now for such a scene, yet hers was a deadened, hopeless longing, for the scene which she visualised was no longer for her. The figure on the sofa, which had such a remarkable resemblance to herself, was her twin sister, the stranger who disappears from cradle at a time long before Act One and who reappears, full of hopes and desires, in the banal crisis. The man at the big table, who so slowly turned his head and smiled gently towards the girl, while his lips formed an inaudible amiability, was a character she did not know. In her heart she called his name, Charles, Charles, but he, in his own world, could not hear her. He rose from his desk and walked across to stroke the black hair of the girl on the sofa.

Reality returned as Louise snapped shut her compact. For a moment she stood, listening to the loud music and the bubbles of unintelligible conversation. Then, closing the lavatory door carefully behind her, she walked back to the table.

As she approached, Rivière rose to his feet. Oliver, glancing round, did likewise. Katherine remained, the only seated figure.

"Where's he gone?" asked Louise.

"We sent him home," said Katherine.

"Oh." Louise sat down.

It was nearly closing time. Henri was walking around the room, urging his customers to drink up and go.

Katherine stared at Louise. "Why don't you say something? It's your evening, after all."

"Katherine," said Oliver: "For God's sake shut up."

He saw her gesture as she reached for her glass. He knew her well enough to be enabled to duck at the last possible moment, thus avoiding both the indignity of premature evasion and the inconvenience of being hit. It missed him, sailing a good foot over his head.

"I told you they were better thrown when full, didn't I?"

The glass sailed across half the bar, smashing against the wall close to the head of one of the painters under the clock. He looked up mildly, and then with distrust towards his companion. Baffled, they both decided that it was time to go home, and swallowing the last of their bitter they fumbled into heavy overcoats and were gone.

A moment of silence fell over that part of the bar where the incident had occurred. A high pitched voice was heard saying:

"So I told him to take his bloody harpsichord and do the other thing."

A few drops of whiskey had fallen on the sleeve of Henri's double-breasted, grey flannel, Lesley and Roberts suit. He was patting at his cuff with a red bandanna as he hurried up to the table where Oliver and his friends were sitting.

"What goes on here, eh? What sort of a place do you think this is, eh? A fine lot of gentlemens you are, brawling here like you was in some low place in the East end, like a common pub."

Oliver, Louise, Katherine and Rivière all felt for a fleeting second as though they were back at school. The people seated at the adjoining tables were enjoying the scene, an elderly air marshal even clicking his false teeth in disgust. Henri was quite red in the face. Oliver laughed.

Katherine said, "Marvellous sense of humour, you've got." Then she turned to Rivière, "I shall go home. Would you please accompany me?"

Henri stood partially in her way.

"Come on," she said to Rivière. "Let's get out of this awful place."

Henri was working himself up towards a tantrum.

"Yes and please not to come back to my bar any more, any of you."

He glared at them with pig eyes, including for good measure a blond, inoffensive Norwegian sailor at the next table.

"What goes on here, then, like it was Stepney?"

"Oh, get out of the way." Katherine pushed at his fat stomach. He grabbed her wrist. He was becoming incoherent. Rivière tapped his arm and Oliver rose to his feet. For a second it looked as though there would be a real fight and one of the barmaids began edging towards the telephone. Then Henri dropped Katherine's wrist, and she and Rivière walked on towards the door. Henri turned back, still enraged but a little frightened, towards Oliver and Louise. Oliver had sat down again.

"Get out of here, you too."

"When we've finished our drinks," said Oliver mildly.

Henri grumbled and walked away. Immediately he began shouting at his other customers to get out, closing time, bar closed, no more, go home.

Oliver said to Louise, "I'm very sorry. I hope it hasn't upset you too much."

Louise smiled at him, a tired, rather silly smile. All around them the sheeplike, half-drunk people, whom Henri so deeply despised, were getting up and dutifully trailing away. Oliver and Louise swallowed their drinks and he helped her to her feet. She said:

"Oh, Oliver, that poor girl."

Walking out behind her, watching her thin shoulders, he thought of Katherine with a guilty animosity, an unkind regret. His thoughts were scarcely more clear, and if anything less kind, than those of Henri—she should not behave like that towards me. And yet Oliver knew, in fact, that Katherine should; he knew that the whole of their not unhappy affair had been based by himself on an understanding by which they would behave towards one another exactly as they chose. Furthermore, he knew that her noisy jealousies and ruthless desire had been in the past a delightful flattery. No, his present animosity towards her was based solely on his desire not to frighten Louise; besides, it was so much easier to mingle distaste with his feeling of guilt. Not, he told himself, that he had any reason to feel guilty. Katherine was grown up, knew her own mind, had come to him without illusions—the whole string of inapposite clichés was on his side.

During the two years of their spasmodic cohabitation she had always been entirely at liberty to do what she wished. The fact that her only true desires were centred in him was her business, or so Oliver had tried to tell himself. They had had a fine time together. Why then must she spoil the ending? Surely they could part friends, linked by a happy memory? Even as he said these words to himself, in the back of his mind he could imagine Katherine's loud comments on such hypocrisy, and he knew that she was right. It was for her truthfulness that he had first wanted her. He would always want such truthfulness.

All this passed through his mind in the fraction of a second, and he lived again the scene in her flat, three weeks before.

She was lying naked on her couch, her face to the wall, the big line of her hip and the small line of her back hard and great in outline against the crimson silk. Oliver had awakened and was sitting before the electric fire. Without turning, she had said:

"Would you like me to make you a cup of tea?"

"No, I'd rather have a drink. Go back to sleep. I'll help myself."

When he reached up from the cupboard, with the gin in one hand and the French in the other, she was leaning on one elbow, watching him.

"Want one?" he had asked.

"Oliver, is this really the last time?"

"Until I get back from India."

"Do you think it can last after such a parting, our thing together?"

"That depends on you."

"On me? You mean you would like me to be faithful to you?"

"Here, have this."

He handed her the gin and vermouth. She thought, how awful that he does not care.

She swung her feet down onto the floor, and as she took the glass she felt out with her other hand and touched his hip. Then she thought of those other women, the ones in India and elsewhere, whom he did not even know now and whom she could never know. She would rather he had another girl, right before her eyes, here on her couch, rather that than the dark and certain uncertainty of absence.

"Kiss me, Oliver."

He kissed her, and in his kiss there was already the first step of departure. The gang-plank was lowered, waiting for his feet; the ship's whistle had already sounded. And in his lovemaking there was an exhausted reluctance which he did not intend. He knew of course that she could sense it, and yet he could not dispel it. He had already gone.

Then they had dressed and she had become again his trusted companion. They had gone to the pub, and after a couple of drinks it was time for him to go to Paddington. She had kissed him goodbye without apparent fear, and with no more anguish than was sufficient to justify his vanity.

As Oliver and Louise went out of the bar and turned to the right up the stairs, he dismissed the shameful scene from his memory.

"Damn her," he thought. "Damn her, the poor little bitch. She should at least have hit me with that glass."

Taking a long step, he was beside Louise as they mounted the stairs that led up into the open night. Just before they stepped out into the blackness of the unlit streets, he glanced down at her. She was staring straight ahead, her face taut.

"Where are we going, Oliver?"

He had taken her arm and was leading her away from her flat, down sidestreets towards the Royal Hospital.

"This way."

The action of walking soothed them both. The fresh, damp air was very soft after the desiccated cigarette smoke in the bar. The rain had almost dried out of the pavements; the airplanes had all gone home. At midnight, the beginning of tomor-

row, the people from the cinema had boarded the last bus, and
for Louise and Oliver the conspiracy had returned.

It had returned from its torturous, man-made convolu-
tions, battered as a chewed mechanical hare. There was no
moon and the last clouds closed imperceptibly from constellation to constellation. Away on either side the occasional bombed
flatness lent an unnecessary poignant certainty that this is the
end, this is the last chance. Louise heard their heels, clicking
on the stone.

They walked on, as it seemed to Louise, for miles. The
houses stood, close and shuttered, giving out no emanations,
being but irregular roofs against the less black sky. A cat
crossed. They turned into a sunken garden square, a place of
dying where the red houses leaned backwards in disproportion-
ate, unnatural embraces. Some had cardboard windows; some
were sullied with the refuse of stray dogs; in one an Indian was
playing a gramophone. They turned away from the square and
into the fattened Chelsea of the nineties, so heavy with the
ghosts of hock and seltzer that the very streets seemed to offer
an odd welcome.

"Oliver."

"Yes, Louise."

"Oliver, I must go home."

They turned again, down towards an open space where
the big clustered branches of leafless oak trees blew in the star-
light.

"Louise, let's sit down."

It was a low wall this time. It was very like that stone on
which they had once sat together. Louise looked at Oliver for a
moment before she seated herself. She could see only the outline
of his features, his high cheekbones and the darker places where

were his eyes. She knew now that she must remember very carefully. She knew, too, what it was that she must not forget. The syllables were in her head, see, on the tip of her tongue. Charles first, then Katherine. She sat down beside Oliver on the low stone wall.

"Louise, you asked me earlier this evening if I had ever been in love, and I gave you a silly answer. I have. I have been in love with you since first I saw you. I've wanted you, always, awake and asleep, and that's why, since your marriage, I've had to force myself not to see you. Not seeing you has been painful. I'm going away now, and therefore I can tell you. I love you, Louise."

She sat upright. His words had very little reality for her; they were so much less than those she had expected. So much less that she turned against him in the dark.

"It is not fair of you to speak to me like that, Oliver. You're cruel to talk that way, cruel and selfish. I'm married to Charles. Katherine loves you."

"Louise, please try to understand me. I'm not talking of Charles or Katherine, nor of any other stranger. I'm talking of you and me, here in this dark night."

A slight gust of wind blew out the big oaks. Their voices were low. They both stopped talking as a man walked by with a cigar, calling to a dog.

Louise thought, in a minute he will kiss me. She said:

"You're so cruel. You've been so cruel to that poor girl. Now you want to break my life. Oliver, you must not. Can't you be satisfied? What do you want with me? I have nothing for you, nothing to pay for all the pain and suffering."

"There is no profit and no loss. If we love each other, that's one thing. If we hurt each other or break the web of our society, that's another. Cause and effect are not true here."

Louise scarcely listened to his words. She was trying with all her strength to hold on to some wisp of dream which lingered in her memory, some fragment of stability, a kind smile or a gentle word. But those acts of kindness are difficult to grasp. They are the grasses which make the smooth lawn or cover the sweeping hillside. They are not readily tangible, as are the strong trees of passion or the impenetrable undergrowths of misery.

The hot wind from the furnace was blowing Louise rapidly across the careful countryside, the tidy pastures and the dimpling streams; it carried her, now more and more swiftly, over the broad and simple expanses of farmland. In the distance she could hear the high seas pounding against the last escarpments of her land. There was nothing for her to hold to, no trusty rock or sure defense.

"I . . . ," she began.

Oliver took her in his arms and kissed her. The man with the cigar walked back, casting a cursory glance at the urban lovers. When Oliver let her go, she said:

"I love you, Oliver. Oliver, I love you."

She was beginning to cry. Oliver drew her to her feet and kissed her again. In silence they began the walk, back to her flat.

CHAPTER SEVEN

LOVERS are cardboard figures, forever enraptured of their pseudo-classic attitudes, preys to the ravening dullness of biology. For all the ingenuity of man and pliability of woman, each enamoured pair merely poses against the quaint axiom that one and one make three. A magnet, locked for ever against another magnet, with its mysterious electric current happily circulating, forms an immobile pattern, the scrutiny of which soon becomes tedious. It is the solitary force, as it grasps at the rusty pen-nib or makes the iron filings to jump for snow-flakes, that provides more than passing interest. Let us, therefore, return to Charles Monroe, alone before his electric fire.

The bomb that had fallen on Cale Street, and had so nearly frightened Louise, had shaken the flat. Charles had heard the glass tinkling down to the street a few hundred yards away. He walked around, looking at his windows. None were broken. Then, drawing the curtains in the bathroom a little closer, he had returned to the drawing room. Oliver's uniform, scattered on the bed as he passed, had lost its symbolic quality. It had become just old clothes, fit for a scarecrow.

He sat down again in his chair, and picked up the anthology through which he had been glancing.

> Troop home to silent grots and caves,
> Troop home and mimic as you go
> The mournful winding of the waves . . .

He let the hand holding the book drop to his lap. Was that a distant all clear? He listened carefully. It must have been a motorcar. He began the poem again.

> Troop home to silent grots and caves . . .

But he was already at home. He glanced around the room. This was home, this was the warm place for which he had longed while sitting in the brown train, and walking through Paddington. It did not look so lovely, now that he was here. In fact, he thought, his eye following the banal line of the standardised sofa, in fact it was positively ugly. He wondered if Darley would have urged his readers to troop home to this. The electric fire glared over the greenish carpet. The room looked untidy but not inhabited. It was as though a respectable family had camped here for two days and then gone on, leaving their unwanted possessions behind.

Charles read:

> In bowers of love men take their rest,
> In loveless bowers we sigh alone . . .

This, he supposed, looking around him with distaste, was for the moment a loveless bower. At least he had sat here sighing for quite a while. Despite the poet, though, a loveless bower was a fine place for a rest. The rooms at Oxford, which he had occupied prior to his second marriage, though loveless in the extreme, were none the less—or all the more—very restful. He

read the poem again, and decided that the antithesis was foolish, even though the final line seemed to atone for earlier folly.

He closed the book and replaced it on the shelf. Yes, this
loveless bower certainly was a depressing place, made even
worse by the clothes scattered over the bed. He looked at his
watch, and saw that it was after half past ten. Were it not for
that uniform, he would be tempted to go to bed without waiting
for Louise. The thought of Louise returning with Oliver depressed him. He decided to go for a walk. It would be better to
arrive when they were here, rather than appear as an unwilling
mentor, timing their return. Switching off the light, but leaving
the electric fire, he went down the staircase and out into the
night.

As he stepped into the street the all clear began. He
thought for a moment of the coincidence. As he arrived, earlier
in the evening, the warning had gone. As he left the all clear
sounded. Yet it was an untrue coincidence, for a walk could
hardly be worth a departure. He turned out of the mews, and
went in the direction of a red glow, rising from the fire in Cale
Street. Back in the empty flat, where the electric glow went
on, the only evidence of Charles' recent presence was the canvas
bag in the corner behind the hall door.

When he reached the top of Cale Street he could see busy
figures around the burning building, silhouettes against the
redness, torches flickering. He was enjoying his walk, reacting
against the gloomy thoughts which had sprouted in the ugly
flat. He said to himself that he had been foolish, making
miseries, piling ridiculous guilt on senseless fear. What, after
all, did it all matter? Why fuss so? He was as bad as the poet
peeping with anguish at the copulation of seals.

He decided not to go down Cale Street, and turned instead

towards that labyrinth of square and garden that carries the
name Cadogan. Deviously, through Rawlings Street and Dray-
cott Avenue and the backs of Harrods' warehouses, he made
his way towards the Fulham Road.

These purposeless night walks were familiar to him, although for the last few years he had taken none. What miles he
must have covered in his time, walking as though over some interminable, half-lit street, strung across Europe from Edin-
burgh to Athens. As he thought of that long, solitary striding,
it was a night walk in Paris, in 1915, that he remembered. He
had been on leave from the army. He thought with passing
nostalgia of those half shuttered cafés at the corners of little
streets, from which, as one hurried by, one could hear the quick
explosions of foreign conversation or the soothing rattle of
dominoes. It had been a wrench, in 1915, to pass each one, and
really, looking back on it all, he wished that he had then been
less intense in his quest for an undefined Utopia.

Soon he was in the Fulham Road, where the hospitals for
incurables cluster, overground catacombs. The smell of anti-
septic is always pungent in this street, and the strictest blackout cannot conceal the light in the room where death is awaited.
Charles walked on, across Old Church Street, down which a
grumbling taxi lurched, its tail-light glowing red. His thoughts
went back to Paris.

He had been to Paris many times, but it was three visits
which identified the city for him. The most recent of the three
was twenty years ago, and time had played one of its usual
tricks, merging all three into one identification of a city—the
visit to Paris. The first had been with his mother, just before
the war, the spring before she died; the second was in 1915;
the third, ten years later, was memorable to him because it was

the last time he had seen Helen. Now, as he walked at night in London, he found that it needed an effort of thought to disentangle from that confused memory of Paris any one of the three visits which were the elements of its composition.

He remembered, perhaps more clearly in its implications of Paris than any other occasion, the morning in 1925 when he was trying to pass the hours before meeting Helen for lunch. He had woken early and, after eating his breakfast in bed, had lingered in his bath. He felt again the wooden handles of the taps and saw the profusion of thick towels hanging on their rack. Slightly groggy from too much hot water, and scrubbed perfectly clean, he had sat by the window before getting dressed. He wished to refresh his skin. So to sit naked was something he would scarce have done in England. He had fingered the rough, white lace curtain, and a little dust had remained on his hand. Then, after brushing his teeth a second time, he had dressed and gone down into the sunny street.

He walked out along the Rue de la Paix, looking for a shop which sold ties. The one he was wearing, a dun coloured thing bought in Manchester, had revolted him when he put it on. It still carried the creases of its previous wearings and permitted only of one specific, soggy knot. It was altogether most unsuited to his mood, a delicate mood of poised anticipation. He did not know what this luncheon with Helen would bring, and in fact he expected it to be nothing. Nonetheless, he certainly would not meet her at the Crillon with this muddy looking rag about his neck.

The shops of the Rue de la Paix looked, as always, totally forbidding. Their windows were filled with improbable eye-catchers for the very rich—gigantic bottles of scent; huge, ornate silver bowls, at whose purpose Charles could only dimly guess; a length of crimson damask scattered negligently across a High Gothic prie-dieu; a model of the Mauretania; a Bokhara rug almost of a size to carpet a football field. Here was clearly no tie for Charles. Yet it was an agreeable street, and he found pleasure in speculating about the possible future purchaser of an Etruscan sarcophagus which stood, flanked by jade Buddhas, in one great window.

Charles felt that the elegant shop walkers eyed him slightly askance. After all, it was only ten o'clock, and the man to buy the sarcophagus would barely be awake at this hour. Well, let them look at him with contempt if they so wished. He could tell them, with truth, that he would not accept their old coffins as presents. Furthermore, he had a secret which they could never share.

Yet when he came to inspect his secret, it hardly seemed likely to interest the tail-coated figure rearranging those great Javanese sponges. The fact that an English chemist, no longer in his first youth and with the gold dust of promise brushed from his wings, was going to lunch with his ex-wife, was not really an excitement for anybody except himself. He watched the man in the sponge-filled shop pick himself up from the grey floor in the window—his face was red from bending. He gave the central sponge one last tap, and brushed the dirt from his striped knees. Charles noticed that he wore a pearl grey stock with a pin in it. Should he too perhaps buy a stock? He grinned happily at the sponge man who, fearing mockery, hurried into a dark corner of his shop.

Charles strolled on, up to the big Boulevards. Here traffic was in earnest, urged on not merely by its own lemming-like desires, but even compelled to accelerate by the sharp whistling and fierce gestures of the policemen in their short capes. He stood for a moment, gazing at the Café de la Paix across the street, and was almost knocked down by a pretty girl with a hat-box. She smiled gaily at him in the sunlight and for a moment he quite forgot his ugly brown tie. Then she was gone. The Café de la Paix remained, a faint echo of an old elegance.

There was plenty of time. His luncheon engagement, that magician's stone, was not until twelve-thirty. The tie, though, the tie. There was, he knew, some fashionable shop for ties. The name escaped him. Chabert, was it? Or Farnot? Somebody had been talking about it only the other day. It was, he thought, somewhere near the Louvre. He walked past the shiny office of Thos. Cook, down the Avenue de l'Opéra.

In the Avenue de l'Opéra the shops are much the same as those of the Rue de la Paix, much the same, but in 1925 a little more vulgar. In the latter street the eye glides over a patina of imported American shine, which, at that date, was glossy with novelty; the older ostentations of the Second Empire seemed a little tawdry by comparison. The great glass globes in the Avenue de l'Opéra, each on its ornate standard, have since then acquired a delicacy of their own—twenty years ago they were little more than a last high-water mark of a turgid tide.

Charles noted the vulgarity of the Avenue de l'Opéra, but not with displeasure, for, box within box, it carried him back to his visit to Paris with his mother, before the war. And now in London, in 1944, walking slowly along the King's Road, his mind switched to that other Paris which he had also known, that Paris which, though other, was yet the same.

In 1911 there still lived many old people for whom the Second Empire was a reality. Cramped and chalky, they drove in open carriages. For Charles, then a boy, they were living proof that the Paris of his reading, the Paris of Flaubert and young Maupassant, existed. Then, at night, when those great bowls of light led in perfect perspective to the fantastic Opera house, then he felt that here indeed was a city to move men's hearts. The carriages and the cars that hurried by were filled with laughter, the scent of fair women and the throaty wit of dark men. They bowled up the broad avenue, doubtless headed for a dull dinner or for some boring opera. To the sixteen year old English boy, walking with lonely contentment, they were all the lovers of the mysterious world.

He and his mother were staying at the Grand Hotel, a dull building which, designed to be impressive, merely succeeded in being uncomfortable. During the first days of their stay in Paris, she had taken Charles to dine with respectable families of her acquaintance. It was done to improve his French, to enable him to pass that diplomatic examination which the war had subsequently made unnecessary. After a week, gently and quietly, she had fallen sick of that mysterious internal malady which was to bring her to death in the following spring. Charles would sit by her, while she ate a little dinner. Afterwards she would urge him to go out and see Paris. And he, too shy to talk his bad French, too poor to buy the pleasures which the city spread before him, would walk the gay streets and build for himself a palace of solitude.

The Avenue de l'Opéra leads on, down to the Théâtre Français. He had once visited that august institution, to assist at a performance of Racine's *Britannicus*. Even though he had read the blood-thirsty play that very afternoon, it was difficult for him to follow the French. And from where he sat, high up and to one side, the actors were foreshortened, quaint. All that he carried away from the performance was an atmosphere of heroics amidst dusty cardboard and fake jewellery, and in his head the lashing of the long-rolled Alexandrines. As he crossed towards the Louvre, he felt the tautness of Nero's stage leap.

For that young boy the Louvre at night was a place of luxurious and incredible evil. Merimée's Charles IX peered from behind his curtain at the massacre below. In hoarse fury, the harridans of the revolution tore through long corridors, while in nearby Notre Dame the naked prostitute was crowned the Queen of Love. He walked a little way along the quai, past the boxes of books and prints, now closed for the night. Then, turning to the right over the bridge, he was on the island, and in another visit, in 1915.

That second summer of the war was still a time when action was unnatural. A year or two later the trenches had become truth, peace and improbable dream. But in 1915 it was the war which was crazy, and Charles still strove to pursue a sane existence despite the encircling madness. When he received three days' leave, he decided to go to Paris on his own. He wished to be free of his dull military friends, and he thought to recover, if only for a few hours, that mental detachment which the war was in danger of destroying. He went to Paris, not to do anything, but to look.

The first day had been all he wished. He sat in the Luxembourg, watching the fountains play, and later, outside Fouquet's, he drank a champagne cocktail while the lazy crowd gaped at itself in the violet evening. He slept for fourteen hours.

The second day was somewhat disappointing. He had not realised that Parisians, a fickle race, were already weary of British soldiers. Assuming, from his uniform, that he knew no French and was therefore half-witted, a policeman answered his polite question with shouted monosyllables. A café waiter overcharged him, and tried to bluster when Charles objected. That afternoon he walked through the Latin Quarter and sat outside Soufflot's. The Boulevard Saint-Michel was empty of its students gone away to the armies of Flanders and Champagne. It is always, perhaps, a sad street. The spectacle of frolic and high ambition inevitably suggests a regretful question. Empty, a student quarter provides its own answer. Charles finished his drink and walked on up, past the statue of the two chemists, past Ney with his lethal sabre, up even past the Lion de Belfort into a part of Paris which was to him quite new.

Tired, he found a small café-restaurant, and going in ordered a simple meal: onion soup, a herb omelette with sauté potatoes, a salad, brie and a bottle of Rosé d'Anjou. The café was almost empty and the girl in black, who laid the place and brought the soup, stayed for a moment to talk.

"This is a delicious soup, Madame."

"I am glad." She smiled at him: "It is always a pleasure to be able to feed a man well when he is so far from home."

It was no set speech. To her he was a lonely soldier, as he might have been had he come from Marseilles or even from Thuringia. And she knew that it was her duty, a pleasurable duty, to feed lonely men, as it was their duty, doubtless no less pleasurable, to admire her curly hair and well turned figure. She was that admirable type of woman, more common perhaps in France than elsewhere, who gives out such a warmth of feeling that everywhere she goes, in a bus, at dinner, in the by-the-hour room of a railway hotel, she creates the passing illusion of a comfortable, bourgeois home.

"Monsieur is on leave?"

"Yes, three days."

"My man is there. It is terrible, the war."

That was to her a statement of fact. Commonplace though it be, she had not simply accepted it from the newspapers. It was to her a discovered truth, and one worth imparting to the English soldier. It was an invitation, not without dignity, to share for a moment the cosy furniture of her little mind.

She fetched Charles his omelette, and at his request pulled up a chair, drank a vermouth cassis. As they talked, of rising prices and the sins of politicians, of marriage and the cruel partings of war, the grating irritations of Charles' day disappeared. Even the deeper hardships seemed softened by the good food in the warm corner of the bar.

"Monsieur is not married?"

"No, not married."

"Engaged perhaps?" She showed clearly that she believed any man a fool who fled the joys of domesticity.

Charles did not like to disappoint her:

"No, I am not engaged, although I may be before long." It was his turn to smile at her now.

"And might I ask what is the young lady's name?"

"Helen."

"It is a charming name." She picked up her glass: "To la belle Helène!"

"To la belle Helène!"

Every now and then she would get up to serve a customer, usually a tired looking fellow with rheumy eyes and a cloth cap, once three Zouaves who tried to engage her in bantering flirtation. For a moment she played with them, but disappeared through into a back room. She returned to Charles' table. Her mother, a forbidding figure in black bombazine, emerged from

the private part of the house to control the Zouaves, who soon
left. Charles sat over a brandy while their conversation ambled
slowly along.

At last he felt that he must go. The bombazine figure at
the cash register was yawning pointedly. He paid his bill, and
after accepting their sincere wishes for his good fortune, he
left them, soothed and happier. He had walked back to his
hotel, past the half-lit cafés of the domino players, down
through that great city where there is never absolute silence.

During his visit to Paris in 1925, he had attempted to
retrace his steps of ten years before. The scientific business
which had brought him to France had been completed that
afternoon at four o'clock. He was returning to London the next
day. On the way back to his hotel he remembered the 1915
dinner. He had nothing to do that evening, and with a glimmer
of excitement, he recalled the warm handshake of parting, the
stray meeting which suddenly stood out like a fully lit steamer
on a dark ocean.

He left his attaché case with the porter at his hotel. He
did not now wish to see that uninhabited bedroom of his. He
called a taxi, a red Renault with a pointed snout, and told the
driver to take him to the Lion de Belfort. As they rattled
across Paris he noticed a clock in a postoffice window. It was
only five. It was too early. Last time it had been at least half
past seven before he entered the restaurant. For a moment he
thought to stop the taxi and walk. That implied too positive
an action. Also he was not quite sure of the way, starting from
here, for the taxi was now turning into the Rue de Rennes.
He leaned back in his corner and lit a cigarette. When they
reached the Place Denfert-Rochereau, where the Lion de Belfort stands, the driver turned, a look of enquiry on his face.

Charles told him to stop against the curb, by the newspaper kiosk. He paid him hurriedly, adding too large a tip. He felt that all the crowd, for there was a crowd, was watching him.

Which way now? He glanced at the Lion, and the Lion, that most Gallic looking King of Beasts, gazed impassively towards the Rhine. The crowd was really quite thick. It took Charles a minute or two before he noticed the cause. There was a small street fair in progress, just off the place. He still felt that it was too early for him to start looking for the café, the café which he now thought of as "his" restaurant. He walked down to the fair.

It was a simple place of entertainment. A small round-about turned noisily in an alley. Nearby was one of those large revolving wheels from which, for five francs, the lucky man can gain a hundred franc ticket in the National Lottery. There were a couple of shooting booths. A game of skill, which consisted of throwing soft balls at pyramids of bent and shiny cans, completed the fun. In addition there were vendors of ice-cream with their yellow barrows, and a ferocious looking individual who was snipping new-made candy into cushion-shaped lozenges.

The majority of the small crowd was merely there to watch. They strolled slowly from booth to booth, loud in admiration if a youth knocked down the pyramid of cans or scored a bull's-eye with the twenty-two rifle. Charles joined them. The number of actual competitors was few, and the proprietors of both shooting booths looked haggard and tired. Charles strolled to the end, where normal street life resumed, save for an occasional couple washed up from the little lake of gaiety. He retraced his steps. There was now no one at the first shooting booth, and the proprietor looked so utterly miserable among his dangling clay pipes that Charles was overcome with charity. Besides, he liked shooting at a target. He glanced at his watch. It was still only five-and-twenty past five. He put down his money and the man, his expression as wretched as ever, handed him the five little cartridges.

The rifle was sighted wide and low. He grouped his five shots quite well, in the outside rings at about four o'clock. He pulled out another crumpled five franc note, as the man handed him his target. This time he aimed high left. The first round entered the centre bull without so much as touching the line. A small gasp of admiration went up from a boy at his side. The second did likewise, and at the end he had shot a perfect score. When the man gave him his target, the spectators craned over his shoulder to admire.

The proprietor looked more unhappy than ever, for he must now hand out one of his prizes. Charles would have liked not to take one, but he thought, quite untruly, that the man might resent this. Besides, it would disappoint those hot and garlicky breaths behind him, whose owners were now all eyes to see what he would choose—a green china cup? a white toy bunny-rabbit? two forks and a spoon, tied together with pink twine? an ominous-looking bottle labelled champagne? It was a hard choice. He decided on the champagne, and the proprietor gave it to him with a shrug. The crowd gazed after him as he walked away with his trophy. They looked disappointed. Surely a china cup would have been more useful?

Now he set out to find his restaurant. The search was not easy. After all, it was ten years since he had been this way, and then only once by daylight. New buildings had been put up since then, and shops had changed hands. He thought he knew the turning from the Place Denfert-Rochereau, and he followed a street for a little way. It twisted—he remembered no such twist—to become a long vista of tall grey apartment houses. He turned back. The second street he tried seemed familiar. He recollected a turning to the left, quite near the Place. In this street, the first turning to the left was a cul-de-sac, where there was no café. The second was several hundred yards further on. He took it. Almost immediately he came on the Café des Amateurs, a dirty grey place, with a zinc bar running the whole length of its short rear wall. He walked on, much farther, until he came to the Café de la Fusillade. It looked familiar, but then it resembled in its lay-out so many other Paris cafés that the familiarity was suspect. Surely he would have noticed such a curious name, if this were indeed the place he had visited before? Besides it seemed too far from the Place Denfert-Rochereau.

He looked through the door. There were four or five marble-topped tables and in the corner two more, covered with fly-specked red and white cloths.

"Monsieur?"

A heavily built man with black handle-bar moustaches leaned across the bar towards him. Charles was in doubt, and seated himself at the nearest marble-topped table. He placed his trophy bottle before him. The face of the man behind the bar clouded:

"You wish to drink that here?"

"No, no. Give me a Pernod, please."

A wizened old man, leaning against the zinc, cleared his throat and spat, prior to resuming his conversation with the owner of the bar. Charles sipped his Pernod and tried to reconstruct the room. There was, indeed, a door through to the back, somewhere near the place he expected it to be. But the cash register, which had stood isolated on a dais, was now behind the bar between the bottles.

Charles realised immediately he sat down that the only way he could identify this bar as the one of 1915 would be the appearance of the girl. Even so, after ten years. . . . Certainly he could not find out from the proprietor. There was no way of framing the question. Perhaps she might appear, or the old mother. But even if she did. . . .

He drank his Pernod slowly. The wizened customer, after a final paroxysm of coughing and spitting, had gone. The proprietor—was he the man who had been at the front?—rinsed the used glass and polished it. Charles ordered another Pernod, hoping to engage him in conversation. But before his drink had been poured out, three men came in, their shoes clopping on the ground, distinguishable as masons by the white plaster which clung to them. Charles drank this second Pernod quite quickly. The bar was beginning to fill up. There was no sign of anyone in the back part of the house. Through a lace curtain he could just distinguish what might be a potted palm on a round table.

He had paid for the drinks as he got them, so that now, swallowing the last of his Pernod, he simply got up and walked out. He was a few yards down the street when he heard the proprietor's voice:

"Monsieur!"

He turned eagerly. The man stood on the threshold, the bottle of champagne in his hand:

"You forgot your bottle."

Charles was embarrassed.

"Oh, it is of no importance. I don't want it."

The man looked at him doubtfully.

"As you wish."

He turned back into his café. Charles looked after him. Then, a taxi passing, he called it and gave the address of his hotel. It turned around and once again he drove past the café. If only he could be sure that it was at least the same one.

Yet, if it had been, what then? The soft lights and the gentle voice, the pink and merry complexion, that would all be gone, all blown away. There might once have been the offer of such a life, but even that was unlikely. Charles leaned back in the corner and thought of his mother, dying as had his father, among vile smelling medicines and to the clink of a spoon against glass.

"A message for you, Mr. Monroe."

He took the folded piece of paper from the hotel porter and walked over to the lift. His mind was still vaguely occupied with faint regrets. The elevator had reached his floor and he had not yet looked at his note. He tore it open in the corridor.

"4:30. Madame Monroe requests Monsieur Monroe to phone her at Elysée 65.14."

He read it again and then unlocked the door and entered his empty bedroom. Although he could not think how Helen knew he was in Paris, nor could imagine why she should wish him to telephone her, he accepted her message as fitting into the pattern of his present emotions. He had sought domesticity in Montrouge. He returned to his hotel and found that his wife of five years ago still wished to see him.

His hand was reaching for the telephone when something stopped him. He sat down on the bed. It was, indeed, five years since last they met, and that meeting had been one of pure formality, at a solicitor's office, called to decide the future of the baby. This note then meant what? He had never thought to see Helen nor to hear from her again. He had imagined that she was married to someone in America, for he had heard that she was in New York. Yet here were their two names, if not side by side, at least on the same piece of paper—Monsieur et Madame Monroe—almost like an invitation to a dinner, or an entry in a hotel register. And in the back of his mind there still lingered the warm lamplight of the unfound café. At least she had not married again.

Yet was it safe? Would it not be better to pack his bags immediately, move to another hotel tonight, and catch the first train to London in the morning? Suppose she did really want to try it again? Suppose they did live together for a little while? Would not worse misery than ever resolve from such an attempt, born like diphtheria from the festering cesspools of old jealousy? He shook his head. He was being stupid, going off again into those absurd daydreams. A request to telephone was hardly a proposal of remarriage.

He unhooked the earpiece, and asked for her number. The hotel operator dialed it, and Charles listened to the distant ring, heard away in some Paris room where Helen was perhaps now sitting, waiting for his call. It rang again and again. He was too late. She must have gone out, gone back even to New York. He was about to replace the receiver, when it clicked, and a voice said, "Hello?"

It was a man's voice, rich and deep, with a slight American accent.

"May I speak to Mrs. Monroe, please?"

There was a second's pause. Then the rich voice enquired, "Who is it speaking?"

"It's her husband."

There was silence at the other end. Charles wished he had

said Mr. Monroe. After all, he was her husband no longer, or so the lawyers had told him.

"Hello, Charles?"

It could be no one else than she, and yet her voice, her sweet voice, sounded strange. Perhaps it was only the telephone. He gripped the black earpiece a little tighter. He had never become accustomed to telephones and always had to restrain a desire to shout.

"Hello, Helen. How are you?"

He wondered what made his voice so hard, and why he had asked such a foolish question. She said:

"I heard from Duvivier that you were here."

"Duvivier?"

Her voice had perhaps the slightest edge of irritability. "The chemist man you came over to see."

"Oh, Duvivier."

"Yes. He gave me your address."

"Oh."

"I wondered if I could see you before you go back to London?"

Watching himself, as he talked and listened in a frigidity of impotent awkwardness, he saw a little dam break, high on the mountains, and waters which might grow to a flood come tumbling down towards the plain.

"I'd love to, Helen. Any time you say. Tonight?"

"I can't tonight. How about lunch tomorrow?"

"Certainly. Where shall we go? Weber's?"

"That's always so noisy. How about the Crillon?"

"All right. Say twelve o'clock?"

"Twelve-thirty would be better for me."

"All right then. Twelve-thirty."

There was really nothing more to say, yet Charles was loth to cut the tenuous cord.

"How are you, Helen?"

"Oh, I'm all right. We'll talk tomorrow."

The little stream, high in the mountains, had disappeared. There would be no flood. He said, "Yes. Tomorrow then." There was a short pause.

"Goodbye, Charles."

"Goodbye, Helen."

He heard her ring off. He replaced the receiver on the hook. His own voice, and hers so distant, seemed to re-echo from the papered walls of the small and chilly bedroom.

The following afternoon, still wearing his brown tie, and carrying a battered leather portmanteau, Charles walked the windy expanses of the Gare Saint Lazare, on his way to London. It was all over, then, and sitting in the train he felt a relief that it had so finished. He was tired, too. The luncheon had been a strain. Helen, in five years, had changed considerably. She used more make-up than he remembered and of a more violent type, particularly about her eyes. Her cloche hat was of canary yellow. Her dress, of the same yellow and irregularly striped with crimson, seemed to Charles hideous in the extreme.

She was already at the Crillon when he arrived, and he recalled her unfailing punctuality. She was chatting with two men at the bar. When she saw Charles she left them, and he and she sat at a table half darkened, in the corner by the stairs. They talked in generalities, she simulating gaiety, a sort of cocktail party conversation in which he followed her lead. She treated him with a familiarity which he somewhat resented, though he sensed nervousness beneath her manner.

She laughed a little too heartily at his small attempts at wit, and when they walked towards the dining room she laid her hand on his sleeve. He would have liked to brush it off.

They ordered. She explained about her diet. Then:

"But my dear Charles, where *did* you get that tie?"

"In Manchester."

"It looks it. Why haven't you bought yourself some new ones at Charvet's?"

"I don't like Charvet ties."

Not now could he tell her of his morning long search, for the elation of the morning was all gone out of him. Was this the woman who had peopled his dreams and lain her shadow across every waking hour? Was this the girl who had sat beside him in the Gloucestershire garden? He doubted it. His dreams, even his nightmares, had been his own. He had made them for himself. She had been merely useful, a stage property. He could know that now, looking at her across the white cloth, the glass and the silver.

He had purposely asked her no questions about herself. She was apparently expecting him to do so, for at last, and with a certain lack of ease, she said:

"I've taken a villa on the Riviera."

"How nice for you." Charles cut another mouthful off his tournedos.

"Yes, it is, isn't it? It's a lovely place on top of a little cliff. The pinewoods almost reach into the bedroom windows."

Charles remembered the rich voice on the telephone, and saw Helen in a Mediterranean garden, the sun on her bare shoulders. But it was his Helen that he saw, not the woman across the table. What this one did or left undone was no concern of his. She said:

"I wondered, Charles, whether you would let Oliver come and stay with me for a part of the summer."

He looked up at her, and said with his mouth full, "Is that why you wanted to lunch with me?"

"Oh, Charles, don't be silly. I wanted to see you."

He smiled at her. "Quite. You haven't hurt my feelings."

It was much more difficult than she had expected.

"How about it then?"

"Oliver?"

"You have become dense. Yes, Oliver. Will you let him come? It would be such fun for me, and he could learn some French."

He liked her honesty for putting her pleasure first, but he said, "French in the South of France?"

"I know I signed that thing at the lawyers. But if you agreed . . ."

It was hard for her. She usually took what she wanted. Requests came to her uneasily. For all her attempts at party conversation, she had succeeded only in reconstructing for Charles the atmosphere of the solicitor's office. It was odd for him to think that only yesterday, on the telephone, he had referred to himself as her husband.

"Well, Charles?"

"I don't think it's a very good idea."

He did not in fact care deeply about Oliver. The boy was staying with his cousins and Charles barely saw him more often than once a year. Yet why should he give him to this canary-coloured woman who was masquerading as Helen?

She tried another approach, the worst, perhaps, that she could have attempted. She talked of old times, of the days just before their marriage, of Charles' return from France after the war, of Oliver's birth. Charles replied in monosyllables. This probing into the past was utterly offensive to him. To her such recollections might be pleasant. For him, the pleasure was so deeply covered by the slimy pain of his Paddington years, that it had quite disappeared. That she should fail to realise this, filled him with contempt for her.

She brought the conversation back to Oliver. He knew she would not drop it now, and therefore, with a perfectly clear conscience, he told her a straight lie:

"As far as I'm concerned he can certainly come and stay with you. But I'm not really responsible for him any more. If my cousins agree, I'll agree too. If not, well, they've taken over the boy's upbringing. I wouldn't go against what they think right."

"Shall I write to them?"

"I doubt if that would be a very good idea." Charles' voice was dry.

She looked at him, haggard, and saw no sympathy in his face. She realised that this was the end. He wondered, as he looked at her, whether she was wishing him dead. The bill was paid. They walked out into the sunlight and said goodbye. He had her address and he would write. He had just enough time to pack and catch the afternoon train.

His feeling of relief in the train was considerable. It was now, definitely and forever, finished. He had seen her. He had ventured into the cruel jungle and had found that it was no longer dangerous. He was going back to London, back to that solitude which had at first been so hateful, but which now beckoned with irresistible charm. He was returning to the carefully regulated life which he had built up for himself. He knew it, that lonely palace whose foundations he had laid while still a child. He knew every room of his own building; every stick of furniture was there by his own choice; and the ghosts that walked it, the ghost of Helen more prominent than any of the others, could now never be disturbed. For him the lamplight of a winter's evening would be of his own lighting, the late night miseries would be his own constructions. From the flesh-and-blood Helen, from the unfound restaurant, from all the turbulent dangers and the siren calls, he was going home, back to his own home, back to where he was safe.

And now in London, as he walked the streets of 1944, the danger that hung over his head was understood in the terms of that earlier encounter.

He had covered a wide circle, and was only about a half mile from his flat. By the chink of light from a traffic control standard, he looked at his watch and saw that it was half past twelve. The memory of Louise returned suddenly, superimposed as it were on that of Helen—the real Louise on the real Helen, not the fantastically desirable wraiths of his imaginings.

He realised, as he walked home, that he was very tired. It was considerably less than twenty-four hours since he had left Casablanca, and the turbulence of the emotions which he had experienced that evening was in itself an exhaustion. He felt his feet dragging, and had he seen a taxi he would have taken it. Furthermore, he knew that on his return he must confront Oliver as well as Louise. He had lost the strength to see her as he had pictured her in the train. It was too much for his tired brain. He wished he were returning to an empty flat. Yet what if the flat were empty? That was another problem. He brushed it from him as a man might push, ineffectively, at a mosquito.

And then Oliver. Well, he would simply ignore Oliver. And

in the morning there would be breakfast, and, if he could, he would ignore Oliver at breakfast too. He and Louise would catch the eleven o'clock for Oxford. How interminable was Ebury Street! If Louise were not in the flat tonight, then he would go alone to Oxford. He would never see Louise again. Or if, just suppose, Helen were there waiting for him? If he should step back into the restaurant and the beliefs of thirty years ago?

> Troop home to silent grots and caves.

On, on he walked. Was there nobody awake in this stony sea? He turned into Eaton Place, an odious square, pompous without being self-assured. Louise, then, was waiting for him at home. He tried the magic touchstone again, but again it failed to respond. Louise was there, smooth comfort. She would always be there, darning on the sofa, while he, at his desk, turned and smiled. The palace of solitude was now only his weekend home, an occasional place for a summer's day visit. Louise sat on the sofa, dropping cigarette butts into ashtrays, and he must imitate the "murmuring seal." Imagine, at his age, pretending to be a seal!

He turned into his mews. A chink of light through the curtains showed that Louise was home. Oliver, too, would be awaiting him. He slowed his steps. From the depths of his being he attempted to pull forth the energy which he knew he would need. He put his key in the door, and, as he did so, he wondered for one confusing moment whether he would recognise Louise. Yet he knew her voice, as she cried:

"Who's there?"

He began to mount the stairs. "It's me. Charles."

CHAPTER EIGHT

LOVERS may indeed be cardboard figures and Oliver, returning with Louise to the flat, may have felt the gradual constriction of desire. His knee joints seemed stiff, awkward; he was conscious of a curious friction when his fingers bent inwards to the palms of his hands. The hiatus between the unspoken promise and the consummation is a time of indignity best cloaked in silence. Neither he nor Louise spoke. He looked at her, where she walked half a yard from him, and divined in the darkness that her head was bowed. Her attitude was one of sacrifice, and Oliver might have felt pride in his eventual mastery. Yet, in imminent achievement of an old desire, the desire itself, a certainty of many years, seemed to shrink and crack, almost to disintegrate.

What caused this premature disillusionment? Was it for this that he had lost Katherine? He had nothing to offer Louise, for in two days he would be gone to India. Would the corruption of her marriage be accomplished in this atmosphere of a vow fulfilled too late? The question almost emerged in his mind, walking now beside her. He dismissed it before it had been posed. But later, in India, he did try to answer it.

It was January of the following year. Oliver sat, in his shirt sleeves, under a naked electric light. This small room was now his home, but his few intimate possessions hardly scratched its ugly personality. He looked at his hairbrushes on the fake marble washstand, his slippers beside the sagging bed. He had never decided which was the least uncomfortable, the dusty grey armchair or the hard yellow one before the table. The armchair was indeed stuffed, but it had an unpleasant smell. Oliver sat on the hard chair and rested his arms on the table.

It was in this atmosphere that, remembering Louise, he tried to arrange his recollections of her, to discern some pattern or causal chain in the confused emotions with which she had inspired him. The high peaks stood out clearly enough, but they were inexplicable without their surrounding foothills. Then, too, he must not confuse the finished mountain range, wooded and snowed, with the elementary Freudian geology hidden below. Indeed, he thought, that metaphor can be taken further. The Himalayas do not require to be understood; it is quite satisfactory that standing there, leaning across Asia, they should remain large and incomprehensible. But the busy men who have, as best they could, mapped them, photographed the accessible parts and analysed the construction of the whole, have at least made it unnecessary to repeat those labours. Oliver doubted if he would ever fully understand the Gothic emotions which he had felt, and to a certain degree still did feel, for Louise. None the less he felt that it was time he made an attempt to search for or to invent some pattern to which he could in the future refer. He wished to shut up those dead or moribund emotions in the files of his mind; there they would remain, accessible and neatly ticketed. He had had enough of the way they kept fluttering about his littered desk, interfering with every new emotion he experienced.

He picked up a pencil from the table before him, and turning it over in his fingers, tried to visualise Louise, and to recall the sensations of years gone by. Her face was misty and not remembered; he could no longer see the dark blue of her eyes; and though he told himself that her hair was black, its blackness no longer possessed any quality of its own. When he tried to think of Louise at Oxford it was Peacock's dumpy face and harsh flat voice that usurped the centre of his private stage.

It was as Peacock's mistress that he had first noticed Louise. Their juxtaposition had seemed odd, and he had been intrigued that she should have chosen that half-farcical figure. It was as though Heloise had wandered off from Abelard and had taken up with some Punchinello from a Commedia del' Arte troupe. It was, in its way, rather shocking, though Oliver realised now that it had been no concern of his.

He remembered that summer of 1939 as a particularly futile time—just one year more futile than 1938. There were some people who continued to live in a planned and orderly manner—he supposed, in fact, that most people had done so. At Oxford the grey men who were to get firsts went on with their reading. Others were careful not to overdraw at their banks. Oliver had felt, when he saw such mundane and praiseworthy activity, as though he were watching an animated Pompeii. Besides, it was irritating. There was Stanley Hampden, for instance, a contemporary of Oliver's, whom he had met through his father. Although Charles had, as was his habit, made no direct statement, Oliver suspected that his father drew an unwelcome comparison between Hampden's leathery

persistence, and his own selfish acceptance of impending catas-
trophe. One evening in May Oliver happened to walk into
Hampden's rooms in Wellington Square. Hampden was sitting
under a powerful reading lamp, in a dark shot-silk dressing
gown. As usual he was suffering from what he called heavy nasal
catarrh. By his elbow stood a glass of hot rum and water.
Over the mantelpiece hung a Medici print of Van Gogh's sun-
flowers. He was reading Jane Austen. Oliver sat and talked to
him for a while. Hampden had arranged for everything, even
including the coming war. He had arranged well. He got a first
class degree; he took an examination for the Civil Service which
he passed with high distinction; as soon as the war broke out,
he began training for an airforce commission. Two months
later he was sliced into rashers by the propeller of a training
plane.

During that long summer of 1939 Oliver would have been
delighted had he had a preview of Stanley's nemesis. It would
have reassured him in his certainty that his manner of life was
the only one which a reasonable young man could follow.
Rumour invariably has it that the condemned man ate a hearty
breakfast. While the German generals peered at their time-
tables, there still remained plenty of good wine and innumerable
handsome women west of the Rhine. Oliver, in London and
Paris and later in the South of France, took the best that he
could find. He remembered in particular a little Danish girl at
Antibes, not a day over sixteen. . . . But he was wandering
from his train of thought.

Those simple pleasures were not all that he enjoyed, waiting for the thunder. Many people he met during that time were
actively unhappy, others puzzled and lost. Some, like Stanley,
made the most careful and elaborate preparations, as though

the coming cataclysm could be negotiated by careful study of
the bus routes, could be equipped against with the hampers
from Fortnum's and *All You Want to Say in Dutch.* Oliver
preferred a frame of mind based on macabre amusement com-
pounded with awe. For there was, in the anticipation, a funny
side, a sort of cosmic revenge. He visualised whole trainloads
of bank clerks, still worrying about their insurance or over-
draft, as the carriages hurtled over the precipice, down
into the dry ravine where distressed gentlewomen scrabbled in
a refined manner for crusts. The spectacle of the collapse of
cities would have an impressive timelessness and grandeur that
would blot out, once and for all, the niggling and inanities of
the age, the pained righteousness of the *New Statesman and
Nation,* the literary gossip in the Café Flore, the squalid search
for a middle-class God in California, the snobs and the bores,
the people who said, "Do you see what I mean?" and those who
replied, "Surely you must agree," the smug and the smart, the
good and also, he supposed, the evil. And afterwards there
would remain the fantastic ruins, the broken metropolis silent
save for the dripping of acid from the huge containers in the
power station. Oliver contemplated the future with a cheerful
grimness.

During that last summer term at Oxford Oliver had not
seen a great deal of Roger Peacock. They had never really
been close friends, and now Peacock's flirtation with the priests
at Campion Hall, his pretence that he wished to join the Catholic church, struck Oliver as an absurd performance. But they
still spent an occasional evening together and Oliver found Peacock's car useful. Oliver preferred Peacock when the latter was
drunk. Sober he found him rather annoying, with an irritating
habit of dragging in to all conversations the names of celebrities

whom he knew less well than he implied. Cocteau, Yeats and Maritain would be wedged, sideways as it were, into subjects where they can scarcely have felt at home. Oliver's attitude to Roger was one of mild contempt—he was so desperately fond of ceremonial and his intellectual's Debrett was so thoroughly thumbed. Yet he was not the sort of man with whom Oliver could quarrel. One June morning Oliver met him in the High. It was suggested they drive out to Woodstock that evening for dinner. Oliver, having nothing better to do, accepted.

Oliver had met Louise Collins at one or two parties, but had never spoken to her before that evening when he found her in Peacock's rooms. He had arrived a little early and had entered Roger's sitting room without knocking, for he could hear music. The scene that confronted him was curiously posed and stiff, like those moments in a dress rehearsal when the actors and the set are being photographed. The whole room was elaborately tidy, which was in itself unusual. Oliver assumed that it had just been put to rights. Louise sat in the middle of the sofa—the cushions to either side of her were puffed up and smooth—and Peacock leaned over his radiogram with an air of affected unconcern, as though *Eine Kleine Nachtmusik* were a new and quite interesting experience for him. The whole place looked, in fact, as though something had been going on. Oliver wondered for a second if Peacock had attempted to rape her, but one glance at that unhealthy little man was enough to tell him that such could not possibly be the case.

They talked for a moment or two and Oliver half expected Roger to call off their dinner, but he soon realised that he was wrong. Peacock did not look at nor speak to Louise, and Oliver knew that this was not some obscure manifestation of shyness or guilt. Louise scarcely spoke. Whenever Oliver addressed a remark to her she replied with a monosyllable. Yet she did not appear in any way nervous. Oliver found the whole business quite intriguing.

After a short time she said that she must be returning home. Roger offered her a lift. She declined it at first, but he insisted. Oliver decided that he still wished to impress her, and that he felt more powerful at the wheel of his car, with another twelve cylinders added to his personality. In any case they drove her home, to the hideous red house at the end of the Banbury Road. When she got out Roger said, in an authoritative voice:

"Will you come to lunch tomorrow then?" The engine of the car was still running.

"If you like, Roger."

Oliver watched her turn into the gate. She had a very graceful walk. As they drove off Roger, without looking at him, asked, "Like her?"

Had Oliver been a little older, or had he known Peacock as well as he later did, he would have realised then, as he realised now in India, that the question was an important one for Roger. In this, as in all other matters, he could not rely on his own opinion; he wanted expert confirmation. In fact Oliver might even have felt slightly flattered that he should be regarded as an authority on such a subject. As it was, though, he had interpreted the question in another way. It seemed boastful and rather impertinent. It sounded like an attempt to put Roger and himself on the same footing, to make of them colleagues or even conspirators together. Oliver resented such presumption and gave a non-committal answer.

They had dined at the Marlborough Arms. It was a poor

meal, but a pleasant dinner. Roger talked well; his ideas, always borrowed ready-made from someone else, were well presented and made his conversation enjoyable. After they had finished their meal they motored out to a small and smoky village pub. It consisted only of a room, into which one stepped down from the road. It was loud with rustic oaths and the banging down of cribbage cards. They sat in the corner.

"Have you read Montherlant's recent series?" asked Peacock.

"*Pitié pour les Femmes?* Yes." It seemed an unsuitable topic for the environment. Oliver would rather have discussed pigs with one of the farm labourers or, better still, played darts.

"What did you think of it?"

Oliver assumed that Peacock was working back to Louise, or rather to himself in the light of an intellectual Don Juan.

"As a series of novels, or as a handbook of seduction?"

The soft atmosphere of dung and beery sweat was soothing. Peacock ignored the question.

"It seems to prove that the emancipation of some women has left most of the others to do exactly as they're told. One wonders what Mrs. Bloomer would have thought of *that.*"

"I should think," said Oliver, bored and less than half attentive, "that she would want to know what it was that the women were told to do."

"My dear Oliver, there's only one thing that a woman is ever told to do. Horace Walpole sums it up, 'Lie down'."

Up to that point Oliver had spent as pleasant an evening as many others passed in Peacock's company. But suddenly this curdled nonsense disgusted him. Now, in retrospect, it just seemed silly undergraduate talk, but there, in the simple pub, Roger's loud flat remarks had stuck in his gullet as thoroughly as if they had been lumps of distasteful matter swallowed by error with the clear amber ale. He remembered wondering just how much Peacock disliked women and whether Louise was merely an object of revenge for him. That, he now realised, should have been a warning. Perhaps unconsciously he had accepted it as one. In any event he had said nothing. After a great deal of beer they drove back to Oxford. That night he had speculated about Roger and Louise with a vague distaste before he fell asleep.

Next morning he decided that he had seen enough of Peacock to last him through the summer. Once or twice they had met, as was inevitable at Oxford, and Louise had usually been with Roger. Oliver had avoided deepening his acquaintance with her. He felt, in the presence of her and Roger, an awkward malaise, a mild disgust, a desire to be elsewhere. He did not at the time make any attempt to analyse the sensation of faint decay with which their liaison affected him. As far as he was concerned they could all go to hell their own way.

Now, in India, that emotional background seemed very remote, even though the war still went on. Then, before the war, violence had seemed about to destroy all the minor irritants. Now that the violence of destruction was known, Oliver realised that the confusion of 1939 could, for him, have been resolved. The fact that he and Peacock might and probably would die, Oliver now saw, was no reason for him to have refused the cross currents of other emotions. If he had felt pity for Louise, as he now thought he had, he was wrong to deny her that pity merely because he felt that the whole generation was doomed. That evening, India seemed less strange than the Oxford which he was trying to reconstruct.

Shortly after the end of the summer term Oliver found himself living in a tumbledown hotel in Charlotte Street run by an unprejudiced and amiable Armenian. Annie told him that she had to go to Oxford to collect some things which she had left there. Oliver, as usual, had overspent his allowance and decided to accompany her in order to touch his father. Working on approved business principles, he had asked his father for more money than he actually needed. To his surprise Charles had given him what he asked. Next morning he and Annie had hangovers. There was a nasty scene, too, with the manager of the Mitre, where they had stayed. In fact they were thrown out.

So there they were, in the middle of an Oxford Sunday, surrounded by the awful and unending pealing of the seven hundred bells. Annie was alternately whining and laughing idiotically. She kept asking for champagne. Although it was a point of pride with Oliver never to admit to a hangover, he too felt that a bottle of iced wine would be, at the moment, a sort of perfection. But it was only eleven o'clock; the pubs would not be open for a full hour. Further, since term was over there were few men in residence whom Oliver knew. Of those few, most, like Stanley Hampden, could be relied on not to have any champagne. On others, Oliver did not feel sufficiently callous to inflict Annie. There remained Peacock. Although the idea of his company did not please Oliver, he felt that there was nothing else for it. He wished now that he had remained in London and written to his father. But, since he was here, he had best make what he could out of the situation. The idea of walking once again around the Radcliffe Camera with this giggling, sobbing girl was out of the question. There was nothing for it but to drink Peacock's champagne.

He left Annie in the front hall of the tall dark house of which Peacock's rooms occupied the third floor. It was a relief to get away from her for a few minutes, and he walked upstairs slowly. The large amount that he had been drinking during the past few weeks had made his nerves very sensitive, but in a curious, inconsistent fashion. Some things appeared suddenly very bright, and a piece of ugliness which one would normally ignore took on a doom-like quality of horror. Those dark steps, after the bright sunlight of the High Street, seemed cool and soothing as an icepack.

Oliver had been entirely unprepared to find Louise in Roger's sitting room. He remembered most clearly the strange sensations which had gone through him when he entered the room and saw her standing there alone. It was, in retrospect, one of the clearest moments of his life. She was by the mantelpiece, beneath a Cocteau drawing of which Peacock was very proud and which Oliver had always thought fatuous. She was lighting a cigarette, and when Oliver entered the room she turned towards him. There was for a moment an almost tangible silence, like the silence between the end of the overture and the raising of the curtain. But it was stronger than that. It was, for Oliver, as though a whole, loud city, a gigantic and vulgar Corneville, had slipped quietly beneath the sea. He and Louise were left standing on the edge of the cliff, she turning towards him, he coming to take her away.

He stopped by the door, reluctant to move and thus endanger the pagan world which had been created between them. But it was to last only a few seconds. Roger called from the bedroom and immediately the glassy sea was broken. Like a noisy version of Poe's city the brassy metropolis rose again between Oliver and Louise, reasserting itself harshly to tell

Oliver that he had been drinking too much and that such smooth moments of silence are illusory. Yet, he thought, that moment had remained in his memory, and for him it must have contained a reality. It was almost uncomfortable to recall it, even now.

Looking at the pencil between his fingers, slowly he scratched out Peacock's name and began to make a large and elaborate capital L. The yellow chair on which he sat was too hard; he took a couple of turns up and down the room. Sitting down again, he scribbled in haste, "Alcoholic mysticism."

They drove out to the country for lunch. Oliver remembered how he had sat in the back with Annie and had tried to work out what it was that he had felt that morning. He did not succeed. Worse, he felt the vision slipping away from him, as a clean beach is trampled by a mass of ill-shaped feet that turn towards the sea after the ebb tide.

When lunch was over they sat on the terrace overlooking the river. Annie had had a lot to drink and had regained that state of semi-intoxication in which she felt at home. Peacock seemed to be inspecting her with slight lechery. Louise sat back in a low chair with her eyes closed. The conversation was between Roger and Annie, and it went grinding on, prowling like the hosts of Midian, circling their mutual acquaintances, edging towards that easy obscenity which was Annie's badge of friendship. When they decided that they wanted to go swimming Oliver made an excuse. Louise was apparently asleep.

Watching her sleeping there, she seemed to make it clear to him that he had indeed reached a dead end. There was nothing more for him in the life Peacock epitomised. Louise attracted him, for he thought to see in her an antithesis to that vulgarity.

Now, in India, he had no doubt but that he had been deluding himself. What he had admired in Louise had been her cool and tidy aloofness, her ability to preserve her calmness even in such company as she found herself in that day. That had filled Oliver with a sort of respect and a desire to achieve such disentanglement for himself. Perhaps he could learn it from her. Then he had imagined the two of them setting off together, standing at the rail of some big liner while the clamorous coast of Europe sank to a smudge on the horizon. Somewhere there must be another land, where together they could lead a fresh and magnificent life.

> Kennst du das Land, wo die Zitronen blühn,
> Im dunkeln Laub die Gold-Orangen glühn,
> Ein sanfter Wind vom blauen Himmel weht,
> Die Myrte still und hoch der Lorbeer steht,
> Kennst du es wohl?

Twaddle? Undoubtedly. Yet a dream, if it be not an ambition, can never be entirely nonsensical to the man who has dreamed it, can never, in fact, be quite as ridiculous as the sillier aspects of his reality. Oliver supposed that during that afternoon he had been, as they say, in love with Louise, and had attempted to account for that preference by identifying her with his desires. But still the fact remained that it had been she, from among so many, whom he had chosen so to identify.

Kennst du das Land . . . Of course she didn't. Oliver now wondered whether whatever Lotte or Lili had inspired Goethe with *Mignon* had known it any better. But that day by the river Louise had become for him a symbol, and a complicated one. She had become a sort of hybrid—part Gretchen, part

Virginie, an altogether extraordinary creature. And with this strange projection of his own mind, he wished to fly to Persia or Peru.

So he had found himself in a quandary, made slightly more confused by the fact that Louise was Peacock's mistress. He realised now that he made about as incompetent a mess of the situation as he well could have. Obviously he should either have taken her away or left her alone. His own vision of their future relationship was, however, so strong, that he assumed she too must know that it was to be. Kennst du das Land? Had she not as good as told him so, not three hours before, as she stood there in silence by Peacock's mantelpiece? Confused with alcohol and symbolism, Oliver had therefore made a half-hearted and naturally unsuccessful attempt at seduction in a wood infested with gamekeepers. Then, satisfied by his own dis-satisfaction, he had played a grotesque role of self-denial. As though performing some gallant act, he had renounced Louise. He had sacrificed himself to Armagnac, Danish girls and such. With the morning's queasiness, though, he would remember Louise as a symbol of what he might have been.

My only excuse, he thought gloomily, is that I was very young. And with annoyance he took off his boots and threw them into the corner of the room.

For certainly that attitude of Oliver's had not lasted be-yond the summer of 1939. This made him now think that it must have been largely inspired by the environment. When the war radically changed the background against which he saw Louise, her figure lost its importance for him. He remembered, in the following summer, her visit to Tidworth after his re-turn from France. Then only the pity which he had had for her remained, but a pity of the bored rather than of the amorous sort. He had felt about her as though she were an old mistress of five or ten years before—as if they had had a pleasant but unimportant affair from which the last drop had been squeezed, the last emotion long since worked out. Certainly he had then had no feeling that Louise belonged to him by right of myrtles and laurels and Sunkist oranges. He had given her a few words of comfort, told her what he thought she would like to hear about Roger Peacock, and had made no further attempt to see her again while he was in England. It was, in fact, all over. It was then that he met Katherine.

What then had revived his feeling for Louise in this nagging way, so that it had become almost an obsession with him? He knew perfectly well. It was the letter from his father which had told him of his intention to marry Louise. Had she chosen any other man, Oliver doubted if he would have had more than a passing interest, perhaps the very small regret which he supposed most men feel on such an occasion. For example if he had heard that she was to marry her office boy, who he imagined might well have made her an excellent husband, he would probably have given the matter no further thought.

But the news which he had received in Egypt, that she proposed to marry Charles, had awakened, in a much more violent form, all the desire he had had for Louise while Peacock lived. It was more than jealousy, it was anger. Since that anger would not have existed had she chosen to marry any other man, it must, Oliver thought, have been inspired more by his father than by Louise. Yet he did not actually dislike his father, and never had done so. He realised that if he was to understand his feeling for Louise at this time and later, it was important that he try to remember how he had felt towards his father during those years.

He wrote down his father's name—Charles Monroe. As he stared at it, half visions of his father floated up out of the past towards him.

He was a child at his cousins' house. A thin man sat on the sofa, the man he knew to be his father. Oliver had been brought in by an aunt. She had said to the thin man:

"He gets to look more like you every day."

Charles had turned his melancholy eyes on Oliver and, embarrassed, had given him a paper bag of liquorice squares. How could he know that Oliver hated liquorice, hated not only its taste, but its texture and its colour, that he identified liquorice squares with the dirty nose of the postman's son?

"He has something of his mother's eyes," Charles had said.

Then the two grownups had spoken French, and Oliver had felt, though he had not recognised, the despair in his father's voice. He believed it to be Charles' fault that he had no mother. He did not blame his father on this account, but he resented the hopeless, clumsy kindness of the man. When he got out into the garden again he hurled the liquorice high into the thick rhododendrons and tore at the leaves.

During the last three years of pre-adolescent savagery, Oliver had frequently spent the holidays with his father. From those days he remembered little. On one occasion they had gone to Lord's to see Bradman, but Charles had fallen asleep. Once in the summer, there had been a distant thunderstorm, and Charles had said, more to himself than to Oliver:

"That is how the Flanders guns must have sounded from the Essex coast."

When Oliver had asked about the guns, Charles had been evasive and had left the room. Oliver, too, remembered the incident at the school, when the black bombers had flown so low overhead.

During late adolescence, his relationship with his father had been almost shamefully false, each pretending towards the other a polite affection which was to both of them patently insincere. Oliver felt a reproach in his father's attitude, and against that reproach he cultivated an armor of indifference. He made even fewer attempts to understand Charles and, as he grew older, saw him less and less frequently. By the time Oliver was twenty he and Charles were practically strangers.

Perhaps the last occasion on which that gulf could have been breached was one autumn day in 1938, when Oliver had gone to call on his father in the latter's rooms at his college.

It was a raw October evening, Dickensian weather, the wan street lamps half shrouded by the cold mists which rose from the rivers of Oxford. Oliver hurried along the street past the muffled figures of his fellow undergraduates. Charles was out when Oliver arrived, but the coal fire blazed cheerfully and the servant brought tea. It was just the room for such weather, and when the curtains were drawn Oliver felt pleasantly filial, as he glanced at the books and the incomprehensible lecture notes on the desk. This atmosphere of scholarship, shabby but well fed, filled Oliver with a sort of comfortable respect. He was glad that he had come to see his father and that there was no financial or otherwise utilitarian motive behind his visit.

Yet almost as soon as Charles entered the room he destroyed Oliver's frame of mind. He greeted his son with limp affection. He looked damp and cold, and his nose was blue. His clothes smelt strongly of tweed, and he drank the lukewarm, overstrong tea, rather than ring for his servant and order fresh. It seemed then to Oliver that the comfort and quiet dignity of the room could not possibly be the creation of this nervous, colourless chemist, but must derive from the patina left by its previous inhabitants which Charles' weak character could not even scratch.

Oliver's respect and affection of the moment, superficial as they were, dripped away. They talked for a little in generalities. But it became increasingly clear to Oliver that his father was expecting him to ask for something. At last he brought it out, avoiding Oliver's eye: Was there anything he wanted? It gave Oliver a now wholly malicious satisfaction to say that there was nothing, that he had come only for the pleasure of talking with his father. Charles seemed at a loss to know what to do next. Perhaps he thought that Oliver had come to him for advice of some sort, for he said:

"It's none of my business, Oliver, but the Vice-President of your College told me the other day that in his opinion you were drinking rather too much."

Oliver did not reply and again Charles looked away.

"As I say, it's none of my business."

Then why had he mentioned it? Oliver had rather be ordered about than expected to accept hints which were as foolish as they were half-hearted. There was a moment's uncomfortable silence, and then Charles rather laboriously opened a conversation which seemed to Oliver, both at the time and now looked at in retrospect, to typify his father's weak foolishness.

Charles had an acquaintance dating from his school days, one Sir Wilfred Rumbold, a Liberal politician whose loud and pompous pieties had reverberated, diminuendo with the decline of his party, through the twenties and thirties. Sir Wilfred had always, plainly and outspokenly, advocated peace, wealth, godliness, cleanliness, faith, hope and charity. It appeared that

Charles had recently received a letter from this elderly desperado which dealt with the recently concluded Munich pact. It was to this that he now turned. Apparently Sir Wilfred deplored the agreement, commenting on the babyish and hysterical reception with which the Prime Minister had been received in the House of Commons when he returned from selling his country's honour to the Austrian house-painter. (Oliver assumed this was Sir Wilfred's amusing way of describing Hitler.) On the other hand Sir Wilfred seemed to express pleasure that war had been avoided. Charles put the letter away and made one of his customary non-committal statements. He was plainly relieved to have steered the conversation into such an impersonal channel. Oliver asked him whether he agreed with Sir Wilfred's point of view. He blew his nose as he replied:

"I wouldn't go so far as to say that I agree." He trumpeted into his handkerchief. "On the other hand," he blew twice more, "it does seem a pity that England should be so undignified." He squashed his handkerchief into his trouser pocket. "Don't you agree?"

Oliver said that he could not see that England's dignity had any bearing on the matter. An elected government had plainly carried out the will of the people and had succeeded in avoiding a war.

"You may be right," it was a typical phrase of Charles', "but then, as Sir Wilfred says, if it's just a postponement, just irresponsible, hysteria . . ." He left his sentence unfinished.

Oliver could no longer remember how the depressing conversation had ended. But he knew that Charles' attitude, or rather his lack of attitude, had seemed to him then as it seemed to him now to underline the weakness of that character. Here was a man who really, as Oliver knew, both hated and feared war. His inactive pacifism was no pose, as it might be in the case of Sir Wilfred. Charles knew by personal experience what war meant and could entail, and he had long ago decided that no calamity could possibly compare in horror with the outbreak of another one. Oliver knew that the news from Spain, for instance, had affected Charles deeply. Yet for all that he was not even prepared to take a firm point of view, let alone to embark on a course of action. By such behaviour over a period of years, Oliver felt, Charles and others like him had permitted the world to become the place it now was. In fact, he thought, Charles' superstitious terrors were not only despicable but positively dangerous. Even as he had handed his son over to his cousins, so had his generation by default handed that son's generation over to the war lords and the card sharps of the world. Oliver despised him for it.

While the sour-sweet smell of India drifted in through the window Oliver recalled the momentary amusement and incredulity with which he had first received the news of Charles' intentions to marry Louise. But those feelings had rapidly passed. An unsatisfied passion that has been dormant is capable of a surprisingly quick and strong revival. The symbolic Louise of Peacock's time had become a part of Oliver's private mythology, an important if inactive figure on his Parnassus. That that clumsy-fingered coward should dare to trespass in such a place had seemed to Oliver an intolerable sacrilege. Yet what right had he to complain? What feudal privilege could he advance? He had written to Louise and he had written also to his father, but he had torn up both the letters.

Now the figure of Katherine rose up to confuse his memory. For a moment he contemplated her with a sickened regret. If only, he thought, she had had the ability, that evening at Henri's club, to understand that his desire for Louise in no way detracted from his affection for her. That she had not done so was obvious, since she had answered none of his letters since that evening. He realised now that he should have explained it all to Katherine, about Peacock and about his father. Perhaps she could have seen, then, that Louise was no sort of rival pretty girl, but only the representative of two worlds from which Oliver wished to be forever freed. Louise had become for him a charm, an animate piece of magic from which and through which Oliver desired to make his escape. But at the time he had confused Louise the magician with the girl at the table. If he himself had then been unaware of the subtlety, he could hardly blame Katherine for her failure of perception. Besides, he thought with a smile, women are notoriously lacking in charity about such matters. The only person who might have been expected to understand was Louise.

Oliver took up the piece of paper he had been scribbling on and read the disjointed and meaningless words which he had written. He tore the piece into four and dropped it in the basket by the table leg.

Walking back with Louise to her flat, as Oliver recalled it, was not like going to an amorous tryst. It was rather the accomplishment of a vaguer and yet more positive action, the deliberate breaking of an old power, the end of a long confusion, of a pointless self-denial. It was, in some ways, the shutting of the door against his youth, a sort of inverted gesture of self-discipline. Whether, in truth, such confusion as had been centred in Louise could be straightened by the action of one night, Oliver still did not know. But he thought so. He believed that he was now free of Louise and all that she had meant to him, and that he had received that freedom when she had started from his arms and he had heard his father's voice on the stairs crying:

"It's me—Charles."

Oliver rose from the table. The noises of the Asiatic night flickered like bats against the window screen. He threw his clothes on the floor and went to bed. He dreamed, as he so often did these days, of Katherine.

CHAPTER NINE

THE scene which confronted Charles as he entered the drawing room of his flat was immediately unbelievable to him. It was a scene which should have been framed in heavy gilt and hung on the walls of a provincial gallery—an allegorical and exaggerated canvas after the manner of Géricault or David, a thing all of shadows, pregnant with meaning, and figures representing abstractions.

The main element of light came from the electric fire, for the table lamp, though lit, had been placed upon the floor, between the table and the sofa. The fire's red glare was blackened by the green carpet, so that the very light seemed dark. The sofa, silhouetted by the lamp, loomed like an impending ruin. The far corners of the room were dark. Despite the smallness of space, the atmosphere suggested a Belshazzar's Feast or a Destruction of Samson, scaled down, of course, and with the secondary characters left out. This imagined fever, this suspicion of distant holocausts and crashing masonry, was emphasised by the figures of Louise and Oliver.

At the sound of the steps upon the stairs Louise had risen

from the sofa. Oliver had half undressed her. The buttons at the back of her black dress were undone, and it now hung loosely from her hips. Her brassière trailed over the arm of the sofa. As Charles came in she made an uncompleted gesture to cover her bare breasts with her right hand. Her face was flushed, and over her usually calm features were spread horror and abandonment and fear. She stood in the centre of the room, looking toward the door; her body was turned slightly to one side.

Oliver had not risen from the sofa. He was in almost total darkness, a little light catching his profile, his grey suit apparently black. The artist who never painted the picture would have thought Oliver's figure the sinister counterpart to the pale mounds which were Louise's breasts.

But for Charles, in the first shock of entering that make-believe world, there were no emotional responses. Despite his recognition of his own admittance to the disordered scene, his immediate reaction, characteristic and perhaps pathetic, was for himself. That might be Louise, and the dark figure might be Oliver, but he was always and forever Charles; his first wish was for himself. A panic to escape flitted through his mind, to walk back out of the flat and perhaps so to make the scene disappear. He dismissed it immediately. He might have adopted a bullying, policeman-like tone, but such was not his nature. His first conscious thought was:

I must be careful now. I must not make a fool of myself. And he said, in a soft, unsuitable voice, as though this were an unexpected meeting in a restaurant:

"Louise."

She glanced from him to Oliver. In her mind the words were, This cannot be true. It is impossible. It is not me, it is not Louise, nor is that Charles. I am not Louise. I am a girl who was about to be loved by that man on the sofa. I have no name, no home, nothing but this body which was in a silken web, arranging for itself the love which it was ready to receive. Now something has happened which I do not understand. I am placed here in the cold centre of this room. The breaking of that web is impossible. I must remain unnamed, unknown.

Therefore when Charles said her name she looked to Oliver for help. There was no help from him. At that time he was the only one of the three who understood at all what had occurred, and even in his case that comprehension was for the other two, not for himself. Charles had called Louise's name, not his. Therefore he watched, for the moment as a spectator, the interplay between them.

Charles took half a step back towards the door, and turned the electric switch. The white overhead light dispelled the orgiastic fantasy in which the room had been clothed. Louise was no longer a creation of distant tragedy, but merely a half-naked girl whose white breasts were as incongruous in a drawing room as was the brassière that trailed on the sofa. The dark, seated figure was no soft Medici or sinister prophet, but merely a young man in a crumpled grey suit.

For Louise, too, the bright light brought a return of consciousness. She still did not realise what was going on about her. She only became aware that she was partially undressed, and that it was therefore unsuitable so to stand, in a bright room with two men. With a half cry she ran through the bedroom, her hanging dress twisting as she went and almost causing her to trip. She closed the bathroom door. Charles and Oliver were thus left alone together.

For Charles, it was as though he were rising from the

depths of the sea. The uniform green waters were about him, suffocating him, but now it was becoming lighter. The air was not far away. He did not desire that hot and parching element, that bashing sunlight. Yet he knew that he must reach it or drown.

His eyes had followed Louise. Now he turned back to where Oliver had risen from the sofa. He saw standing there a stranger, the cruel foreigner in this room of Charles' home. Such was the man who had set the torch to Rome; who, a drunken mercenary, had fought back when surprised with his arms full of Chinese loot; he was the man against whom the generations had built walls and dug moats, the man from outside, the power from across the frontiers of the mind. To that man Charles must add the name of Oliver, his lounging son, the boy back from school on the afternoon train, a baby in a Gloucestershire garden, Helen's soft hair in the deep nightingale dark. Charles tried to superimpose the name on the apparition. He looked away and saw the jar of peppermint humbugs that stood on the corner table.

Oliver, watching the direction of his father's glance, saw the bottle. *Sweets!* Charles was therefore abdicating, was not going to do anything. Oliver thought, he has thus given me the keys, the power of action. He cannot even assume the mask of tragedy, but must stand there thinking about sweets. I hope he eats one. Meanwhile, before I decide whether to go alone or whether to take Louise with me, an act of one sort or another must make clear my acceptance of initiative.

His eye lit on the brassière, hanging forlorn. He leaned to pick it up, and was aware that Charles was watching him. Without looking towards his father he carried the strange garment through to the bedroom. He held it, not gingerly, not between finger and thumb, but firmly, with the grasp of property. It was to the observation of that immodest action that Charles broke the green surface of the waters, out into the beast-haunted air.

Louise had heard Oliver's heavy step in the bedroom. She sat on the flat edge of the bathtub, her head in her hands. All she knew was that she wanted help. Help for her meant Charles. Once before that evening, in the club with Katherine, she had longed for his kindness; now, a hundred times more, she wished for a magic transformation, for the uninquisitive, unimpertinent help which Charles had always given her when most she needed it. Immediately on the formulation of that wish, she realised where Charles was. She dropped her hands from her face and stared at the blank white wall that faced her. Slowly she saw rising before her the complicated monster which had been created when Charles entered the flat, a minute and a half before.

She washed her face hastily. The last remnants of her make-up were gone now, and her face, which had been flushed, was chalk white. She heard Charles' voice, muffled, incomprehensible, and Oliver's equally unclear answer. Quickly she pulled up her dress. What was happening in there between the two men? She must hurry lest there be violence. Her black dress felt rough against her bare breasts, and her trembling fingers could not master the many difficult buttons on her back. When she opened the bathroom door, her eyes, in her pale face, were very dark.

Oliver had placed the brassière on a chair in the bedroom, and then, with deliberation, had turned back towards Charles. In that action the two figures whom Charles had seen, the child and the despoiler, merged into one. Charles saw the determination in his son's face, the look of contempt which hid a certain nervousness. Because of that suspected nervousness Charles felt pity for Oliver and with that pity he felt responsibility. He knew that he must not condemn his son for a crime which was still unproved. Later he could judge and decide. Now the imperative was to avoid speech and further entanglement. He therefore said:

"You must go now, Oliver."

Oliver saw the flicker of charity in Charles' eyes and refused it. He required no consolation. He was the stronger, and as such he would surely win. He would reject all but the elements of conflict between his father and himself. Why had this man come breaking in like this, unannounced, when he was supposed to be in Italy tinkering with machines? He was only getting what he deserved. Oliver walked past Charles, over towards the electric fire, and said, with his back to his father:

"I must speak to Louise before I go."

Those were the words which Louise had heard in the bathroom. After he had said this, Oliver turned around. Charles' expression was changing. He had felt pity for Oliver as he would for any man embroiled in violence and fear. He had forgotten that for some men a violent atmosphere is the only air that they can comfortably breathe. He had felt responsibility for Oliver. Now he saw in his son's face that insolence which is the buckler of those who live by the sword, and, from the depths of his insulted kindness, he felt a fury beginning to rise, a fury which was almost a release. He remembered a sensation which for years he had been happy to forget, the sensation of pleasure which he had experienced while bayoneting a prostrate German in France, thirty years before. Yet even though it were a consolation, he wished still to stem that fury. He said again:

"I told you, Oliver, that you must go."

They both heard the click of the bathroom door, and they both turned towards the sound. Oliver said, in a distinct tone which was louder than his normal voice:

"And I told you that I must say goodnight to Louise before I can go."

Louise stood in the door that led from the drawing room to the bedroom. The harsh light from the ceiling accentuated the pallor of her face.

"Yes?" She looked from Oliver to Charles.

Charles now saw, for the first time since he had re-entered the flat, the face of his wife whom he loved; the features which were to him so intimately known that they might have been his creation; the dark blue eyes in which his own essence had so often been reflected; the thick black hair through which, as through a forest, his desires had wandered. He saw it all and all was distorted. Behind him he heard Oliver strike a match.

Louise, watching Charles, felt emotion dry up within her. She had come into the room sure in the knowledge that she could revive that sympathy between Charles and herself which she had previously believed to be total. But when she saw in his eyes that involuntary horror which her own distorted image had inspired, she mistook his reaction for one of distrust and unbelief. Then, too, she had seen Charles as both fugitive and refuge; now he was changed into a grey, unhappy man in a malfitting, semi-military uniform.

Charles spoke to Oliver:

"Go. Don't stand there smoking. Go." His voice was high and cracked.

Oliver addressed Louise:

"Will you come with me?"

She saw them both, standing near the far end of an interminable vista, standing there, moving slowly, Oliver addressing her, Charles' hysterical voice echoing in her ears. Oh God, she thought, they are mad, they are both mad. It is nothing to do with me. I am too tired for this. Taking a step forward, she half fell into the armchair. Both men looked at her apprehensively, but she said nothing, her eyes going from one face to the other. I am too tired to understand these madmen. She buried her face against the back of the chair.

Oliver began to speak again:

"You must come away with me, Louise. You love me. You told me that you love me. You cannot stay here."

With the cigarette between his fingers he made a gesture towards that part of the room where Charles stood.

Charles' expression became more strained and bitter. He had not expected such naked words, nor, even if he had expected them, could he have anticipated the pain that they would cause him. There are many degrees of treachery, many steps on the shameful stairway of deceit. Charles now learned that Louise had mounted that stairway a little higher than he had thought. Oliver had shown himself a little more cruel than he had believed him to be. He did not perceive that Oliver's cruelty was for Louise and that Oliver was the man to whom she had lied. Charles saw the slumped figure of Louise in the chair. Once again he felt his anger mounting against his son.

Oliver blew out a cloud of smoke, and Charles had a spasm of desire to kill him. The traditions of his life were still too strong. He spoke to Louise:

"Answer him. You must answer his question."

Charles' voice had become as hard as Oliver's.

Louise was crying, and, muffled by the padding of the chair, she said:

"No. No."

"No, what?"

It was Oliver who spoke, tense and irritated.

Louise was sobbing now, long dry sobs. Oliver and Charles felt almost drawn together in an antagonism to the spectacle of her harsh tears. With disgust Charles recognized the false alliance towards which he was veering. In reaction he walked over to the chair where Louise huddled, and, touching her shoulder, said gently:

"There, Louise, there. Pull yourself together."

He felt her move, and for fear that she was shrinking from his touch immediately withdrew his hand. She looked up towards him, her eyes puffy in her white face, and said his name. Oliver watched this scene, frowning slightly. He stubbed out his cigarette and put his hands in his pockets.

Charles did not know what her saying of his name implied. Was it intended to show that she would not leave with Oliver? Or was it a regret that by so leaving she must hurt Charles? He did not know, and, at the moment, he did not very much care. His only wish was that this appalling scene would end, that one or both of them would go away. The desire crossed his mind to order Louise out, and thus to end it. Yet if she refused to leave? Perhaps he should walk out himself. He looked at Oliver, standing squarely by the sofa. Charles decided that he would not go, nor would he tell Louise to do so. Even though, at the time, he felt no love for her, yet he knew that he had loved her and he believed that he would love her again. He wished more than anything else for this scene to end.

Louise began to talk through her sobs:

"I don't want to hurt anyone." She had averted her face again. "I didn't think . . . It is all my fault . . ."

Oliver said, "This is too much," and fished in his pocket for his cigarettes.

Charles had been leaning forward a little, straining to catch what Louise was saying. He turned savagely towards Oliver:

"Be quiet."

Louise looked up at Charles.

"What am I to do, Charles?"

Charles felt the room begin slowly to revolve. He took a step backward and balanced himself with his hand against a table by the sofa. He was conscious that his muscles were trembling. As he held to the table physically, so mentally it was his anger against Oliver that supported him.

Oliver said, "I feel *de trop* amid such charming domesticity." He looked pleased with himself. Inside he felt as weak and sick as did Charles, but Charles could not be expected to divine this.

"I gather from your silence, Louise," Oliver continued: "that you are not coming with me."

Louise shook her head slightly. Charles said:

"Then tell him so."

Louise, a dull expression of pain on her face, said, "No. I shall stay here."

"In that case," said Oliver, "I shall go." He glanced around the room. "I need some fresh air."

Charles thought, Now, if he goes now, I can control myself. It is important that I should not kill him, or try to kill him. If he leaves immediately that danger will be past.

Oliver began toward the door. Then he stopped:

"Oh, by the way, there's my uniform. I'll come back for it tomorrow."

Tomorrow. The word fell into Charles' mind. He had forgotten that there would be a tomorrow. At least it must not be a repetition of today. He said, flatly, "Take your uniform now."

"Wouldn't it be more convenient . . ."

"Take your uniform now."

Oliver shrugged his shoulders.

"Very well."

He went through the door into the bedroom. Charles waited until the bedroom light was lit and then closed the connecting door. Louise was looking up at him from the armchair. Charles walked across in front of her, and sat on the corner of the sofa. He lit a cigarette and stared at the electric fire. Louise said:

"Charles."

He did not reply. He was listening to the slight sounds which Oliver was making in the bedroom. If, at the time of his divorce, he had allowed Helen to have Oliver. If, he thought, he had agreed to her request during that luncheon in Paris, he would not now be avoiding the desire to kill his son.

"Charles." It was Louise's voice again.

He looked at her, but said nothing. His eyes went back to the electric fire. It is really very difficult to commit an unpremeditated murder in London, unless one has a gun. Charles' mind wandered about the flat, looking for lethal instruments. Electric fires have no pokers. There were no spare lengths of lead piping in the bathroom, no stilettoes in the kitchen. His eye rested on the half empty gin bottle. It probably would not even hurt. He wondered how men did each other to death

with razors. It seemed unlikely that they would use safety
razors. Charles was launched into those side alleys of specula-
tion which were his substitute for action, at times an unsatis-
factory substitute.

Louise, too, listened to the occasional sounds which came
from the next room. The silence which lay between her and
Charles was as heavy as velvet. She wished that he would speak.
She wished particularly that he would say something disagreeable or cruel. She would have welcomed any form of punishment or harshness, for by accepting such words she could
show Charles that she desired his affection. Against this in-
sulated silence there was nothing she could do. There were no
footholds offered, no path that might lead out of the entanglement. She looked at Charles, where he leaned forward over the
electric fire, occasionally knocking his cigarette ash on to the
carpet. She remembered that he had always been very careful
about cigarettes; he had always used an ashtray.

The phrases that came up in her mind she could not utter.
"I am sorry." She could not say it to Charles. "I love you
more than ever." It was unspeakable. Oliver began to whistle
in the bedroom. Charles looked up, towards the door, frowning.

Oliver had changed into his uniform. He had bundled his
grey suit into the case, and was now adjusting his web belt
and revolver. There could be no more delay. He must go back
through the drawing room where they sat. It was foolish to feel
so weak, as though he had but recently recovered from a
serious illness. What had he done, he asked himself, except
exercise his just privileges? Was he not a free man? If his
father had chosen to make a fool of himself and marry Louise,
then it was his father's responsibility to keep her. Oliver was
sure that he had no cause to suspect himself. He began to

whistle as he tugged at his clumsy web belt. He changed the direction of his thoughts. Tonight he would sleep at the Y.M.C.A. or somewhere like that. He might even go drinking and stay up all night. Tomorrow he must return to camp. India in three or four days.

The very atmosphere of the bedroom was urging him to be gone. Oliver surveyed the room. This contemptible domesticity. Why must they so huddle together? The beast with two backs is one thing. This is the beast with two fronts, back to back for mutual protection against surprise. It is a good thing, Oliver thought, to give them a jolt from time to time. The bedroom reminded him of those small furry animals which can scarcely find time to eat, so busy are they searching the ground and the sky for their enemies. They are food for hawks, and their fear is justification for the hawk's stoop. Yet, if he were here the bird of prey, and it was a pleasing fantasy, why then did his stomach keep turning over? Perhaps it was because he had had a lot of brandy. He picked up his suitcase and opened the door into the drawing room.

The drawing room was heavy with uncommitted crime. Charles rose when Oliver entered. Oliver stood beneath the light. He was reluctant to make an immediate, undetermined exit. He looked at Louise. Charles, with a gesture of modesty which he resented as soon as it was made, moved over to the table by the window where the peppermints were. Oliver said:

"I'll go now."

Neither Charles nor Louise answered him. He made no sign of going. It seemed an eternity of time. Oliver said:

"I shall sleep at the Y.M.C.A."

He was talking for the sake of hearing himself speak, determined not to be strangled by the silent anger of his father. Charles was conscious of the clenching of his own teeth. Controlling his voice as best he might, he said:

"You had better go now, Oliver."

He had intended no threat, but Oliver thought he saw one. He stared at Charles.

"I shall say goodnight to Louise first."

He put his suitcase down beside him. Charles' muscles continued to contract. His right hand gripped the bottle of peppermints. Oliver took a step towards Louise. Without premeditation Charles threw the bottle with all his strength at Oliver's head. It missed. It hit a bookcase and fell to the carpet. The glass was thick. It was not even broken.

Louise looked from Oliver to Charles. Charles was trembling visibly, Oliver merely surprised. The bottle rolled towards his feet. He leaned down and picked it up. Then he laughed.

"Sweets!"

He laughed again before drawing his revolver. Charles stood quite still. Louise cried out:

"Oliver, don't, don't."

Oliver ignored her and walked over to where Charles stood. Oliver's face was serious now. He held the revolver with its muzzle pointing to the floor. He stopped, two feet from Charles.

Charles and Oliver looked each other full in the face, for the first time perhaps in their lives. Charles thought that Oliver was going to shoot. Oliver saw that, and he also saw that Charles was not frightened. Louise sat with both her fists dug into her cheeks. She did not wish to scream. Oliver said:

"Here are your sweets."

Charles took the jar and replaced it on the table. Oliver

unhooked his revolver from the lanyard which was about his neck. He held it out on the palm of his hand to Charles:

"Do you want this?"

Charles looked down at the revolver and then up again into Oliver's face. Oliver's cheeks were drawn in, and his mouth was a straight line, for Charles it was suddenly like looking into a mirror. Somewhere in his life each of the two had met a forked road. Charles had taken one lane, Oliver the other. In this moment that fork was negligible. They were both back at the point of parting.

Oliver was still holding out the revolver.

"Do you want it?"

Charles shook his head slowly:

"No."

Oliver worked the clip in the butt that attached it to his lanyard. He put on the safety catch and replaced the revolver in the holster. He said: "It makes no difference. It isn't loaded."

Turning, he picked up his suitcase. At the door he stopped.

"Goodnight, Louise. Goodnight, Father."

He opened the door and they heard him going downstairs. The front door slammed. They heard his steps in the mews. Then they too faded away. Charles walked over to the door and switched off the overhead light. He lit a cigarette.

Louise said, "Charles, can I tell you . . . ?"

He interrupted her, "There's nothing to tell."

He paused before sitting down on the sofa.

"You must be very tired, Louise. You had better go to bed."

Louise rose obediently. Charles' voice was hard, devoid of feeling or desire, but she wished only to do as he said. She came over to the sofa. Her handbag was there. He was apparently unaware of her proximity, for he made no move. She took her bag and went towards the bedroom.

"Goodnight, Charles."

She stood with her hand against the door. It was the same pose as that which she had held when first she had emerged from the bathroom.

"Goodnight."

Charles did not look at her.

"Will you be coming to bed?"

"I shall sleep in here."

"Charles . . ."

He made a gesture, as though warding her off.

"Not now, Louise. Go to bed. It is too late."

"Too late?"

"It is after one o'clock."

"Oh, I see." She paused before she said again: "Goodnight."

He did not reply, and she went into the bedroom. Charles closed the door between the rooms. When he returned to the sofa, and leaned back with his eyes closed, the inside of his eyelids was a scarlet sheet.

Tomorrow, or some day after tomorrow, he must make a decision. Not now. Now he wished to sleep. Yet he saw the face of Oliver and heard the familiar words: *she loves him, I love you, you love him, he loves her, we love I, me love you love.* It was like Esau on his see-saw. Was that all it amounted to, people banging together like billiard balls, cannoning off and back? He remembered again the girl in the Paris café-restaurant. With her would he have known such senselessness and falsity? Or was he the murderee, guilty of his own blood?

Perhaps his desire for permanence and kindness was an invitation to all the world to slap him. Perhaps his modesty and confession of ignorance were an insult to his fellows.

Helen had once said that the pursuit of happiness was a ridiculous activity, doomed to failure and, apparently for that reason, to be despised. In which case a desire to promote the happiness of others, or at least to avoid making others unhappy, was equally foolish and contemptible. Charles shook his head.

His mouth felt dry and hard from exhaustion. He lit another cigarette. The smoke seemed almost solid in his mouth.

Let us leave out happiness, then. What else is there to desire? That nineteenth century fatalism which sees the development of personality as a worthy pursuit, regardless of what that personality may be or what its development may entail for other personalities? Alternatively a substitute of external personality for one's own, the disciple who accepts his pain and his falsehood for his belief in the truth and beauty of another's ideas? The second motive seemed to Charles incompatible with his own ideas of honesty, the first intolerable in its Teutonic savagery.

He realised, sitting on the sofa, that the only way he could have won Oliver's respect this evening would have been to admit his desire to kill him. He had wished to kill him; therefore, according to his son, it was simply weakness which had prevented him from so doing. Charles did not like being hurt. He asked himself if there were anything peculiar or immoral in that dislike. If there were not, then was it wrong to extend it until it became a dislike of hurting others?

The questions went around and around in his tired brain. He stubbed out his cigarette and wished to brush his teeth.

He saw that there was still light under the bedroom door, but he remembered that his toothbrush was in his overnight bag. While getting it out his fingers touched against the package which contained the cameo and the silk square that he had brought back for Louise. He brushed his teeth in the kitchen. Then, partially undressed, he lay down on the sofa and turned out the light.

Almost immediately the questions began again. Was there no place at all for him in the world? He had tried to live alone: it had been too hard. He had tried to live with two women. The first had left him. The second. . . . He noticed that Louise had put out the light in the bedroom. He would not think about Louise now. He had had a son and. . . .

It were perhaps better had he died in the war. Death and peppermints. Yet dead, how could he know the desirability of death? Maybe the dead have their own society, where cruelty is mocked as weakness and personality is not understood: on the other hand they may live as Aeneas saw them, a crueller, more highly pitched squeak of anguish and dislike—or they may just lie, peppermints in a glass jar.

If he had died he might still not know. He remembered the face of the dying man in the airplane which had crashed so near him in 1918, a face with whose features he had in that short part of a second become so intimate—though of its owner's name or nationality he knew nothing. That face now became slowly confused with Oliver's.

He had been standing in a trench when the plane crashed. It had come from behind him. There had been a battery firing nearby and he had not heard it, which was why he had not ducked. It had suddenly appeared, a few feet over his head, spinning and broken, one wing completely gone. As it landed, perhaps five yards from where he stood, it had crumpled prior to its explosion. During that short time Charles had looked into the face of the man in the plane. The dying man wore no goggles; he had a large, blond moustache and full, red cheeks. His expression was one neither of fear nor of surprise, but of pained interest. Looking at Charles, his eyes had seemed to say:

"Since I must die and you in all probability will die with me, let us now look carefully at one another. We shall never have such an opportunity again."

Charles had been knocked unconscious and badly burned. The other man had presumably died.

The expression of the aviator became confused in his mind with the expression on his son's face as he had seen it that evening over the revolver. It seemed, to his tired brain, to mean that now even the aviator had denied him. And, as he lay on the sofa and contemplated the long rejections which he felt he had received from all the world, Charles wondered, not for the first time, whether he would not have done better to change places with the unknown man.

It might be better to be dead. On the other hand, it might be worse.

CHAPTER TEN

ONLY one major character, of those portrayed in this book, has died. On a hot June day in 1940, Roger Peacock lay alone on a pile of straw in the corner of a far Flemish barn. Since that time, now so long ago, when his sergeant had surrendered to the Germans, he had been marching in a long shuffling line, reminiscent of a girls' school, across the dusty white roads of northwest Europe. He had not tried to escape; he had merely become unable to march any more. The small wound in his shoulder, at first a neat hole like a nail mark in a polite crucifixion, had reddened, swollen, begun to stink, enclosing eventually the whole left side of his body in a stiff agony. They had marched on and on, for days perhaps for years between the poplars, until Peacock had suddenly and quietly fallen into a ditch of nettles. The men who had marched beside and behind him gave him a quick, blank look and were gone. The long procession of nameless prisoners marched on. He could hear them from his ditch; he could hear the occasional motorcycle of the German escorts. Then had come a time of silence, as sleep or fever washed away the untruth. He awoke, cold under the star-hung sky. Next morning the frightened farmer had brought him to this barn. The farmer's wife had fed him. Peacock made little effort to talk to them. He thought that they would hand him over to the Germans if he lived too long, but he did not think that he would live very long.

He was alone in the barn. The door was closed, and what light there was streamed through the fissures between the coarse boards. An occasional fly buzzed over his face, and once a rat had come quite close to watch him. If he lay still he almost forgot the pain in his left side. His shoulder became a large piece of ugly furniture to which he was incongruously attached, a heavy sideboard or Victorian sofa, absurdly placed beside him on the straw. Roger Peacock watched the dust skimming on the rays of light, too tired to notice the rat, and his mind prepared itself for death:

"The image of life, say the symbol of reality that flickers like an old film—a dining-room table, ready for a meal, the knives and forks so—that I know and therefore it comforts me for a second or two. Though they have all forsaken me, all left me here, I am no longer frightened. If, as I know, I am now going to die, I am less frightened than the day when the car stopped on the high bluff and the attempt on the girl had to be made, there among the heather, for the ashy satisfaction of pride. I would rather think of the dining-room table. Yet if this is the death that they talked about, and it must be since there can be only one, by definition, Q.E.D., back to school and the ink-rubbed fingers tracing a map of Africa. . . . Yet if this is the death that they talked about, why did they make such a fuss? It is really quite easy compared to those other things, particularly since I am alone. If I were in my bed, my big four poster bed, with Oliver standing on the one side and Louise on the other, and the shame of my parents bringing goodies up on trays, then it would not be easy. But here, where cowardice is irrelevant, where I am going to die as though I were going to drink a glass of water, where no birds sing in this curious smelling barn, here is no conflict. There is no need for me to be Roger Peacock any more.

"But it is not like drinking a glass of water, stupid. What was it that the priests used to say, talking about death, life after death, death after life, a sandwich jumble of abstractions whose meaning I once thought I understood? I forget now, and it doesn't matter. I am going, quite simply, to stop. I, who was not, still am, but shall not be. Can I put it more clearly than that? I, who was not . . . I was not at the siege of Troy, nor did I listen to the flutes at Sans Souci. I was not at all at the siege of Troy, and if I think I was, if I think that by reading and talking and picturing, that I know Troy and perhaps was a little bit there, I am, as always, cheating, cheating like those who say they know when all they do is guess and juggle metaphors. I that was not at Sans Souci, though I, too, have played the flute, late at night when the long windows opened onto the silver lawns and the tall candles stood against the black mirror. And if, then, I saw the moonlight on the rococo edges of the roof and thought I was at Sans Souci, then it was only because I was too blind or not imaginative enough to see the moonlight on my roof or listen to the notes of the flute which I, not Frederick, held. I was not, and all the sophistries of the Orient can blow away like that dust in the sun.

"But I still am . . . well, what's so wonderful about that? Everybody still is. I cannot tap my head, like Chénier, and say, 'I had something there.' Why should I? Perhaps if, like Chénier, I were dying on a guillotine before the eyes of the world, I, too, should want to tap my head or my balls or my stomach. Perhaps I could even impress myself, as I used to try to do by bullying Louise. But here the heroic gesture would be somewhat silly, wouldn't it? Besides I might get it wrong. No. I still am, that's enough. I should like to know what I am, but that's another question. If I had time enough, say thirty, forty years, time in which to work my way back through the tangled forests of action and reaction, I might find out. But would I? What would I find at the end? A little nut, something about the size of a coffee bean, which I could call identity, a small, shiny black pebble. A lot of good that would do me. Besides, landscape gardening is an art of its own. No, I still am, apart from thinking, and with this right hand I can make a little mark in the dust, see? It makes my left shoulder ache intolerably. The swelling giant there is grabbing at my left side and a screaming sea, unbearable, cruel, is washing against me. There, I must lie still. Now it gets a little better. What symbol now? A bookshelf full of books as it was when I was fifteen. There that's better. The unread, alluring titles, that were to give me smooth knowledge. The sea is retreating now, now the pain is like a honey-comb, full of blank hollows where there is no pain. The bookcase and the books, new, enticing, I can see the titles now as I saw them then, *La Porte Etroite*, a tall, thin, yellow book, *South Wind*, *The Anatomy of Melancholy*, *The Complete Works of . . .*, of whom? Whose complete works? I don't remember. The bookcase fades and the pain is almost gone.

"I shall not be. How funny that sounds, almost like a slogan. 'They shall not pass,' that's what I'm thinking of. Our program: I shall not be. Well, that's that. The others though, they'll go on. They have a different slogan, or perhaps their slogan is 'Peacock shall not be.' Louise, for instance, will go on, kissing and being stupidly silent. Oliver will go on, arrogant, bluffing conceit. I think I'm really well out of it all. The priests will frighten and the wise will pretend they know, and all over the world lovers will call copulation love, and sometimes it will be love, and people like me will, what? What happens to people like me if they still go on being? Marry Louise and be polite to Oliver? Marry Oliver and be polite to Louise? I haven't got much longer to live. There's hardly enough time left for silliness."

Peacock lay still, the dust settling, a fine grey powder on his flushed face and torn uniform. In a detached way he attempted to calculate the time of day from the angle of the sunshine, but soon gave up. After all, what did it matter?

"The book they told me of when I was a child. Kept by an avenging angel, a heavy, leather-bound book, studded with brass buttons, where all my actions were written down, the good on one page, the evil on another. Each action valued in the ledger, and out of this celestial double-entry bookkeeping, came a sort of result, a sum or figure. What foolishness, God and the bankers. But now that I've got the time, what is it that I lose by dying, what do I lose that I regret, what am I rid of that has irked me?

"Louise. Never again to lie with Louise. I suppose I regret that. If I could remember more clearly what it was like to lie with Louise, I might regret it more. But it seems so long ago. I remember what? One night when she stood before the window and the moon made a single thick white line down the side of one uplifted arm, one breast, one swelling hip, one strong leg, and her face was in profile in shadow, and those shadows promised a richness which I never knew. That moment, yes, if I thought that such a moment could ever recur. But what else,

I mean what else about her body? I can't remember anything special. What was it then that made me hold onto her so, and yet allows me now to let her go with so little regret? I suppose the fact that she wanted Oliver and probably didn't know so herself. That was the chief reason, not a very creditable one for me. Yet they had no business to make me fat, ugly I suppose. Damn them, all of them. Still, I fooled them. I kept Louise from that sardonic Oliver. He couldn't even let me die in peace, he had to come and sneer at me even in that farmhouse. But fat, silly Peacock kept cool, clever Oliver and simple, sexy Louise from their natural consummation. All right then, that's why I held on to Louise, I just didn't want her to have Oliver. But of course that's not all of it. I'd have married her. And anyhow I wanted her to love me long before I knew anything about her and Oliver. Not long before, really, a couple of weeks. The time before we went swimming with Annie. By then it was obvious that there was no ecstasy in our affair. Why didn't she go off with Oliver then? It would have been better for me, really. I should have told her to go or thrown vitriol all over her. And I think I would have told her to go if it had been anyone but Oliver.

"I wonder if she'll live with Oliver now? Maybe he'll be killed in France here. Would I like that? I don't think I'd care much. But if she does go to live with him, I hope he makes her suffer. And yet I don't really care about that either. Anyhow I can be sure she won't make a fool about me, pretending she loved me. I can't believe she would do that. Oh Christ, haven't I anything better to think about than Louise and Oliver? I should be cheered up, as my mother would say. Let's see then about Louise. Credit: one moment in the middle of the night. Debit: a lot of time worrying about her and Oliver. Balance:

humiliation for me. Good riddance. No regrets to be free of that.

"But of course it doesn't really add up like that. Stupid angel with his fountain pen. I wanted to love Louise, didn't love her. Why bother more. It was just another step towards this foolish, outlandish death. Learning to box at school, learning merely because I was afraid of being hurt. The square, central fear, like that big black stone they go and kiss at Mecca. Every action seems to have led up to or away from that monument. What then was it, the fear of other people? When I was alone for a sufficiently long time the fear all disappeared. I could build a fantasy world, like I did that winter in Rome, a personal existence of checks and balances, but something within me always drove me out of my private worlds, oh over and over again, drove me out to steal and beg and impress. That's where the fear came from. Where? I don't know.

"At first, I suppose, it was desire for knowledge that sent me out. I wanted to watch them. But I didn't want them to watch me, criticizing, laughing at me behind their sleeves, just as they had done before, at school. So I had to ignore them, insult them, most of them, and hit out at the ones I could not ignore. Peacock's quest for knowledge led to this: if you can't sneer, snap. Well, I've known this for years. Perhaps if I'd thought less, if I'd taken more for granted, broken my heart, joined the Catholic Church, become some sort of harmless madman. . . . But always going into these things with my eyes so wide open. Now I'll do Peacock falling in love. Now I'll do Peacock getting religion, getting drunk, getting a double first, getting clap. Peacock dying isn't like that.

"Why not? What was it that fool don said, something about identifying oneself with society. Peacock dying is identi-

fied all right now, identified with his moribund society. Put that
in your psychiatrist and smoke him out. My society was made
for this war. They wanted it, they, the same ones that made me
ugly, made Louise stupid. Ever since I can remember they've
been pushing us gently towards this cliff. It began with hero-
worship for the dead, armistice day, greater love hath no
man, hope and glory. The fathers of the race were killed, sorry,
they weren't exactly killed, they died facing fearful odds, a
smoking revolver in either hand. You, my boys, must follow
that splendid example. That's what we were taught to admire,
courage, self-immolation. Jesus Christ, what a society to
identify yourself with. Well, I made it, at last. Perhaps they'll
put up a plaque to me in the school chapel. He died that you
might live. The hell he did. I'm dying because I didn't have the
sense to be a conchie, because being a conchie would have been
just another gesture of refusal, another of a long train of
refusals. Refusal had become as automatic and unthinking as
acceptance, and I wasn't getting any happier for it.

"So they got their war and now we can all identify our-
selves with their society. 'Your courage and so on will bring us
victory'; at least they've got the honesty to plaster that all
over the walls of England, home and beauty. When they've at
last got my name on that plaque in the school chapel, they will
forgive me for having been ugly and they will forget about how
I cheated to Louise. Nor will it matter about the flutes of Sans
Souci, not to them, and I won't be here to care. I am now. I still
care, but it won't be much longer. I can feel that pain beginning
again, a new one now, heavier, closer to me, like an unwanted
embrace. The barn seems to be changing its shape. The pain is
very close to me now, it seems to be almost climbing over me. I
wish I had a glass of water to drink. I wish . . ."

CHAPTER ELEVEN

OLIVER was alive, and being alive he walked down Piccadilly. He was relieved that he had missed the victory celebrations. There was no heroic welcome, only bedraggled bunting and a few rain-soaked stands at which men were busy with tools of demolition. It was his first day out of the army. The papers headlined the forthcoming explosion of an atom bomb at Bikini. It looked as though it were going to rain shortly. It was June, 1946.

There was, then, no greeting for him. He expected none. He had told himself that all he desired was a quiet return to normal life. The double-breasted grey flannel suit, which he had last worn over two years ago, still fitted. In the inside pocket he had found a crumpled ten shilling note. There was no difference. Others were dead, but he had won out. He had become a civilian again.

Around the bus stops the little queues stood, waiting to go home, sad in the placid knowledge that they would be standing here tomorrow and next week and probably on into 1947 and the 1950s. Bedraggled women in grey trousers sporting plum-coloured overcoats, men in much patched suits, an occasional khaki soldier with his heavy boots, already beginning to feel awkward and conspicuous in his uniform. Oliver attempted to define for himself the present atmosphere of London. A man awakening from sleep? No, that was not it, for it had not been a sleep. A man coming out of an anaesthetic? That was more like it, with its connotations of sharp scalpels and bored, white-coated nurses. A man coming to, after unconsciousness in an oxygen tent, the weakened organism attempting once again to absorb its sustenance from the normal air? A neat image, Oliver thought, neat but effective. He looked again at the queues by the bus stop. Of course it was all rubbish, that about oxygen tents and so on.

Meanwhile, what was he to do with his evening, now that he had himself escaped from the killing-bottle? It was a problem. He could scarcely remember any friends in London. The two or three whom he had thought to find were, as he knew by his afternoon telephoning, gone away. The idea of trying to get in touch with Louise had crossed his mind, but he did not know her address since she and his father had separated. In any case he did not particularly wish to see Louise, at least not this evening. He wanted to see somebody with whom he could talk. It would be pleasant to run into some man he had known and liked, in a pub, say, or in the Café Royal. He would go to the Café Royal, later. Meanwhile he turned down White Horse Lane, towards Shepherd's Market.

The first two pubs he came upon were closed. In the early evening, the streets of the little village which is Shepherd's Market were half empty. A youth, leaning against a wall, eyed a very pregnant cat, which stepped with heavy daintiness among greengrocer's rubbish. A yellow-haired girl walked from the paper shop across to a butcher's. Watching her, Oliver remembered a remark of Rivière's to the effect that only French women knew how to roll their hips. He wondered if Rivière was by any chance in London. He turned up a narrow street, between the shuttered houses, to the corner where the two red telephone booths stand. He rang the number of Rivière's club.

Yes, Mr. Rivière was in the club. Who was it speaking? Would he hold on a minute? Rivière's voice, when he came to the phone, sounded more fruity, more self-satisfied, than Oliver remembered it as having been. When Oliver suggested that they meet for a drink, Rivière hesitated a moment:

"I am going out to dinner."

Oliver asked him if he would not care to join him in a cocktail, and again there was a slight pause before Rivière said:

"Yes. Come around here. You know where it is, don't you?"

Oliver hung up and began to retrace his steps towards Piccadilly. He felt that somehow he had blundered in telephoning to Rivière. The Frenchman had sounded as though he half expected Oliver to try and borrow a fiver from him. And, indeed, Oliver, too, had a suspicion that perhaps he was coming to beg, as he walked up the steps into the club. He touched his wallet to reassure himself, as he crossed the threshold.

Rivière was waiting for him, standing rather stiffly just inside the door. It was as though Oliver might commit some indiscretion or act of violence should Rivière not keep him under close observation from the moment he entered the club. Their greeting was rigid, recognised words falling like stones into a deep well, a slight splash, followed by silence.

"Let us go through to the bar."

They walked down a narrow corridor, Rivière half a pace

behind Oliver. Now Oliver's sense of maladjustment became tinged with anticipation of possible calamity, a vague military memory of ambushes and booby traps. When, after what seemed a long walk, they emerged into the little, well-lit bar, Oliver felt that he had escaped from an unknown danger.

They drank Martinis. Rivière looked prosperous in a new blue suit with a faint red stripe. He informed Oliver that he was working at the French Embassy, and that he was to dine there that evening. By the tone of his voice, Oliver suspected that Rivière found this piece of intelligence impressive.

"When were you demobilized, Oliver?"

"Today."

"My congratulations. And what are you going to do?"

"Do? I have no idea."

Rivière shook his head at this. He had become quite plump in the past two years. His manner was both avuncular and reluctant; it struck Oliver as odd. At any moment he suspected that a slab of advice might appear upon the bar, or the offer of a job be brought in on a tray. It was not for this that he had telephoned. He switched the conversation slightly.

"Are you planning to become a career diplomat?"

Rivière took a swallow of his drink before replying.

"No. I shall stay here for a few more months and shall then return to Paris. My father's business is reviving. Diplomacy is too badly paid."

"What is your father's business?"

"It is connected with banking."

"But what do you want in a bank?"

"Frankly, the money."

A somewhat chilly smile crossed Rivière's face. There was no doubt that he was being patronizing towards Oliver. Pulling a gold watch from his waistcoat pocket, he observed that he had time for just one more, before dressing for dinner. He spoke to the barman with authority, and then turned to Oliver again:

"And your father?"

"I've no idea. He was in America. I imagine he's back at Oxford now, fiddling with his test tubes."

"I saw your step-mother a month or so ago."

"They are separated, you know."

Rivière raised his eyebrows, showing slight disgust rather than surprise.

"I did not know. I merely spoke to her for a second, between the acts of a play."

Again there was an awkward pause in the conversation. Oliver, somewhat illogically, said:

"And when are you going to marry your heiress?"

"My heiress?"

"Well, any heiress?"

"As a matter of fact I am getting married at the end of this month."

"My congratulations."

"Thank you."

"What's her name?"

"Katherine Farr."

There it was, then. That was it, the name with the long strings that had ensnared their meeting. Oliver wondered why Rivière had been such a fool as not to tell him in the first place. Rivière's curious mixture of nervousness and superiority became immediately understandable. For one thing, he now saw Oliver through the mist of old conversations held with Katherine. Then, too, he was marrying a girl whom Oliver had not wanted.

Finally, he would have liked to kill Oliver for the sin of having been loved by his future wife. Since he could not kill him, he must make him feel inferior with any weapons which came to hand.

This whole Latin conspiracy annoyed Oliver. But if that was how Rivière wanted it, Oliver was prepared to play the game the whole way.

"How very fine. I'm sure that you and Katherine are well suited to one another."

"Thank you."

"Oh, don't thank me. It's nothing to do with me."

"I suppose not."

There was faint unhappiness in Rivière's eyes. Oliver was without mercy.

"I hope I can come to your wedding."

"We're not having a wedding here. Just the registry office formalities. We shall be properly married when we return to France."

"Naturally, if that's the way you feel about it. But would you have any objection to my seeing Katherine? Taking her out to dinner, say?"

"My dear Oliver, I have no control over whom Katherine dines with. She decides whom she wishes to see."

"This is all rather awkward, isn't it?"

"Is it?" Rivière was returning to his previous frigid manner.

"I mean that I want to ask you for Katherine's phone number."

"Oh, I see." Rivière took another swallow from his drink, before pulling out a little green leather book from the waistcoat pocket above his watch.

"Surely you must know Katherine's number without having to look it up?"

Rivière pursed his lips and did not reply. After considerable thumbing of pages, he finally read out the number. Oliver borrowed a pencil from the deferential barman. While still writing the figures on the back of an envelope, he said:

"You must be wanting to go and change for your dinner."

Rivière pulled out his gold watch again, even though there was a clock behind the bar.

"Yes, I should be dressing in a minute."

"I'll go along now, then."

"You're sure you wouldn't care for another one?"

Oliver laughed. "No, really, thank you. Don't bother to see me out."

Rivière had risen to his feet. There was a mute appeal in his eyes, but Oliver remembered his sloppy insistence on banks and embassies and gold watches. He said:

"Don't worry, Rivière. If Katherine has said that she will marry you, you can be sure that she will."

With that he turned and left the bar, walked down the long passage and out into Piccadilly. While talking to Rivière, he had remembered a drinking club off Rupert Street. He took a taxi there immediately.

This barroom was very dirty, with old cigarette packets scattered on the floor. An ugly middle-aged woman accompanied herself on a bashed-in upright piano. A frowsy blonde with an Oxford accent did not remove the cigarette from her mouth, as she said to Oliver, "Yes?"

"I used to be a member here."

A man sitting at the bar, the only person in the club apart from the woman behind the bar and the pianist, looked up and sniggered. The bar-woman said:

"We've changed hands. You'll have to join again. One guinea."

Oliver put a pound note on the bar.

"I said a guinea."

He took out a shilling. The blonde woman pushed a form towards him. He signed his name and gave a fictitious address.

"I'll have a large pink gin, please."

"Not tonight, dearie," said the woman, in an unconvincing Cockney accent.

Oliver frowned at her. The man on the stool sniggered again. Oliver turned towards him, "What goes on here?"

The depressed gentlewoman behind the bar was staring at her fingernails.

"You'll get your membership card through the post."

"Oh, come off it," said Oliver. "Do you think I joined your club for its social appeal?"

"Ask him," she said, nodding towards the crushed individual on the barstool. "He owns this place."

The man who had sniggered looked up.

"Bertie Myers is the name. Late of the R.A.F."

"Do you think I could have a drink, Mr. Myers?" Oliver attempted to be polite. Mr. Myers sniffled and blew his nose.

"*I* can buy *you* one."

"That's very good of you."

"If *you* slip *me* the money."

Oliver handed him a pound note, and asked the blonde if she would like to be included in the round. She poured out three drinks and passed Oliver half a crown change.

"That's six shillings each for the whiskeys and five and six for the gin."

"How much does it cost to sleep with the pianist?" Oliver asked.

Myers sniggered again. A man in a teddy-bear coat came in.

"Evening, Dorothea. Evening, Bertie."

"Hello, Mr. Evans. This is Mr. Monroe, another Irishman. Mr. Evans is in the film business too."

Mr. Evans looked at Oliver with bored interest. He asked, "What part of Ireland are you from?"

Oliver said, "I'm from North Audley Street, if it's anything to you."

Mr. Evans frowned, but Mr. Myers laughed heartily. He went over and repeated the witticism to the pianist. The barwoman began telling Mr. Evans about a weekend she had spent at the house of the Marchioness of Abbeyhurst. Apparently she had not enjoyed it. They had had fish for breakfast, skate.

So this is the return, Oliver thought; this is the place to which one comes back. A dirty room, a glass of gin, a pompous Frenchman, and beyond the tideless sea of human faces. He remembered the rachitic children of India, the bursting black corpses of the African desert, the haggard return from France six years ago. After a man has been killed in a war, another man is killed in a revolution. It would have pleased him, had he been able to see some connection between the two sets of phenomena. But, he thought, the phenomena are their own connections, unless they be boxed away from each other into doubtful generalisations. Since the second death follows on the first, it may be said to be caused by the first. Thus the fact that Oliver had seen Peacock frightened in France was the cause of Oliver's ordering another pink gin.

The man in the teddy-bear coat asked Oliver for a match, the preliminary to conversation. Mr. Myers stared up into Oliver's face as he produced a box.

Oliver thought, for example, two things have happened. First there was the evening with Louise, and now there is Katherine's forthcoming marriage. Those two events are probably only distantly connected. Yet everyone, including myself, must see a connection; of the half dozen people involved in the first, three, at least, are involved in the second. So in practice it is impossible to ignore the connection between them. The release of magic which took place when Rivière mentioned her name is sufficient to disprove my belief in casual action.

Mr. Evans, the teddy-bear coat, said, "So you're in the film industry too?"

"No," said Oliver. "No, I'm not."

And another thing that disproves it, Oliver thought, is the undeniable fact that at this moment I am annoyed with myself for not having married Katherine two years ago—or, at least, for not having made it possible for me to marry her now. Or, if not to marry her, then to live with her.

The pianist had stopped playing. Mr. Myers sang, in a high, cracked voice:

"I'm a rambler, I'm a gambler, I'm a long way from home."

Mr. Evans moved a little closer to Oliver, and said, "Bertie says you are."

"Says I am what?"

"In the film industry."

"Oh, for God's sake stop pestering me with your film industry."

Mr. Evans took hold of Oliver by the sleeve. "Now then. Who do you think you're talking to?"

"I neither know nor care. Leave go of my sleeve."

For half a second he thought that Mr. Evans was going to hit him, and felt an intense desire that he should do so.

Nothing at that moment would have given Oliver greater pleasure than to smash his fist into an ugly, red face; a blow for Peacock, a dozen for his father, half a score for Katherine and twenty for Louise, he could have gone on fighting happily for hours. But he was not to get his fight. Myers stopped singing, hastily, in the middle of a word, and, running up, separated the two.

"Now, now, now, now," he said. "Don't let's lose our tempers."

Mr. Evans dropped Oliver's sleeve and muttered a couple of obscenities. Dorothea, the bar-woman, looked a little less bored for a minute or two. Bertie Myers said:

"What's the matter, eh? What's the matter, Mr. Evans, eh?"

Mr. Evans did not reply. Mr. Myers said, "Let's all have a little drink then, and settle down quietly."

The drinks were brought and paid for by Mr. Myers, who smiled happily. Oliver decided that Bertie must be a little weak in the head. The pianist settled down to beating out the *Warsaw Concerto.* Mr. Evans, with a great attempt at amiability, said:

"I like a film with plenty of good music in it."

Oliver thought, Even though I can now not marry Katherine, nor live with her, why should I not spend this evening in her company? If I am condemned to pass the rest of my life in grimy lunatic asylums such as this, I should like to have one last pleasurable evening before beginning my sentence.

Mr. Evans said, "I'm sorry if I offended you by assuming that you were in the film industry."

"That's all right." Oliver managed a smile.

"You see, most people are, nowadays, since the war."

"That's interesting."

"It is curious, isn't it? It's Mr. Rank, you know."

Oliver said, "Could you tell me where the telephone is?"

Mr. Evans was all friendliness now.

"I'll show you. Come this way."

They ascended half a flight, amidst a growing smell of drains. Mr. Evans said:

"Wonderful the way the telephone works, isn't it?"

Oliver said:

"Yes. Most mysterious."

Mr. Evans said, "Got your tuppence?"

Not even a grown-up lunatic asylum, Oliver thought; a children's one, with Mr. Evans for nurse.

"Yes, thank you."

Mr. Evans paused for a moment.

"Well, you should be all right now."

He sounded doubtful, but apparently decided to risk it, for he left Oliver and returned to the bar.

Katherine's voice was lower and softer than he remembered it to have been. She expressed no surprise at hearing that it was Oliver speaking. He wondered if Rivière had already informed her of his arrival in London.

"Would you like to come to dinner with me?" he asked.

"Where are you?"

He mentioned the name of the drinking club. She said, "I don't like that place."

"Neither do I."

He named the first restaurant that crossed his mind.

"All right, then, Oliver. I'll meet you in the downstairs bar of the Café Royal in about a half an hour."

"Don't be late, sweet."

She said, in a level voice, "But, Oliver, no trying to make ghosts walk."

"I'll try. I don't know if they will, though."

There was a moment's silence before she said, "Unless you promise me not to try, I won't come."

"I promise."

He heard her laugh at the other end of the wire. "You'd promise a girl anything, wouldn't you?"

"Almost anything to you."

Then she had hung up, and he was walking downstairs again towards the bar.

Mr. Evans was waiting for him anxiously.

"Get through all right?" There was real concern in his voice.

"Yes, thank you."

"I'd like you to meet two friends of mine, Betty and Sally."

Oliver had already examined the two women. Both were blonde. Both wore dark suits from which appeared plump, rounded legs in salmon-coloured stockings. Betty was about thirty-five, her face somewhat lined with those occasional triangles of puffy flesh which one associates with elderly prize-fighters. Sally was probably some ten years younger. Her dead blonde hair, blue eyes, creamy skin and curved pink mouth were as standardized as a tube of toothpaste.

Oliver explained that he must, regretfully, go. Mr. Evans said:

"One for the road then, eh?"

Oliver paid for the round and began talking to Miss Sally.

"Are you in the film industry?"

"We-ell, not actually."

"How so?"

"I'm a dramatic artist."

"A what?"

"I'm on the stage."

"Oh, I see."

Sometimes, Oliver thought, sometimes it is like mountaineering, all crags and precipices; at other times it is a long walk across a desert. This was clearly one of the latter types. He said:

"Are you in a job at present?"

"Not actually."

It was plain that she was struggling to say something. Oliver waited, and at last it broke surface:

"Mr. Evans says you're not in the film industry."

"Not actually," he replied. He went on, "I'm sorry, but I have to go now."

"I'm sorry too," she said.

"Perhaps we shall meet again. Will you be here later?"

"I may be. I come here often, in the evenings. It's so sort of cosy, don't you think? And Bertie's so amusing."

Oliver glanced around the room. Bertie was dusting a hard-backed bench with a piece of rolled up newspaper. The woman behind the bar was cleaning her fingernails with a match stick. The pianist played *The Stately Homes of England*, humming quite loudly.

"Yes, it is cosy. Well, I must go now."

He had difficulty in persuading Mr. Evans that he really did not wish for another drink. Eventually he escaped with a promise that he would return later. Remembering Katherine's remark on the telephone, he decided that that was one promise he would not keep. The *Ewig-weibliche* was all very well, but surely even Goethe could hardly be expected to pursue the feminine through such a habitat as this.

When he reached the Café Royal, Katherine was already seated at a corner table in the bar. She was wearing a red pointed hat, but apart from this she looked so exactly the way he had remembered her, that he felt real embarrassment as he apologised for his lateness. He thought it best to make his position quite clear, immediately.

"I saw Riviére this afternoon. That's how I got your telephone number."

Katherine looked at him mildly.

"I didn't know you were going to marry him. You should have written and told me."

"I didn't think it was any concern of yours."

"That was unkind of you," he said.

"What has kindness got to do with it?"

"Nothing, I suppose. Let's eat. This bar is too full."

They sat against the wall, in the big room, side by side on a red plush seat. After they had ordered, Oliver said:

"I'm going to ask you not to marry Rivière, but to marry me instead."

"Why?"

"Because I want you to marry me."

"Why do you want me to marry you?"

"Stop pretending to be three years old. Because I love you, of course."

Katherine laughed aloud.

"Thank you for the 'of course,' but my dear Oliver, I wouldn't marry you if you were the last man alive. So you can save yourself the trouble of trying to persuade me that you love me."

Oliver swallowed a mouthful of soup. Katherine said:

"Anyhow, if you think that that is the way to resurrect ghosts, you're very much mistaken."

"I don't believe in ghosts."

He took another swallow of soup, and then asked:

"Tell me, since you're so hard boiled about me, why did you come out to dinner?"

"Curiosity, chiefly. Also there are a lot of things I used to like about you."

"Thank you."

"Not at all."

Their second course was put down before them, and two pints of beer. Katherine smiled cheerfully and said:

"If I am not being indiscreet, Oliver, what are you going to do, now that you are out of the army?"

"I've no idea. Perhaps I should go into the film industry. Your fiancé asked me the same question. What do you suggest?"

"You might become a journalist."

"I might." His expression became quite wretched. He let himself feel as unhappy as he could. "But it hardly seems worth while, does it?"

"Because you cannot marry the girl of your choice?"

He turned towards her and put his hand on her knee.

"Oh, Katherine, it's all such a bloody awful mess, isn't it?"

"I thought that that was the way you liked things to be."

"Did you?"

"At least in the time that I have known you, you have never made any effort to tidy them up. Rather the contrary. For example, if you're so intent on getting married, why not marry Louise? You love her; she is alone, and probably unhappy. But oh no, not you, you have to want to marry me.

Just when I've got rid of you at last and am preparing a proper life for myself, you have to come back and try to smash it up. I know you too well, though, Oliver. It won't work with me, not twice."

They sat in silence for a minute. Oliver told the waiter to bring their coffee with their sweet. Then he said to Katherine:

"I know what you mean, but it's not right. It isn't fair, what you have just said. I don't want to live in a boiler factory for the rest of my life. I'm nearly thirty now, approaching early middle age. I asked you to marry me because it is my belief that we could live what you call a proper life together, better with each other than with anybody else. But I won't ask you again, I promise you. Though do believe me when I say that I wasn't merely trying to exercise power over you."

"Perhaps not. Maybe I spoke too harshly, Oliver. But you did, at one time, have a lot of power over me, and I don't want to be a marionette in your puppet-show ever again. In fact I don't believe in puppets or puppet-masters any more. It's like you not believing in ghosts. That, Oliver is why I am getting married. At least François is trying to make something, if it's only a bank and a family."

"Those sound to me like two pretty good things to make. But I should like to make something too, Katherine."

"Maybe. That remains to be seen. I hope you do. Personally, I doubt it. I think you will sit around for years, getting an occasional job, sleeping with a lot of girls, pretending on occasion that you loved me and on other occasions that you loved Louise, drinking too much and generally becoming rather dull. You'll spend the peace waiting for the next war."

She stopped for a moment. Oliver stared into his coffee cup. She went on:

"I'm sorry, Oliver. I hope I'm wrong. But I thought it as well to make you realise why I am marrying Rivière. Last time I saw you, I told you not to come back looking for me, because I wouldn't be there any more. You didn't believe me. You must now. It's not the same Katherine."

"You've become quite a moralist."

"Yes, I have, haven't I?" She smiled. "It's rare in one's lifetime that one gets the opportunity to make a speech which one has been rehearsing for a year."

"Will you have a drink?"

"No, thanks. You do, if you want one."

"I hardly dare, after your sermon."

"All right then, don't."

Again they sat in silence for a short while. Oliver said:

"Would you like to go to the pictures?"

Katherine laughed aloud.

"I don't think we need go to quite such extremes as that."

"I don't know what to say to you, you see."

"No, I don't either."

"Perhaps you had better go home, Katherine?"

"Yes, I think I should."

He escorted her as far as Piccadilly tube station. When he re-entered the club Mr. Evans and Betty and Sally were in exactly the same positions in which he had left them. He noticed by the clock that it was only one hour since he had gone to the Café Royal.

"So you're back," said Betty, the elder blonde.

"Hello, hello, hello," said Mr. Evans.

Sally sat on her barstool, looking rather stuffed. The pianist, having doubtless run through her repertoire, was back at the *Warsaw Concerto*. Oliver bought a drink for each of the people to whom he had previously spoken. There was no longer any question of his right to buy drinks. He had returned and was now a 'regular.'

He was too tall to lean on the bar with comfort. He pulled around a stool, and sat beside Sally. She said:

"You *are* sunburned, Mr. Monroe."

"Oliver," he said.

"You *are* sunburned, Oliver."

He thought, If my pleasures are the standards for my behaviour, then I suppose I might as well call myself an anarchist. And if I am that sort of anarchist, Katherine may be right. Perhaps I am just waiting for the next war. My type of anarchy is more immediately satisfactory during a period when the anti-anarchists are dropping atom-bombs on each other. He said:

"Are you married, Sally?"

"What a funny question!"

It was clear that she now felt entirely at ease with Oliver.

"I dare say. Are you?"

"No. I was engaged, but my boy got killed."

Her baby face assumed a solemn look, suitable for listening to the King's speech on the wireless. Oliver had a momentary hope that she might squeeze out a tear, but in this he was disappointed. She said:

"We mustn't think about the war any more, must we? At least that's what I say."

"You're quite right to say it," said Oliver. "We mustn't."

What was it, then, that Katherine expected him to do? It is all very well to talk about anarchy and disillusionment and so on, but such talk can hardly be the basis of behaviour. For instance, what sort of a job should he get? Where should he live? How? He suspected that Katherine might be merely doing the old female trick again, making of home a moral obligation. He would put it to Sally.

"Would you like to get married, Sally?"

She giggled and looked at him in what she doubtless imagined to be a coy manner. Unfortunately her features were incapable of expressing even so simple an emotion as coyness. He went on:

"Wouldn't you like to have a nice little house—at Barnes, say—with a nice little husband, who never beat you, and two nice little children, little kiddies, and a nice little car? Wouldn't you?"

Parodying Katherine in this way relieved him. He wished she were here to listen, but then he thought perhaps it was as well that she was not. It was not a very close parody of what she had said. And she would have had some more to add too, in all probability. Sally replied:

"I don't like short men."

Oliver drew himself up a little, and thought, In fact that was not at all what Katherine had suggested. She had merely said that if he must marry someone, it had better be Louise.

He leaned across Sally and called to Mr. Evans. The latter replied:

"Yes, old boy?"

Oliver asked him if he knew his prayer book. Mr. Evans, apparently finding the question funny, laughed heartily. Oliver insisted:

"I want to know whether a man is allowed to marry his ex-step-mother."

Mr. Evans, still laughing, said:

"Shouldn't think the question has ever arisen."

Bertie Myers interrupted.

"He cannot. It says 'A man may not marry his step-mother.' She's number eleven in the Table of Kindred and Affinity."

"Does that table hold good for civil marriages too?" Oliver asked.

"I don't know." Myers had lost interest. "I only know what's in the Book of Common Prayer."

"Thank you."

Mr. Evans, his mouth slightly open, was watching Oliver, fascinated. He turned back to Sally. She said:

"You are a funny fellow!"

"Am I?"

"Why do you want to know that, about the Prayer Book?"

"I was thinking of marrying my step-mother, if you're interested."

She smiled, an uncertain smile.

"Why do you want to marry your step-mother then?"

"I don't, much."

Sally laughed a little. Oliver reassured her, by buying them each another drink. He remarked that it was odd the way no one else came into the bar. Sally explained that it was Monday.

Oliver thought, On the other hand, Katherine may have had some idea that I should do penance, that by my previous actions I have made it essential for myself to marry Louise. Something like Byron going off to Greece, but in reverse. Though I have always suspected that Byron was more bored with Italy than begeistered with the Greeks. Looking at it another way, Katherine is obviously talking a certain amount of sense. The satisfaction which I shall derive from going to bed with this Sally will be small, the interest nil. A protracted affair or even marriage with Louise would at least give me something to think about while waiting for the next war. The idea of atonement, though, is rather odious.

There was a telephone directory on the end of the bar. Oliver reached for it and looked up his own name. There were few Monroes, and there could be no doubt that Mrs. Louise Monroe, who still lived in the mews flat, was the Louise he was after. He glanced at the date of the directory. It was April 1946.

"Excuse me, Sally, I must telephone."

"Oh." There was a note of disappointment in her voice.

"I'll be back in a moment. Order me another drink."

He patted her bottom, where it curved out over the top of the barstool. As he walked up the evil-smelling stairs he realised that he was more intoxicated than he had thought himself to be.

He felt the blood pounding in his head as he dialed her number. She must have been sitting by the phone, since she answered even before the first ring had finished.

"Hello."

"Louise?"

"Hello? Who is it?" Her voice sounded tired and puzzled.

"It's me—Oliver."

He wished that he had not had so much to drink. He shook his head slightly, as though to clear it.

"Louise, I . . ."

There was a click, followed by that purring noise which shows that the connection has been broken. Oliver stared at the black machine. Then, digging in his pocket for two more pennies, he dialed the number again.

"Hello, Louise. Don't ring off. I must talk to you."

"What is it?" Her voice was small.

"Louise, I must see you. When can I see you?"

There was half a second's silence. He began again:

"Could I meet you tonight somewhere?"

She said, "I don't ever want to see you, Oliver. I don't want to talk to you, ever again." She rang off.

He stood looking at the useless black instrument in his hand. He was tempted to call her name into it, but did not do so. Instead he jiggled the rest up and down. He searched his pockets for more pennies, but found none. Then he replaced the receiver in its cradle.

He stood in the half-lit corner of the stairs, feeling dazed. As he was reaching for a cigarette, he heard heavy steps mounting towards him. It was Mr. Evans. Mr. Evans said:

"You all right, old boy?"

Oliver looked at him blankly, not quite understanding what was meant. Mr. Evans repeated his question. Oliver said, "Oh yes, I'm all right. Just been telephoning, you know."

Mr. Evans looked at him closely.

"You're sure you're all right?"

"Quite sure."

Oliver lit his cigarette and started down the stairs. In the bar, Sally was on her stool, watching the door by which he entered.

"There you are," she said brightly.

"Yes, here I am," said Oliver, and, as an afterthought, "what a pretty girl you are."

CHAPTER TWELVE

DINNER at the house of Sir Wilfred Rumbold, the Liberal politician, was a long and gruelling affair, even in wartime. Sir Wilfred was not only a stickler for etiquette, but also prided himself on being a brilliant conversationalist. As a result, even after the interminable meal was over, the gentlemen were constrained to drink vast quantities of port while listening to their host's rodomontades. Charles did not care for port —it did not agree with his liver—and his interest in politics was slight. He was therefore relieved when Louise told him that the dinner party to which they had been invited that evening had been cancelled.

Charles was taking off his light overcoat. Louise went on:

"But he wants us to come around after dinner for a drink. He seems very anxious to see you before you leave for America."

"There are not many people in the streets."

"He says that tomorrow will be the official V-E day. Do you think that that will interfere with your airplane?"

"No, I don't think so. What time does Wilfred want us to come?"

"About nine. He has a letter of introduction for you to take to the Governor of New York State."

Charles walked through the bedroom to the bathroom. Louise watched him go.

The last year had changed Louise. The flesh on her face had begun very slightly to fall away, giving the hint of a haggard look to come. It had not been an easy year, since that night with Oliver. For the first few days after that episode, she had expected some sort of scene or explanation between herself and Charles. There had been none. Charles had never alluded, even indirectly, to Oliver or to that evening. His manner towards Louise had been, as always, courteous and thoughtful. The only noticeable change had been his increased reticence. He had been working hard, both at Oxford and elsewhere. Once he had had to go to Cambridge for six weeks. Louise would normally have accompanied him, but Charles explained that he would be working fourteen hours a day and that it would be easier for him to live in a college. Louise had spent the six weeks with her mother in the Banbury Road. Last month, when he had received the offer of a trip to America, he had not discussed it with Louise. He had simply informed her that he would be away about a year. She had asked him whether he thought it would be better for her to live in Oxford or in London while he was away. He had told her to do as she wished.

Charles came out of the bathroom, drying his hands.

"Did you say New York?"

"Yes. The Governor of New York State. Who is he?"

"I have no idea. In any case, since I am going to Arizona, it is unlikely that I shall ever meet the gentleman."

He went back into the bathroom and hung up the towel. When he returned to the drawing room, Louise asked him whether he would prefer to go out to dinner or eat at home. He said:

"I expect the restaurants will be crowded and unpleasant. If it's not too much trouble for you . . ."

"It will only be a scratch meal."

"That would suit me perfectly."

Charles sat down in the armchair and picked up a book. Louise looked at him sadly. It was not that he wished to spend his last evening in England with her; it was merely that the restaurants would be full and uncomfortable. She remembered a Victorian couple, of which she had once read; the husband had discovered his wife in an infidelity, and for the rest of their lives they had never spoken to each other except in public.

Charles turned a page. Louise felt that it irritated him to have her sitting opposite, doing nothing. Yet she was unwilling to surrender this final evening. Tomorrow he would be gone. If the barrier between them were not lifted this evening it might well lie between them forever. It was a quarter past six, and she asked him if he would care for a drink.

"No thank you," he replied with a slight smile. He returned to his book.

She watched him again. Then she said:

"All your things are packed, aren't they?"

He half closed the book, marking the page with his index finger.

"Thank you very much, my dear. I believe you have already attended to all that. Aren't my bags at the air terminal?"

He looked at her mildly. She could think of nothing further to say. Charles returned to his book.

Such was the life that they had lived together for the past

year. There was no apparent change, nothing with which
Louise could tax Charles. His manner towards her had always
been courteous, and he had throughout all their married life
preserved a slight reticence. But now, even in moments of intimacy, she felt a distance between them, an intangible screen,
soft and glassy. It was as though they were two fish in neigh-
bouring tanks of an aquarium.

Sir Wilfred Rumbold's house was on the Chelsea embank-
ment. It had once belonged to George Borrow, but that noisy
genius had left no trace of his eccentric personality. Sir Wilfred greeted them at the door, rubbing his hands together in an
expansive manner. He was dressed in a bottle green smoking
jacket, and his monocle, suspended from his neck by a thick
black ribbon, waved from side to side over his plump stomach
as he walked. He led them through to a room which he described
as his den. There were half a dozen people sitting about. The
ladies were drinking madeira.

"So you're off to America, Charles!" Sir Wilfred began,
as soon as the introductions were over.

"Tomorrow morning."

Charles took the whiskey which Rumbold handed him.

"Well, you'll have seen the end of it over here."

"The end of it?"

"The war," said Sir Wilfred. He gave a large smile. "It's
hard to realise we've won it at last. I can scarcely believe that
the Pacific war will last much longer. The Nips have too much
sense. I was talking to the P.M. only day before yesterday,
and he said . . ."

Sir Wilfred's voice rolled on, gradually gaining in pitch
as the habits of thirty years' oratory won control. The sentences became rounder, more mellifluous. Sir Wilfred was cele-

brating the armistice with a busman's holiday. Charles overheard Louise talking to Lady Rumbold. She had been asked
whether she would be joining Charles in America. She replied
that at the moment it was impossible, but that later she
hoped to be able to do so.

Charles frowned slightly. He had missed a few of Sir
Wilfred's sentences, and did not know why his host had given
a hearty laugh. Sir Wilfred said to him:

"And where were you on November 11th, 1918, Charles?"

"I was in a military hospital in Scotland."

"Not like Piccadilly, then." Sir Wilfred slapped him on
the back. Charles decided that his host must be rather tight.

"No, not really. We all had a lot to drink. I remember
that some flying corps officers tried to persuade the nurses to
do a can-can, but nothing came of it."

"Ah well, it was a great night in London. I doubt if there'll
be anything like it this time."

"No, I don't suppose there will."

Rumbold had begun talking again. Charles' mind went
back to the white hospital in Scotland, and then, inevitably,
to the anniversary, the 11th of November 1919.

He and Helen had come up to London from Gloucestershire
the day before. Helen's grandfather had died recently and had
left his estate to her, which included a small house in London.
They were planning to live in it, for the winter at least, while
Charles attempted to find himself work. His ideas about work
were vague. He felt too old to undertake the course of study
necessary in order to enter the diplomatic service, as he had
intended to do before the war. But then he had no qualifica-
tions for any specific immediate employment. He had spent
the summer in Gloucestershire with Helen, accepting the life of

leisure there offered him as the due of a wounded man, tired after four years' soldiering. He had taken it for granted that Helen and her family would make the necessary allowances for his nervous condition, and they had done so. He had sat for months, reading novels, watching the gentle countryside change from late spring to early winter. He had asked Helen to refuse all the little country invitations, to dinner or bazaars, since he felt that he lacked the strength to see strangers. When her parents invited guests, Charles frequently dined alone in his bedroom. His dreams were preoccupied by men who were mostly dead.

At last the question of his future could no longer be postponed. Charles decided that he would like to become a publisher. He had little idea of what publishers do, but he had a few thousand pounds which he was prepared to invest in a firm, and he imagined that the work would be light and agreeable. They therefore came up to London on November 10th. The journey had tired Charles. They were to stay for a few days at the Ritz Hotel, while Helen's house was made ready. Oliver and the nurse were to follow in a few days.

Charles went to bed immediately after dinner. Helen had sat up in their drawing room for a short while, and by the time she came to bed Charles was asleep. Next morning she went off to look at her house. Charles was lunching with a man who was to introduce him to another man who might be willing to take him into partnership.

Charles had read the *Times* and dressed slowly. There had been a memorial service of some sort, but by twelve o'clock when Charles left his hotel room, it was over. It had been a long luncheon. When he returned to the hotel, it was after four. Helen was not back, and he wondered vaguely where she could be. He sat down, without switching on the lamp, and watched the grey square of London sky darken over the park.

He remained thus for half an hour, a cloud of self-pity surrounding him. He had no wish to embark on a career in the company of the man he had met at lunch. His possible future partner was a forceful individual with strong views, a man to whom the word duty came easily. Charles thought that perhaps he was right to speak so of a publisher's responsibility to the nation, but he did not believe that he could feel any such compunction himself. He would rather return to Gloucestershire. Then he turned on the light and saw an envelope on the mantelpiece.

It was addressed to him, in Helen's writing. Even before he opened it, he felt a sudden, balloon-like collapse. Where then was Helen? What had she been thinking about for the past few months? He had not bothered to find out, convalescing in Gloucestershire. He opened the letter.

Dear Charles:

This letter will surprise you, but when you come to think it over I am sure that you will see that it is for the best. I do not wish to live with you any more. Since I think that you really feel the same way about me, it seems better to finish now, before the quarrels start.

I have moved my things to the Berkeley. I shall of course see you if you want to, to discuss what arrangements should be made about Oliver, etc. I shall go abroad soon.

I have not run off with anyone, as you might suppose. If you want a divorce, though, I shall give you grounds, if you so wish.

You may want to keep Oliver. If you do, you can have the London house.

I don't know how to finish this letter. It seems hypocritical to say 'God bless you.'

HELEN.

Charles passed his hand over his forehead. What on earth . . . He read the letter again, carefully. They were the same words that he had read the first time. He got up and looked about. All her things were gone. Of course she was temporarily out of her mind. "Since I think you really feel the same way about me." What nonsense. From panic Charles subsided into irritation. It was a silly, tasteless practical joke. Why, they had never even had a cross word during the summer in Gloucestershire. "Before the quarrels start." There was no reason that he could see why quarrels should start, unless Helen were to persist in pranks of this sort. If she had fallen in love with somebody there would have been a reason for her so to behave, but she stated quite clearly that she had not done so. In any case, with whom could she fall in love? No, no. It was some sort of bad joke, in the worst possible taste, particularly now, when he was tired. When he relied on her more than ever. No, it could not possibly be serious. If she really meant to leave him, she would surely go a little farther away than to a hotel immediately across the street. Nor would she be so casual about Oliver. He knew from his reading that women always love their children. And that bit about the divorce. He knew that gentlemen always give ladies grounds for divorce, so that the mother can keep the children.

He rang down for a whiskey and soda, and while awaiting its arrival, decided what he must do. He would ring up Helen, adopt a gay, bantering manner. She was probably bored, poor girl. After all, he had not been lively company during the summer. He would pretend to accept this letter as a serious decision—this might frighten her a little, which would be all for the good—and he would invite her to dinner and a theatre. He had no doubt that at the end of such an evening all this nonsense would have disappeared. He read the letter again. "Go abroad." Where on earth could she go? The whiskey arrived, and in an ugly mood of self-confidence Charles phoned the Berkeley.

Mrs. Monroe was in. He was put through to her.

"Hello, Helen. It's Charles."

"Hello, Charles."

"I got your note."

There was silence at the other end. This was more difficult than he had imagined. He struggled on:

"Since we are now separated, I wonder if I might invite Mrs. Monroe to dine with me tonight?"

The light touch was going wrong. His words sounded to himself merely facetious.

"No thank you, Charles."

He dropped the gay manner altogether.

"Look here, Helen, what is this all about?"

"I wrote it to you in my note."

Her voice was entirely matter of fact.

"But Helen, you *can't* mean that. It's so silly."

"Is it?"

"Listen, Helen. I must see you."

There was a pause. She said:

"Tomorrow, then."

"No, tonight."

"I'm sorry, Charles, but I don't want to see you tonight. Come around here at eleven tomorrow."

"But, Helen . . ."

"No good, Charles."

He felt an icy grip around his heart. There was nothing for it but to ring off. He did so.

He could not sit alone in the hotel room. He drank his whiskey and went over to the Berkeley. The porter rang up to Helen's room. Mrs. Monroe was out.

Sir Wilfred Rumbold was finishing a funny story. Charles had heard none of it, but with Sir Wilfred it was always easy to know when he had reached the point of his anecdotes, for he guffawed so heartily himself. Now he looked to Charles for appreciation, and Charles managed to give a polite imitation of a laugh. Sir Wilfred went on:

"In my opinion it serves the fellow quite right. Don't you agree?"

"Serves him entirely right," said Charles.

A young woman in the corner of the room raised her glass, "Here's to victory!" she said in a small, vanquished voice.

They all raised their glasses and drank. Charles found gestures of this sort somewhat embarrassing. He drained his glass none the less, and poured himself another one. Louise had moved away from Lady Rumbold and he went over towards his hostess. That placid lady smoothed a place beside her on the sofa. Charles sat down.

"And how long will you be in America, Charles?"

"About a year, I expect."

"You have been there before?"

"Once. Fifteen years ago."

"Ah well then, you know the country. You must not neglect to look up our friend, the Governor of New York."

"That is very good of you, but I doubt if I shall be in New York."

Lady Rumbold's mind had strayed from what he was saying. Charles could see that her eyes were on her husband. Sir Wilfred, with much characteristic gesticulation, was holding forth to the young lady in the corner. Lady Rumbold sighed.

"Wilfred gets so excited on occasions like this."

Charles smiled at her. "They are not frequent."

"They are for Wilfred. If you only knew how rapidly the country alternates between disaster and complete success. A perfect see-saw." She gave a slight laugh. "And it all seems to depend on Wilfred and the Liberal Party."

She turned back toward Charles. She had apparently been thinking aloud, for she laid her hand on Charles' sleeve, a gesture of confederacy. Her eyes were soft, but they were shrewd. She went on:

"And who knows? Perhaps it does all depend on Wilfred. Or on *you* and your science business. Who knows? Louise looks peaked, Charles, as though she were not getting enough to eat. You must not starve her, even if you are remodelling the universe."

Charles could not follow her train of thought at all, but, obediently, he looked over towards Louise. She was standing, talking to a spotty-faced man by the fire. Later this evening he would once again be alone with her. The thought depressed him. It was only for this evening, though. Tomorrow he would be gone. Lady Rumbold's next remark was such an exact echo of the question which had just crossed his own mind, that he gave a slight start. She asked:

"And how is your son, Oliver?"

"He's in India, you know."

Charles felt uncomfortable beneath the clear look she gave him. But she could not have divined how often, when looking at Louise, he now thought of Oliver.

Their talk wandered on, until Sir Wilfred came over to join them, pushing Louise in front of him. He wished to drive to Piccadilly, to see what he called the fun, and he wanted Charles and Louise to accompany the party. Louise had explained that since Charles had to rise early the next morning, she thought it would be unwise. Charles agreed with her. Shortly after this Charles and Louise left.

Sir Wilfred saw them out, standing in the doorway, filling his lungs with the fine night air. He had forgotten the letter of introduction. Charles did not remind him of it. It was a clear evening, and Louise suggested that they walk home. They heard Sir Wilfred's door slam behind them. The Thames flowed, black and oily, at their side.

They walked a little way in silence. From the occasional groups of people who passed there emanated a subdued excitement. Louise asked Charles if she might take his arm.

"Yes, of course."

He felt the light drag of her pressure. It echoed another such pressure. He sought for the memory. The lunch at the Crillon. Helen had taken his arm on the way from the bar to the dining room. Had his relationship with Louise reached that dead end? Charles supposed that it had. And was this the way Helen had felt about him, that morning after armistice day in 1919, when he had gone to see her at the Berkeley? Again, he supposed that it must be so. Perhaps, therefore, Helen had been right to leave him without fear or reproach.

Louise spoke:

"Charles . . ."

"Yes, Louise?" He turned his head, as though he were slightly deaf.

"Charles, I wish I could come with you to America."

"But you know that that is out of the question."

They walked for a few yards without speaking. Charles' mind wandered off. If Helen's uncompromising attitude was in reality that of a *preux chevalier*, what a curious inversion had taken place! Louise said:

"Charles . . . do you still love me?"

He felt his own heartbeats. He waited until they were stilled, before he replied. He had been avoiding this question for months, but it might be for the best.

"No, Louise. I am afraid I don't."

"Afraid? Oh, Charles."

"I was going to write to you from America, but perhaps it is better to tell you now."

Better? It had not been better when Helen had told him in the Berkeley. They had sat in her bedroom, Helen on the unmade bed. Charles on a small hard chair by her dressing table. Her personal possessions, her brushes and her bottles, had seemed to reassure him with their familiarity. Only at the end had he understood that he would never see them again.

Louise said, "What were you going to write to me?"

"I was going to say that I thought it would be better if we did not try to live together any more."

"But, Charles, I love you."

That is what he had said to Helen, "Helen, I love you."

She had replied, "That may or may not be so. It is hardly the point. The important thing is that I don't love you."

Charles said to Louise, "You see, Louise, I don't love you."

They turned up a sidestreet. Louise was still involuntarily holding his arm. She said, in a low, controlled voice:

"Is it because of Oliver?"

He had said to Helen, "Surely, then, you must have fallen in love with someone else?"

Helen had replied, "No. But if you find it easier to think so, then do."

And he had realised that she was speaking of his pride.

He said to Louise, "Not entirely, not even principally. But if you want a cause, then that is as good a one as any, isn't it?"

Louise let go of his arm and stopped. He waited for her words. She said:

"Can we not try again, Charles, when you return from America? Must it be so definite?"

Charles did not reply. Louise went on:

"I cannot understand. I cannot understand what has happened."

Charles knew that to a lover the disappearance of love is incomprehensible. He had said the same words to Helen. She had replied:

"There is nothing to understand. It is just that I don't love you any more. I thought when I married you that I did. I see now that I was mistaken. I simply made a mistake. And so did you."

"But how? What is there about me that has changed?"

"Nothing, Charles. It is only that when we were married I thought you were strong. Now I realise that you are weak. It is not your fault. It is just the way you are."

Charles said to Louise:

"It is not your fault. It is just the way I am. I made a mistake. When I asked you to marry me I thought that I was a stronger person than I, in fact, am. I thought that I could stand the buffetings and struggles of a shared life. I cannot."

"Charles, I have tried . . ."

"I know you have. But you see the contract that I made with you was that you should be my wife, not my trained nurse. I do not need a trained nurse. I am perfectly healthy and I am not insane. The only thing that is wrong with me is that I am not, as they say, the marrying sort." He gave a dry laugh. "Or rather I am not the sort that stays married."

Helen had said to him:

"You think now that you love me. I doubt if you really do. But even if you do, you will have the choice of luxuriating in a broken heart, or of trying something else."

Louise said, "I had no wish to offend you, ever. I wanted to help you, because I love you and because I need you."

"I think you need me more than you love me. And you are wrong to allow yourself to need anyone. One of the few things I have learned, Louise, is that there is no permanence in human relationships. The only thing that lasts, and that is ultimately sustaining, is solitude."

"Charles, you are hurting yourself."

He was genuinely surprised.

"Hurting myself? Not at all."

"Charles, I cannot believe that this is really the end between us."

He said nothing. They were nearing home. At the far end of the square down which they were walking there was a small public house, bedecked with flags. Outside, in the street, there stood a piano with two oil lights on it. People were dancing to celebrate the end of the war. The thin music trickled down the square. There were no railings. The oak trees growing from the lawn seemed immense and immutable.

Louise went on, "I won't believe you, Charles. I won't believe that it is all finished. You're going to America tomorrow. When you come back it may be quite different."

"I doubt it, Louise. Meanwhile, while I am away, if you meet anyone else . . ." He would see now if the scab above the healed wound were ready to come off. "If Oliver should return from India . . ." Yes, it had come off painlessly. He would try another one. "Or if Peacock should turn out to have been a prisoner of war . . ."

"Oh, Charles, please don't talk such nonsense. Haven't I made it clear that you are the man I love?"

He looked at her, almost whimsically.

"Yes, Louise, but I merely wanted to make it clear that I free you from any promises, spoken or unspoken."

Helen had said:

"The only thing I want you to understand, Charles, is that from now on I owe you nothing and you owe me nothing. You will of course think of me as you please. For me you will be a stranger whom I once knew well. You have no responsibilities toward me whatsoever."

Louise said, "Charles, would you please buy me a beer?"

"Of course."

They entered the circle of light around the public house. The atmosphere of the impromptu celebration was as different as could be from that which they had recently left, at Sir Wilfred Rumbold's house. The pub around which it centered was a small house, away from main roads. Before the war it had been patronised almost solely by the men and women who lived in the nearby streets. Its saloon bar was cramped, but it had a large public bar. The beer had always been good, and during the recent shortage the spirits had been fairly divided. The publican was proud of his house; his wife kept the brass beer handles polished, and the oak tables in the public bar were scrubbed white with sand every morning before opening time. On winter evenings there was always a deep coal fire in the public bar and a smaller one burned in the saloon. The shove ha'penny board was smooth and true; the darts were sharp, and the publican himself soaked the dartboard once every three months to ensure that it kept in good condition.

The people who were now gathered here, dancing and drinking, had in most cases been coming in for their pint or their glass of port every night for years. Many had dropped in for a nip of spirits after a bad air raid. Charles felt almost an intruder as he pushed his way through to the bar. He had only been into the pub half a dozen times before, and he was therefore surprised and gratified when the publican recognised him, and asked him by name what he would have. When the two glasses of beer were handed over, Charles attempted to pay for them, but the publican would not hear of it:

"Not tonight, Mr. Monroe. It's all on me tonight," and he went on filling glasses with amber beer.

Louise was waiting for him outside. On his way through the bar he spoke to the publican's wife. He congratulated her on a fine party. She was pleased, and said that now that it was all over she hoped to be able to get some glass to replace the blasted windows.

"Shocking, it looks," she said: "all that cardboard. And so dark you can hardly keep the place clean."

For these people, Charles thought, the end of the war means something more than it can for us. For me and Rumbold and Louise, we who live mostly in the past and partially in the future, it is only a transference. If I really belonged in a street, I might know that the end of bombing is an end of fear.

As he came out of the pub, he saw that across one of the small houses opposite was strung a piece of white cloth, on which was written, in alternate letters of red and blue: WELCOME HOME JIM OUR SON. Charles suddenly felt ashamed.

Louise was standing by the door, talking to a soldier. The conversation that she and Charles had had, his decision to leave her and her refusal to accept that decision, seemed now part of a dusty and incomplete antiquity. Charles gave her a glass of beer. The soldier said:

"I've been asking your wife for a dance, but she won't, not without your permission."

He smiled frankly at Charles. Thus, Charles thought, thus she denies my refusal of responsibility. The pianist played an army song, and two old women, giggling and tipsy, sang the words in high, cracked voices. The soldier said:

"Not that I'm much of a dancer any more."

Charles was about to speak when one of the tipsy old women, a happy red-faced little gnome of a creature, came up to them with two glasses in her hands. She said:

"Here you are Jimmy. A glass of Guinness for you." She looked at Louise and Charles.

"Thank you, Mother," said Jimmy, and took a deep swallow, wiping the foam from his mouth with the back of his hand. "How about a dance now, eh?"

Louise looked at Charles. The indefatigable pianist played a waltz, banging out the rhythm. Charles was left alone with Jimmy's mother.

Immediately he felt the old, irritating constriction. He wished to say something to the happy little woman, but the sentences he formulated seemed foolish or condescending. He knew that he would have felt equally awkward with any strange woman, but it was the fear that he might be thought proud which galled him. Desperately he said:

"You have a handsome son."

She laughed up at him, showing her small, broken teeth.

"It's good to have him back. Four years in a prison camp he's been. Well, it's all over now."

Charles wondered how often he would hear that phrase in the next few days. Again he felt the stupid inability to speak. But something occurred to him. Conversations of this sort were like jumping from log to floating log on a sheet of water. He asked:

"Is that for him, the sign over there?"

She looked up at him vaguely. He pointed across the street.

"Yes, that's for our Jim. I made it myself."

Charles watched Jim and Louise dance past, Jim holding her stiffly and carefully, not talking, his face showing his concentration on the rhythm. Jim's little mother had finished her Guinness, and with a hiccough went into the bar. Charles walked a short way up the square, out of the bright patch by the piano. When he was in shadow he stopped and looked back towards the dancers.

From the darkness where he stood the circle of light and the moving figures seemed, with their musical accompaniment, a remote and urban Arcady. Charles could scarcely believe that only a few steps separated him from such enchanted gaiety. Yet, he knew that in fact half a lifetime lay between him and the waltzers, half a lifetime since he had sat in the café-restaurant and had talked with the girl whose name he did not know. It was impossible now to reverse the threads of that half-life. He could only be an intruder among such festivity. He took a few steps further away from the dark, into darker shadow.

He could see Louise and her soldier standing by the piano. Jim was asking for a tune, and when the *Lambeth Walk* began, he and Louise started on an elaborate rigmarole of steps. Charles wondered vaguely where Louise had learned to do them. He was not really interested. Beside him he heard a murmur of voices, and looking down, saw that a few feet from where he stood a couple were sitting on a step, locked in a close embrace. Charles felt embarrassed lest they should notice his presence. He walked out onto the lawn. There was a bench beneath one of the oak trees. He sat on it, and took a swallow of his beer.

The nostalgia which the familiar tunes, the happy people and the darkness inspired was, he knew, its own reward. It was merely because they were strangers that their lives seemed so full of light and gaiety. Charles knew that if he had married the girl in the café-restaurant, his own fears and revulsions would have persisted. He would have had with her the same stresses and misunderstandings that he had had with Helen and with Louise. The lives of strangers may be simple and satisfactory, so long as they remain strangers. Once that aura of the unknown is removed, the inevitable conflicts become apparent. For Charles, since one end of the pole of conflict must remain in his hands, the question to be resolved would always be the same.

By emerging from his solitude, by discarding his anonymity and depriving others of theirs, he had, thirty years before, embarked on a course of action which for him, as for the strangers, had been usually disastrous. He remembered the sensation of guilt which he had experienced that dawn, in Helen's bedroom, after the ball. Now it was immaterial whether that guilt had been real or fictitious. He had felt it, and therefore it had influenced his actions and subsequently those of others. He had believed, or if it were not belief it was at least suspicion, that by taking Helen from a dead man he had robbed a corpse. Had they remained strangers, such an ill action could obviously never have taken place. And had he not believed himself to be a robber he could not, in his turn, have been so robbed, when Helen had left him and taken the train from Paddington to the West country. Nor could Oliver have stolen his affection and despised his kindness.

The debt of guilt which Charles had accumulated in his youth, the knowledge of his own life and his own pursuit of happiness among the dying and the dead, he now felt that he had paid off. It had never existed save in his own mind. Looking at the people dancing for victory, he wondered if perhaps each one of them carried with him such a shame. Sin and atonement, crime and punishment, were but a crude antithesis. Louise was perhaps unhappy now; if she had made Peacock, say, unhappy in years gone by, the method and extent of vengeance was blunt and purposeless. For Charles the only real sin was the original one of having been born.

He looked towards the dancing group. Two figures detached themselves from it and came over towards the dark part of the square. Before they left the light Charles recognised that the girl was Louise. He pulled his glass towards him and sat in the impenetrable shade of the big tree. Louise called his name:

"Charles!"

He did not answer, and he heard her say to Jim:

"Where can he be?"

He did not catch the soldier's reply.

Charles' debt was paid off. Incurred in war and love, it was settled by his renewed acceptance of solitude. In the dark he shrugged his shoulders; he had retreated from Louise, and now she too had become a stranger again.

They passed quite near the bench on which he sat. She called his name again, and again he did not answer. She said to Jim:

"I can't think where he can have got to."

"Maybe he's gone home."

"I don't think he'd go home without me."

"Let's go back and have another dance."

"If he's gone home, I ought to go too."

"Lets have another anyway, and see if he turns up."

Louise stood still. The soldier's voice went on:

"Come on, Louise. He might be inside, in the pub."

He put his arm around her shoulders and they went back to the piano.

Charles watched them go. Louise has gone, the last link of the chain. Louise and Oliver, at Oxford, before the war. Oliver has gone. There will never be a welcome home for him, for Oliver, my son. Should I meet him again he will only be Oliver, as Louise will only be Louise, as Helen in the Crillon was only a person with a name. The chain stretches back, through Paddington to Gloucestershire, and from Gloucestershire, to that other war, where a man died in an airplane and another man who had lost a leg once called me a prig. It goes back to my childhood, to the first clear memory that I have, the taste of peppermints. It seems strange that that first sensation should have been pregnant with a knowledge of death.

Tomorrow I shall board an airplane again. I shall go to an unknown country, among strangers, and all these names and faces, loves and jealousies, will take their place behind glass, in the museum of my solitude. It will be interesting to catalogue them, to be one's own curator once again.

Charles looked at the dancing figures. He could not be sure if that were Louise. It might be, but he did not know.

He finished his beer and put down the empty glass on the bench. It would be found in the morning. Getting up, he walked off along the dark side of the square. He would take a round-about way home.